D1499964

J
FIC COOPER C
The lost treasure of
Annwn
4

The Adventures of Brenin

BOOK
FOUR

THE LOST

TREASURE

OF ANNWN

FEB - - 2013

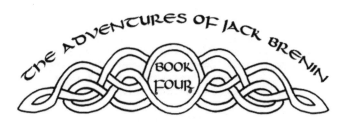

THE LOST
TREASURE
OF ANNWN

CATHERINE COOPER

ILLUSTRATIONS BY
RON COOPER and CATHERINE COOPER

infiniteideas

PERU PUBLIC LIBRARY
100 East Main Street

Copyright text © Catherine Cooper, 2012
Copyright illustrations © Ron Cooper and Catherine Cooper 2012
The right of Catherine Cooper to be identified as the author of this
book has been asserted in accordance with the Copyright,
Designs and Patents Act 1988.

First published in 2012 by
Infinite Ideas Limited
36 St Giles
Oxford
OX1 3LD
United Kingdom
www.infideas.com

All rights reserved. Except for the quotation of small passages for the
purposes of criticism or review, no part of this publication may be
reproduced, stored in a retrieval system or transmitted in any form or by
any means, electronic, mechanical, photocopying, recording, scanning or
otherwise, except under the terms of the Copyright, Designs and Patents
Act 1988 or under the terms of a licence issued by the Copyright Licensing
Agency Ltd, 90 Tottenham Court Road, London W1T 4LP, UK, without
the permission in writing of the publisher. Requests to the publisher
should be addressed to the Permissions Department, Infinite Ideas
Limited, 36 St Giles, Oxford, OX1 3LD, UK,
or faxed to +44 (0) 1865 514777.

A CIP catalogue record for this book is available from the British Library

ISBN 978–1–908984–04–3

Brand and product names are trademarks or registered trademarks
of their respective owners.

Cover designed by D.R.ink
Typeset by Nicki Averill
Printed and bound in Great Britain by
TJ International Ltd, Padstow, Cornwall

MIX
Paper from
responsible sources
FSC
www.fsc.org   FSC® C013056

FOR GEORGE AND EMILY
A GREAT NEPHEW AND NIECE

CONTENTS

THE MAP
OF
GLASRUHEN VILLAGE

NEWTON GILL FOREST

TO NEWTON GILL

THE BRENINS' HOUSE

THE BACK LANE

GROVE FARM'S PASTURE

THE PLAYING FIELD

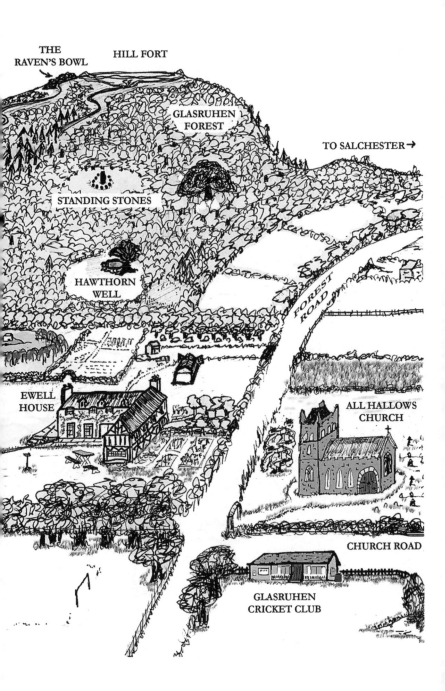

THE
RAVEN'S BOWL

HILL FORT

GLASRUHEN
FOREST

TO SALCHESTER →

STANDING STONES

HAWTHORN
WELL

FOREST ROAD

EWELL
HOUSE

ALL HALLOWS
CHURCH

CHURCH ROAD

GLASRUHEN
CRICKET CLUB

MONUMENT HILL

IN LILLERTON VILLAGE

NW

W

SW

MEADOW MOUND

NEAR THE OAK, ASH, AND THORN

THE ISLAND

IN THE GELSTON RIVER

NE

E

SE

THE TOWER

IN THE RUINS OF FALCONROCK

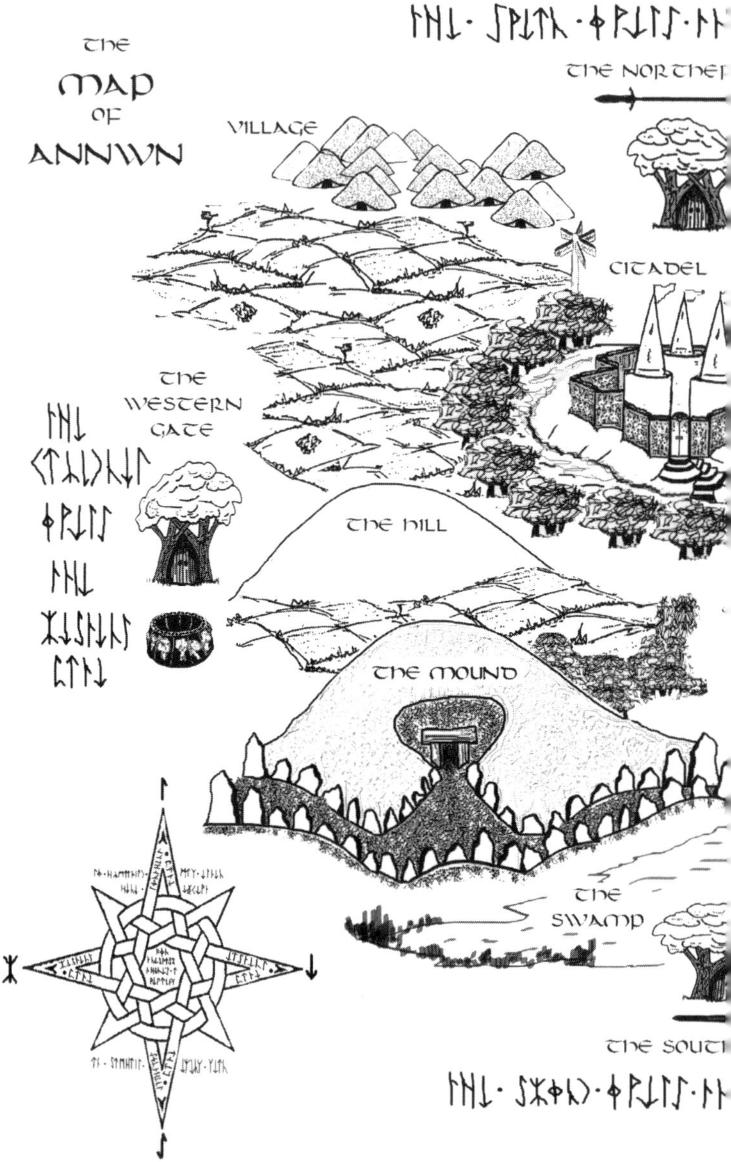

The
MAP
OF
ANNWN

VILLAGE

THE NORTHE

CITADEL

THE
WESTERN
GATE

THE HILL

THE MOUND

THE
SWAMP

THE SOUTH

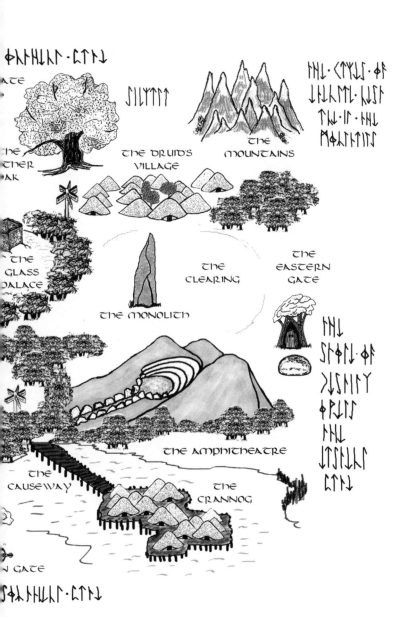

ᚦᛁᚱᚻᛁᛚᚱ · ᚴᛏᚱᛚ

ᚨᛏᛖ

ᛏᚻᛖᚱ
ᚦᚦᚱ
ᚨᚴ

ᛏᚻᛖ
ᚷᛚᚨᛋᛋ
ᛈᚨᛚᚨᚴᛖ

ᛋᛁᛚᛏᚱᚱᚱ

THE DRUID'S
VILLAGE

THE
MOUNTAINS

ᛏᚻᛖ · ᚴᛏᛣᛚᛋ · ᚢᚠ
ᛋᛁᛚᚨᚱᛏᛁ · ᚻᛁᛋᛏ
ᛏᛁᚢ · ᛁᚱ · ᛏᚻᛖ
ᛗᚢᛁᚾᛏᛁᛁᛏᛋ

THE
CLEARING

THE
EASTERN
GATE

THE MONOLITH

ᛏᚻᛖ
ᛋᛏᚢᚱᛖ · ᚢᚠ
ᛞᛁᛋᛗᛁᚱᛏ
ᚦᛈᛚᛁᛋ
ᛏᚻᛖ
ᛋᛏᛋᛁᛚᛋ
ᚴᛏᚱᛚ

THE AMPHITHEATRE

THE
CAUSEWAY

THE
CRANNOG

ᚾ GATE

ᛋᚦᛏᚦᚻᚢᛚᚱ · ᚴᛏᚱᛚ

IT CANNOT BE RULED

AND CHOOSES ITS OWN PATH

PROLOGUE

Jack sat bolt upright in bed. His heart was pounding in his chest and beads of sweat trickled down his back. He told himself it was just a dream but everything had felt so real. He'd been back in the caves in Annwn with Velindur standing before him, holding the diamond key in the air for all to see. He could still hear Velindur's laugh as it echoed around the cavern. He'd felt helpless as Velindur hurled the key against the rock before vowing he'd have his revenge. Had he called out in his sleep? He didn't think so. He held his breath and listened. Only the reassuring sound of Grandad snoring broke the silence. Jack reached for his wand and made the tip glow brightly. Orin was asleep in her hammock and nothing in his room had changed. He

1

let out a long sigh, lay on his back and went over the dream again.

He'd woken as Velindur began yelling, '*Vengeance is mine!*' Jack tried to remember what Mortarn had said. He'd thought crystal magic had been responsible for Velindur's disappearance, but no one knew where he'd gone. Jack shuddered as he remembered Velindur's screams. Where had the whirlwind taken him? If it was true that crystal magic never destroyed it meant Velindur was still very much alive. The dream had shaken him and he knew he wasn't going to get back to sleep for a while so he reached under the bed for his Book of Shadows. He needed to know more about crystal magic. Jack ran his fingers over the trees on the cover.

'Tell me about crystal magic.'

The book almost leapt out of his hands, the covers opened and the pages flipped furiously until they were nearly at the end. As the book became still, writing appeared.

Crystal magic is the oldest and most powerful kind of magic throughout all the lands.
It cannot be ruled and chooses its own path.

This wasn't anything new, Jack had been told this already. He read the answer again. Surely there was a mistake? What did *all the lands* mean? Why hadn't his book said Earth and Annwn?

'Which lands?' he asked.

The Earth where mankind and other creatures live,
Annwn where the fair folk and Druids dwell,
and Elidon, Land of Shadow, where secrets are hid.

Jack had never heard of Elidon. If Velindur had been transported there he hoped it was a long way from Glasruhen.

'Where is Elidon?'

It's in the here and now but nowhere to be seen.

'How can you find something you can't see?'

Knowledge is needed from the Druid's library, and the
labyrinth beyond,
before Elidon can be found.
Only those with the key may find and unlock the door.

Jack yawned. The answer must lie inside the palace library in Annwn. Elan had said there were many ancient books in there. He'd ask Nora about it in the morning, maybe she had a book about Elidon at Ewell

3

House. He was too tired to ask any more questions or try to work it out now. He dimmed his wand, returned his book to its hiding place and hoped he wasn't going to dream about Velindur again.

SURPRISES

A loud buzzing woke Jack. He felt something land on his nose and flicked it away. A squint at the sunshine streaming through the gap in the curtains told him he should probably be up and eating breakfast but it was the first day of the summer holidays and he didn't think Grandad would mind. Jack could still hear the buzzing. He looked around the room and saw a fly heading back towards his bed. It landed on the sheet, on top of his knee. He was about to move his leg when he realised the fly was wearing a pair of glasses.

'Hello, what are you doing here?' Jack asked the Dorysk as he reached for his wand so he could understand the reply.

There was a loud popping sound, and where the fly had been, a prickly ball appeared. It rolled down Jack's leg.

'Ouch! Careful, your spines are sharp.'

'So sorry, didn't want you swatting me again. Thought it would be better to transform so we can talk. Your window's closed so I had to use the kitchen door and come through your keyhole.'

'Nora told me to keep the window shut.'

'That must have been before you got used to your magic; you don't have to be frightened of anything now, not with your powers.'

Jack didn't know what to say. He had no idea what he was capable of doing because he'd never really tried. Magic was still new to him. The Dorysk grinned and continued.

'Nora sent me with a message.'

'A message… Is there something wrong with Camelin?'

'No, he was his usually grumpy self when I left Ewell House a few minutes ago. I'm only obeying instructions. Nora told me to come over; I didn't think it would be a problem.'

'No, no, it's fine. I was just surprised to see you instead of Camelin.'

'There you go, you've hit the nail on the head, so to speak, that's why Nora sent me. She thought if Camelin came over he'd spill the beans and let the surprise out of the bag. She knows I can be trusted, and now I'm officially a member of the Night Guard, I'm available for duty. You know my credentials already, shape shifter, information gatherer, keeper of secrets, and now, I'm at your service too.'

Jack watched as the Dorysk tried to bow but his round tummy got in the way and he toppled over and rolled across Jack's other leg.

'Ow! Do you think you could change into something a little less prickly if I'm in bed next time you call?'

'So sorry, so sorry, I've delivered my message so I'll be off now.'

'Message? What message?'

'Oh dear me! I thought I'd told you. Nora says you're to come over to Ewell House as soon as you can, she's got a surprise waiting for you.'

'A surprise?'

'Yes, but that's all I can say.'

'I'll be there as soon as I can but it depends on what Grandad's got planned for the day.'

'I'll let Nora know. Oh! I nearly forgot, Camelin

says could you please hurry up as he's not allowed to leave the house until you arrive.'

Jack laughed. Camelin would probably be in a super grumpy mood by the time he got there. He made a mental note to take him a treat, something out of his stash tin, maybe a chocolate cake bar, or two.

'I'll try not to be long.'

The Dorysk nodded. There was a loud popping sound and in the blink of an eye, a small fly, wearing a minute pair of glasses, took off from the sheet. It circled around Jack's head twice before disappearing through the keyhole.

Jack washed and dressed quickly before racing down the stairs to the kitchen. He saw a piece of paper propped up against the cereal box on the table. Jack smiled when he read the three words his grandad had written… *in the garden*. The back door was open and Jack could see dark patches on the soil where his grandad had watered the plants. He followed a trail of wet dribbles along the path to the greenhouse. The sliding door squeaked noisily as Jack slid it open. He stepped inside and quickly slid the door back so the heat wouldn't escape. Grandad looked very hot.

'Ah! You're up!'

'Sorry, I overslept, but I can help you if you want.' Jack stood with his fingers crossed behind his back. He really wanted to go Ewell House and find out about the surprise but he felt he ought to ask Grandad if there was anything he wanted him to do first.

'Hot, thirsty work this. You can help by being a good lad and fetching me a glass of lemonade. There's a bottle in the fridge.'

Jack ran back to the kitchen. In his haste he filled the glass a bit too full and had to be careful not to spill it as he made his way back down the path. Grandad grinned when he saw Jack.

'Just the thing; there's nothing quite like cold lemonade when you're hot and thirsty. Now, what are you going to do with yourself today?'

'Could I go to Ewell House? There's something I want to look up in Nora's library, unless you need some help.'

Grandad laughed and nodded to the deckchair on the lawn.

'Once I've finished here I'm going to get my radio, another glass of lemonade, and then sit and listen to the Test Match. You can get another deckchair if you like but there's a *no talking rule* when the cricket's on. I'm sure you'll have much more fun at Nora's.'

'Thanks Grandad, I'll go and get my bag.'

Jack was nearly at the end of the tunnel, that led into Nora's garden, when he realised he'd not had his breakfast. His stomach growled loudly. It would be rude to ask Nora for food as soon as he arrived, but he didn't want to go back. There was only one thing he could do. He unwrapped one of the chocolate cake bars and nibbled a bit off the end. Unfortunately, by the time he stepped into Nora's garden, he'd eaten both bars. Camelin wouldn't be pleased if he knew, but luckily he was nowhere to be seen. Jack wiped his mouth in case there were any stray crumbs.

Jack saw Medric land on the grass and race towards the patio doors. He was only inside the kitchen for a moment before he rushed back out, hurriedly took off, and headed back to the lake. Something must be wrong. Jack ran to the house.

'Is everything alright?'

Camelin sighed, hunched his wings and began to grumble.

'Medric's a dad, the first egg hatched early this morning; that was the second and there are eight more to go. I hope he doesn't get that excited every time a gosling hatches.'

'He probably will,' said Nora, 'but that wasn't why we asked you to come over.'

'You mean Medric's news isn't the surprise?'

Camelin humphed.

'Hardly, this is something really special.'

Nora frowned at Camelin.

'I thought we agreed: not a word, until Jack's seen it.'

'Seen what?' asked Jack as he looked around the kitchen.

Camelin waddled over to the end of the table and pointed his beak in the direction of the dresser. Jack looked at the shelves. A gold-coloured envelope had been propped up on the bottom shelf but it wasn't addressed to anyone.

'It's for you,' said Nora.

'How do you know? It doesn't say it's for me.'

Camelin sighed.

'Why don't you open it and see what it says?'

As Jack touched the envelope runes appeared. He was left in no doubt the letter was his when he saw his name. Camelin hopped onto the end of the dresser and peered over Jack's arm.

'I can't read it! What's it say?'

'It's my name, it says, Jack Brenin.'

'Can't you hurry up and open it? I've been waiting to see what it says for hours now.'

Jack turned the letter over. On the back was a golden seal; the impression of an acorn could clearly be seen in the wax. A large red arrow, pointing upwards, was underneath the seal.

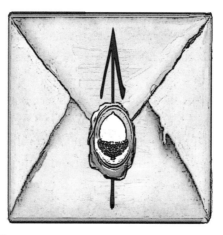

'It's from Annwn,' announced Jack.

'How do you know it's from Annwn? You've not looked inside yet.'

Jack showed Camelin the seal and symbol.

'That's the letter *A* written as a rune underneath the acorn, but how did it get here?'

Nora smiled and nodded towards the garden. As Jack turned he saw Elan walking towards the patio.

'You're back! When did you get here? How long can you stay?'

'What about the letter,' grumbled Camelin. 'I want to know what it says.'

Jack ignored Camelin. He couldn't stop smiling. Elan was back.

'You are going to stay for a while aren't you?'

Elan nodded.

'I can stay until the end of the summer but then I must return to prepare for your coronation. The Druids don't need my help at the moment. A lot of the old ways have been restored. Gwillam and the Blessed Council seem to have everything in order and under control. If he needs me he'll send a message to my Book of Shadows.'

'That's the best news, what a brilliant surprise.'

Elan pointed to the letter.

'That's the real surprise.'

'At last,' said Camelin as he hopped around. 'Come on, open it up, see what it says!'

'Can I use your letter opener?' Jack asked Nora.

'I'm afraid you can't, it's not really an envelope. The letter is written on the inside, you'll have to break the seal then spread it out.'

Jack tried to lift the seal without breaking it but it cracked in two. He spread the envelope out on the table.

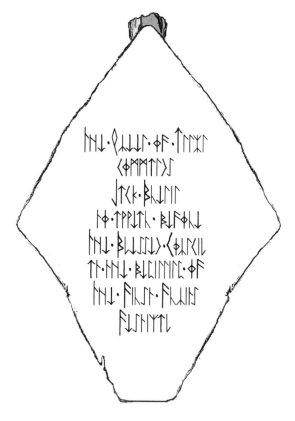

'It's all in runes,' grumbled Camelin, 'I can't read runes. I've only just learnt how to read letters. Can't you magic it into real writing?'

'Camelin,' said Nora sternly, 'it's Jack's letter, he can translate it for us.'

Jack read the contents through to himself first. His stomach filled with butterflies. It wasn't exactly a letter, more like a summons. He sat down before reading it out loud.

The Queen of Annwn
commands
Jack Brenin
to appear before
The Blessed Council
At the beginning of
the First Fruits
Festival

Jack looked at Nora and then at Elan.

'Have I done something wrong?'

'Not at all,' replied Elan, 'you've been invited to Annwn to learn more about your coronation. You'll have to satisfy everyone you're the rightful king. No one doubts you are – it's just a formality.'

'Festival,' interrupted Camelin, 'aw Jack, you know what that means don't you? Sausages!'

'The invitation is for Jack,' said Nora.

Camelin hopped over and leant against Jack's shoulder.

'You wouldn't leave me behind, would you?'

'If Nora and Elan say you can go then it's alright with me.'

'Hmmm!' said Nora as she drummed her fingers on the table, 'I'd say it depends on your behaviour from now until then.'

'When is the Festival?' Jack asked Nora.

'The First Fruits celebrates the beginning of harvest, it starts in eleven days' time, and will last until all the fruits have been gathered in.'

'Blackberry pie,' interrupted Camelin and started his shuffle dance.

Nora laughed.

'We'll make blackberry pie but only if you help pick them and don't eat too many.'

At the thought of blackberry pie, Jack's mouth began to water and his stomach rumbled. Camelin turned and stared at Jack.

'Was that you?'

'I missed breakfast.'

'We could go and have an early lunch in town,' said Elan. 'I was going to ask if you'd help me do some shopping. I've got a list of things we're going to need to take back with us to Annwn.'

'I could manage an early lunch,' replied Camelin.

'Elan was asking Jack,' said Nora. 'You know they can't take you into town.'

Camelin glowered at Elan before shuffling off to the other end of the table. Jack tried not to laugh as Elan rolled her eyes.

'I'll have to let Grandad know.'

'That's fine; we can call in on our way to Newton Gill.'

'And you can help me with some chores while they've gone,' added Nora. 'The herb garden needs weeding.'

Camelin hopped onto the floor and mumbled to himself as he waddled onto the patio.

'Weeding! She could magic all the weeds out but no… they have to be pulled out by hand or beak. I don't know any other ravens who have to do weeding.'

Jack felt bad. He hadn't meant to upset Camelin but he was overjoyed that Elan was back and there were lots of things he wanted to ask her. A walk to

Newton Gill would give them plenty of time to chat. Nora gave Elan some money and then put her hand on Jack's shoulder.

'Don't take any notice of Camelin, he'll be fine, off you go and have a good time.'

As Jack and Elan reached the hedge, Medric flew past them cackling loudly.

'Three and four have hatched now,' explained Elan.

Grandad was pleased to see Elan and was happy for Jack to go to Newton Gill. He fished in his pocket and gave Jack his loose change. Jack and Elan waved from the gate before turning into the back lane. Jack had been to town with Grandad a couple of times but he'd never walked there before. When they reached the stile Jack saw the fairy mound, which lay between the oak, ash and hawthorn trees.

'Have you been here before?' asked Elan.

'Only once. There's a talking door knob in one of the tunnels under that hillock.'

'Ah! The fairy mound. You haven't met the fairies yet have you?'

'No, only the door knob when I was looking for the Dorysk.'

'Fairies are fine in small numbers but when they get together they can be really noisy. It's even worse if they lose their tempers. They instantly shape shift into large angry bees and can only change back when they've calmed down.'

'What do they look like when they aren't angry?'

'They're like tiny dryads. They don't have wings of their own so if they want to fly they shape shift into a small winged insect. Some prefer to be beetles, others butterflies or damselflies, nothing too big.'

As they climbed over the stile into the field a pale blue butterfly flitted past them.

'How you can tell if it's a fairy?' asked Jack.

'You can't, not unless you'd been formally introduced and they decided they liked you. Only those who've eaten fairy food can see them, and only invited guests are welcome to join them for a meal. Once you've been to a feast with the fair folk you can see them in whatever form they may take.'

'Can you see them?'

'Oh yes, so can Nora and the Dorysk too.'

'What about Camelin?'

'Fairy food wouldn't interest him and he probably wouldn't eat it if they offered it to him.'

'Camelin! Refuse food?'

'You obviously don't know about fairy food. It looks revolting and doesn't taste much better. It's a test to see how polite you are. They like people with good manners. The Dorysk doesn't mind what he eats and is quite partial to maggot pie.'

Jack pulled a face. He wasn't sure how polite he could be if he was offered a plate of maggot pie, especially if the maggots weren't cooked.

'Not far now,' said Elan as they climbed over the stile at the other side of the field. 'Once we get to the end of this lane we'll be there.'

'What are we shopping for?'

'Nail varnish, scrubbing brushes and jam covers.'

Jack looked puzzled. It wasn't the answer he was expecting.

'Is the nail varnish for you?'

Elan laughed.

'No, it's for Ember.'

'Ember!'

'She's agreed to take part in the festival and I want

to give her a surprise. We'll need scrubbing brushes to clean her feet and lots of silver nail varnish to paint her claws. I'm going to make sure she lives up to her name. By the time we've finished grooming her she'll definitely look like Ember Silver Horn the Magnificent.'

Jack laughed. He'd never imagined that he would find himself grooming a dragon.

'And the jam covers?'

'They're for Nora, she's going to make lots of blackberry jelly to take with us for the festival.'

'Jelly?'

Elan laughed.

'It's not the kind you put in trifle, this is jam with all the seeds taken out.'

Jack thought that was a good idea. It was annoying when tiny seeds got caught in your teeth. He doubted it would matter to Camelin. The only seed he'd ever heard Camelin complain about was birdseed, especially when he'd been expected to eat it.

When they got to the end of the lane Jack froze. On the other side of the road was the goalkeeper he'd met at the field when he'd tried to join in with a football game soon after he'd come to Glasruhen. The boy had called him names. With him was the tall boy who'd had a bloody nose when Jack had accidentally kicked the ball into his face. Three other boys that Jack didn't recognise were walking with them towards the town.

'What's the matter?' asked Elan.

'That's one of the boys who pushed me. The one who wrecked your bunch of flowers.'

'They're not going to bother us, come on, let's go and get some lunch first, I can hear your stomach rumbling again.'

Jack wasn't sure Elan realised how strong the goalie was. It would be better if they could avoid them altogether. He was going to suggest they waited a while till they were out of sight but Elan had already started to cross the road.

'Come on, it'll be fine, you'll see.'

Jack wished he could feel as confident as Elan sounded but his legs already felt like jelly. He reluctantly followed her into the High Street.

TROUBLE

Newton Gill was busy but Jack managed to keep the boys in sight. It wasn't too difficult because three of the gang were tall. As Elan stopped to look in the window of a teashop, two older ladies came out through the door. For a moment they blocked Jack's view and when they'd passed he couldn't see the boys anywhere. He scanned the High Street but they'd gone.

'It looks really busy in there,' said Elan. 'We could go to the kebab shop across the road or the café in the square. What do you fancy?'

'We'd better not have a kebab, Camelin wouldn't forgive us.'

'He'd never know.'

'He'd smell it. The café sounds better. I've been there before with Grandad.'

They walked down to the town square and stopped outside a black and white timber-framed building. It had several tables outside on the pavement, each with a large green parasol. Elan pulled out one of the chairs.

'There's plenty of room out here, we can sit in the sunshine.'

Jack would have preferred to be inside and out of sight, but the café was full. It wasn't long before they'd given their order to the waiter.

'I think we've been followed,' said Elan.

Jack's heart sank. He looked around but couldn't see the gang.

'Where are they?' he whispered.

'They? You're not still worried about those boys are you?'

Jack nodded.

'Who did you mean?'

'Someone's just landed in the big yew tree by the church gate! Don't let him know you've seen him.'

Jack looked out of the corner of his eye without moving his head. There was a big black shape hiding in the tree.

'I wonder if Nora knows he's there?'

There was an explosion of laughter from behind him.

'Would that be Nutty Nora?'

Jack felt a shiver run down his spine as he slowly turned around. The four boys jostled each other as they each grabbed a chair from the next table. They positioned themselves so they could all see Jack. The goalie, the tallest of the group, didn't sit down. Instead he stood behind Jack, put his hands on the back of his chair and started tilting him backwards. His long greasy hair drooped over Jack's face as he spoke.

'I didn't hear you, Pixie Boy. I said... was that Nutty Nora you're talking about?'

Jack gulped and summoned up all the courage he had to speak.

'She's not nutty. Nora is a very nice person.'

'Ooooh! Get him,' laughed the goalie.

The other boy Jack had seen before joined in.

'Taking your girlfriend out to lunch are you? Aren't you going to introduce us?'

Elan fixed the boy with a look. There was an uncomfortable silence before Jack spoke again.

'This is Elan.'

The goalie released the chair. He laughed as Jack lurched forwards.

'Well Elan, you've got a right wimp for a boyfriend. Has he told you we've got some unfinished business with him? Isn't that right Max?'

The boy who'd had the bloody nose nodded and stood up. Jack could feel beads of sweat running down his forehead even though the rest of his body felt cold. Max took a couple of steps towards their table. Jack was sure he was going to start a fight when he saw his clenched fist. Should he stand up and face him? The decision was taken out of his hands when the waiter came out with their order. There was a scraping of chairs before all the boys ran off. The waiter sighed.

'Were they bothering you? That lot are always causing trouble.'

'We're fine thank you,' replied Elan.

Jack didn't say a word. The boys did bother him. The waiter put their rolls and drinks down and collected two empty teacups from another table before going back inside the café.

'Do you know them?' asked Jack.

Elan laughed.

'Everyone knows them. Your grandad and dad will know them too; they've got quite a reputation. The one who calls you *pixie boy* is Frank Smedley. They call him Tank because he's so big. His dad owns the scrap metal yard on the other side of Newton Gill. There are four boys in the family and Frank's the youngest.'

'What about the one he called Max, the tall one with blond hair, the one who's got it in for me?'

'That's Max Wratten, he lives in one of the big houses at the end of Church Road. The other tall boy with the long dark hair is Danny Westbrook. His dad owns the music shop round the corner. I don't know the other two. It's Max and Tank who usually cause all the trouble. Tank got caught throwing stones over the hedge into Nora's garden not so long ago.'

'He really doesn't like me.'

'He's just a bully. Don't let him bother you.'

'But he's twice as big as me and three times as strong.'

Jack wondered if Elan really knew what the boys could be like. It was alright for her, she wasn't the one who'd been pushed around. If he could use his magic it would be different, he'd be able to tackle all five of them at once and they'd never bother him again. He tried to put the boys out of his mind and concentrate on his lunch. Before he took the first bite he looked up at the yew tree. Thankfully Camelin had gone.

When they'd finished eating they set off up the High Street towards the homewares shop that they thought would sell everything on their list. By the time they got there, Jack was feeling hot and bothered. It was a relief to step inside the cool shop and be out of the sunshine. They loaded up the shopping trolley with six scrubbing brushes, twenty bottles of silver nail varnish, two packs of jam covers and three tubs of beeswax.

'What's the beeswax for?' asked Jack.

'I thought we could rub it into Ember's scales and polish them up. We ought to take some dusters too. They're down the other end. I'll go and get them while you make your way to the till.'

Jack wheeled the trolley to the bottom of the aisle and turned the corner. In front of him stood Max. He turned the trolley to the right only to see Tank standing there with his arms folded. A quick glance to the left told him Danny was blocking his way. Turning around would be pointless; he knew the other two would be behind him.

'That's a big trolley for a pipsqueak like you,' said Max as he grabbed the front and pushed it hard. Jack staggered backwards. Tank pushed him hard on his right shoulder and Danny pushed him back on the left.

'Where's your girlfriend, got fed up of you already has she?' taunted Tank.

Max clicked his fingers and pointed towards Jack. Tank and Danny pulled Jack's hands from the trolley, put their arms under his and lifted him from the ground. Max shoved the trolley down the aisle. Jack heard a crash as it hit the shelving.

'Round the back with him, I owe him a punch in the nose.'

Tank and Danny were about to set off when Elan stepped out in front of them. She narrowed her eyes and looked directly at Tank.

'Put him down,' she said quietly.

Max laughed.

'You can have him back when we've done with him Freckle Face.'

'I said put him down.'

One of the shop assistants appeared at the end of the aisle.

'Is there a problem?' he enquired.

Tank and Danny released their hold, dropped Jack and ran off towards the door. As Jack stood up he noticed only Max was left.

'We're fine, thank you,' Elan replied.

Max glowered and murmured something under

his breath as the assistant started straightening the display on the shelf.

'Now if you'll excuse us,' continued Elan as she brushed past Max, 'we're busy.'

Jack followed Elan to the abandoned trolley. They pushed it to the tills and joined one of the queues. As they waited Jack wondered if Elan had seen the look in Max's eyes. He feared the gang would be out to get them both now.

Camelin was waiting for them on the fence by the first stile.

'Did you save me anything?'

Jack looked down at his feet.

'Aw Jack, I thought you'd have saved me a bit of cheese, it was a cheese roll you had wasn't it?'

'Did you save us any of your dinner?' asked Elan.

Camelin didn't answer.

'We'll see you back at the house,' said Elan. 'Tell Nora we're going to need two glasses of something cold.'

As Camelin flew off Jack thought he saw some movement on the other side of the mound near the hedge.

'What if the gang are waiting for us in the back lane?' he asked.

'They'd be very foolish if they were.'

'Look, the bushes are moving, I'm sure it's them.'

'Come out,' yelled Elan, 'we're not frightened of you.'

'No, Elan, let's get back, I don't want to know if it's them.'

It was too late. One by one the boys appeared from the hedge and stood blocking their way. Max grinned at Jack but his expression changed when he looked at Elan.

'Now we can settle this and there's nobody here to stop us. I don't like girls who think they're better than me.'

Elan dropped the bags and took two steps towards Max. She completely ignored the other four boys.

'Danny, do your thing,' ordered Max.

Jack wondered what Danny was about to do. As he stepped forward he brushed his long hair away from his face before taking something out of his pocket.

31

Jack dropped his bags and moved to stand by Elan. He couldn't let her face the boys on her own. Danny flipped the lid on a small tin and threw the contents at Elan. A huge spider flew through the air and landed on her blouse. The boys laughed. Jack wondered if they were expecting her to scream. They were going to be disappointed if they did. Elan held up a finger and the large spider scurried onto the back of her hand. She turned her hand so the spider settled in her palm. Max looked annoyed. He raised his hand to bring it down on top of the spider. Danny looked horrified and yelled *don't* but he needn't have worried. Elan grabbed Max's arm with her free hand and held it firmly in her grasp.

'Ow! Let go!' wailed Max.

The other boys sniggered as Max tried to wriggle free.

'Do something you lot, don't just stand there. Get her off me!'

Tank had only taken one step towards Elan when a loud buzzing made him stop. From nowhere the largest bee Jack had ever seen zig-zagged in front of Tank's face. He waved his hands around trying to ward it off and protect himself. The others started to laugh but soon stopped when three more bees appeared. They abandoned Max and ran off across the field. When they'd gone, Elan released him. He stood rubbing his sore arm.

'Hadn't you better go and find your friends?' she said.

'This isn't over. You got lucky this time, but we'll get you, both of you.'

Jack and Elan watched Max run off after the others. When he was out of sight Elan went and sat on top of the fairy mound and let the spider run onto the grass. Four large bees buzzed around her head.

'They'll transform soon when they've calmed down,' explained Elan.

'You mean they're fairies?'

'Of course, what else would you expect to find inside a fairy ring? The mound is in the centre and the ring extends to the edge of the trees. They'll not stand for any nonsense, especially when someone tries to kill another creature. Come sit down and watch.'

Jack sat next to Elan. It wasn't long before one of the bees became a bright spark; when the intense light faded a beautiful pale blue butterfly appeared. One by one the fairies transformed, until two butterflies, and two damselflies, were flitting around their heads.

'Oh wow! Will they change again into fairies?' asked Jack.

'Not at the moment, they usually change at dusk. We'll ask the Dorysk to make an appointment so you can be presented to them.'

'I'd like that.' Jack got up and bowed to the circling insects. 'Thank you for your help.'

'We'd better be getting back. I told you not to worry didn't I?'

'Max looked really annoyed when you grabbed his arm.'

'He obviously thinks all girls are weak. Well he picked on the wrong one today.'

Jack and Elan collected up the bags and made their way back to Ewell House. It was only when they got to the stile that he remembered what Elan had said about the fairy food. Would he be offered maggot pie when he met them? If he was, he hoped it would at least be cooked.

Jack went up to Camelin's loft when he'd finished his cold drink. He expected that Camelin would still be in a grumpy mood but instead he was quite excited.

'Watch this,' he said as soon as Jack sat down.

Camelin pointed his wand at a pile of rubbish on the floor. With a flourish of his wand the rubbish rose and flew towards a wicker basket. The basket lid lifted and the rubbish flew inside. When the last piece had disappeared the lid fell back into place.

'That's brilliant!' exclaimed Jack.

'I know, pure genius, I'm never going to have to tidy my room by beak and claw again.'

'How did you find out about that spell?'

'Weeding by beak gives you plenty of time to think and I got to thinking… there had to be a tidying spell. When Nora and I finished in the herb garden I asked my Book of Shadows… and there it was.'

'I wondered if Nora might have put a block on your book until you've had more wand practice.'

'Oh she has, but not for every spell. I asked nicely and said please, and it opened up.'

'That's really good.'

'Don't tell Nora though, I don't want her knowing I'm practising on my own. I promise I won't do anything dangerous, just practical things.'

Jack smiled. He wondered if the things Camelin thought of as *practical* might be things Nora wouldn't approve of. If Jack could only use his magic on the gang it would solve all his problems but he knew he couldn't.

PERU PUBLIC LIBRARY
102 East Main Street
Peru, Indiana

That really would be something Nora wouldn't approve of. Camelin looked expectantly at Jack.

'You won't tell then?'

'No I won't, but be careful; remember you got your wand taken away last time you decided to experiment on your own. Anyway, I've got some news for you, Elan and I saw four fairies this afternoon.'

'Humph! Fairies. Noisy creatures. Never stop talking… they're worse than Timmery.'

'You've seen them?'

'You don't have to see them to hear them, I stay well away.'

'Well they saved Elan and me when those boys tried to ambush us.'

'Ambush! Where?'

'In the field near the stile, they've been bothering us all day in town.'

'I'll get a watch put on them, don't you worry, leave it to me.'

'Thanks but I don't want you getting into trouble.'

'I won't, trust me.'

'I suppose I'd better be off now. See you tomorrow?'

'Are you sure you can spare the time now Elan's back?'

'I'll come over and we can do something together. OK?'

'OK.'

Jack left Camelin admiring his tidy loft. He made his way back to the kitchen and collected his letter.

'I'll be off now.'

'How do you fancy blackberry picking tomorrow morning?' asked Nora.

'Can Camelin come too? I just said we could do something together tomorrow, he was feeling a bit left out today.'

'Of course he can, he likes picking blackberries.'

Jack wondered if Camelin would be pleased. He liked picking to eat but collecting was another thing altogether. Maybe Nora would let him eat a few.

'We'll arrange with your grandad for you to stay at the end of the month when we go back to Annwn,' said Nora as he reached the patio door.

Jack had to sidestep quickly as Medric burst into the kitchen, cackled loudly and dashed out again.

'How many have hatched now?' asked Jack.

'Eight,' replied Nora, 'only two more to go. I was going to take you over to see them but I think we'll leave it for a while, at least until Medric's calmed down.'

37

'Is there anything I can get for them?'

Elan smiled.

'Names!'

'Names?'

'We need ten names but we don't know yet how many are males and how many are females. In his haste to give us the good news, Medric forgot to tell us.'

'Won't Gerda and Medric want to name them?'

'Gerda asked us to do it, as a thank you for rescuing Medric.'

'I'll have a think,' said Jack.

'If we all make a list maybe Gerda and Medric can choose the ones they like best,' suggested Elan.

'That's a great idea,' replied Jack. 'See you tomorrow.'

As Jack went through the hedge he felt grateful that he had a safe way to get to and from Ewell House. No matter what Elan said he was still worried about Max and the others and he knew that if he bumped into them when he was on his own he wouldn't be able to stand up to them. If only there was a way to stop them, but without magic he was powerless. He'd been looking forward to the holidays and hoped the boys weren't going to spoil it. He promised himself he'd try to forget about them and concentrate on other more important things, like names for the ten goslings, and his next visit to Annwn. Elan had said it was only a formality to prove he was the rightful king but he ought to find out more. As soon as he was alone he'd ask his Book of Shadows.

He could hear Grandad's radio before he left the tunnel. The Test Match was still on. At least with the *no talking rule* Grandad wouldn't be asking him any awkward questions. He needn't have worried; Grandad was asleep in the chair. Jack wrote a three-word note… *in my bedroom…* and trapped the corner under the empty lemonade glass. He raced upstairs and got out his Book of Shadows but before he opened it he took out his letter from Annwn and showed it to Orin.

REGISTRATION DAY

'Can I go blackberry picking with Elan and Nora this morning?' Jack asked at breakfast.

'Of course you can, there's nothing quite like Nora's blackberry pie. Could you give me a hand this afternoon at the Cricket Club? It's registration day and I could do with some help.'

'Registration day?'

'For the buggy race, but I'm forgetting, you'd have been too young to remember the last one you went to. It's been going for years, since before I was a lad.'

Grandad went over to the dresser and picked up a sheet of paper.

'Here's the poster. The race takes place on

Monument Hill. The whole village gets closed to traffic for the afternoon.'

'Monument Hill?'

'It's over at Lillerton, in the next village, you know, the hill you can see from my bedroom window with the spike on the top.'

Grandad sat back and folded his arms. He had a faraway look in his eyes.

'Ah! The buggy race! It was the highlight of my year when I was a lad. It would start at the top of Monument Hill and end up in a field at the bottom where the biggest fair of the year always took place. The race and fair are on separate weekends now. It's a lot more complicated these days with all kinds of rules and regulations. There's an entry fee for the race, a form to be filled in, and an information pack to sign for. As I said, a lot more complicated than it used to be. Only ten to fifteen year olds can enter the race but the team is allowed an adult to help with the construction. They use the bridleway now that goes around Lillerton. Runners, and horse riders usually use it, but on Race Day it's given over to the buggies. It's been turned into a cross-country event with lots of difficult terrain. The end's the same though, with a downhill stretch from the top of Monument Hill to the field at the bottom.'

'Did you ever do it?'

'I should say so! Our team won three years in a row. We called each buggy we made, the *Comet*. We would have won four but one year our buggy was sabotaged.'

'Sabotaged! How?'

'Someone loosened one of the back wheels. We'd only just set off down the hill when the back end dropped to one side, I had trouble keeping the buggy straight and the next thing you know, one of the wheels went bouncing past. My best friend, who was riding the tail gate, jumped off and ran after it, but it was no good, we'd lost too much time.'

'Did you find out who did it?'

'Oh yes, they even bragged about it afterwards. It was the Smedley boys and their mate Archie Wratten, they're still around now, always caused trouble they did, and from what I hear, their grandsons aren't much better.'

Jack knew exactly who they were. It made him feel a lot better to know Grandad knew about Max and Tank. Maybe he ought to tell him they'd been bothering him. Jack decided not to say anything, he felt sure if he didn't deal with it himself they might never leave him alone.

'What about Dad? Did he have a buggy?'

'No, your dad wasn't interested in anything sporty, always had his head in a book.'

Jack looked at the poster again before helping Grandad clear the table and wash the dishes. The race sounded great but Jack had no idea how to build a buggy and he didn't have enough friends to make a team. Even without reading the rules and regulations, he was sure, ravens, rats, bats and dragons wouldn't be allowed as team members.

'I'll see you later,' Jack called from the hall as he put on his backpack.

'Bring Elan back for lunch if you like.'

'Can she come and help at the Cricket Club?'

'If she wants to, the more the merrier, I say.'

Jack felt slightly guilty. He'd not be able to invite Camelin back for lunch or to help register the teams. Telling him he wasn't included again wouldn't be easy.

'Take your hat,' Grandad called, as Jack was about to leave. 'You don't want to get too much sun on the back of your neck. It's a slow business picking blackberries.'

Jack picked up the new white floppy cricket hat Grandad had bought him. On the front was the

Glasruhen Cricket Club badge. Jack smiled as he looked at the logo. It was the silhouette of a sturdy oak tree; several grew in the grounds of the cricket club where a great forest of oaks once stood.

'See you later,' Jack shouted back as he put on his new hat so Grandad would see he'd taken it.

Jack thought about names for the goslings as he walked through the tunnel to the bottom of Nora's garden. It was harder than he'd expected, especially since he hadn't seen them yet. The only idea he'd had was to make the last two letters of the gosling's names the same as Medric and Gerda. Finding ten names between them shouldn't be too hard. As he approached the hole in the hedge Jack heard Saige croaking. He was too far away to hear what she'd said but he presumed Camelin would be nearby. He wasn't wrong. As he entered the garden he saw Camelin perched on top of the rockery.

'And how many girl goslings are there?'

'Four,' came Saige's reply.

Jack smiled. If anyone would know the answer to that question Saige would.

'Six boy goslings then,' said Jack as he joined them.

'How do you know? Have you been asking Saige questions?'

'No, it's easy to work out.'

Camelin humphed and looked annoyed.

'You just take four from ten and you get six.'

'I know, I know, it's just that I haven't thought of many goose boy names yet.'

'What have you thought of?'

'Cherry, Honey, Olive and Candy for the girls. Kebab and Bacon for the boys.'

'But they're all food names and you can't have Kebab and Bacon.'

'It's not your choice, Gerda and Medric can choose and I happen to know Gerda likes Bacon.'

'To eat maybe, but I'm not sure she'd choose it as a name for one of her boys.'

'What are your brilliant suggestions then?'

Jack thought rapidly.

'Edric, Cedric and Brodric, Freda, Rhoda and Ada.'

'Oh what lovely names!' exclaimed Nora as she joined them. 'Don't you agree Elan.'

'That's really clever Jack, I'm sure we can think of some more names with those endings. What about you, Camelin? Have you thought of any names?'

'No,' grumbled Camelin, 'I'm not clever like Jack.'

'I'm sure you could think of at least one if you tried,' coaxed Nora.

'Garlic,' croaked Camelin as he fixed Jack with his eye, 'that ends in *ic.*'

Better than Kebab or Bacon, thought Jack, but only just.

'Are you ready to collect the blackberries now?' asked Nora, as she took four bowls out of the basket she was carrying.

Jack hoped they weren't going back to Silver Hill, even in daylight.

'Are we going far?'

Elan laughed.

'Only to the far end of the kitchen garden, the bushes there are laden with fruit but it will probably take us till lunchtime to pick enough.'

'They're for picking, not eating,' Nora reminded Camelin.

'It's not my fault. It's not easy picking blackberries with a beak without squashing them. You wouldn't want me to put squashed fruit in the bowl would you?'

'It doesn't matter today as it's all going to be made into blackberry jelly.'

Camelin didn't look too happy. Jack knew he'd be

even more disgruntled when he found out that he was going to be busy at the Cricket Club all afternoon and that Elan was invited to lunch but he wasn't. Jack got a chance to speak to Elan when Camelin moved away.

'I've got to go home for lunch today because I'm helping Grandad at the Cricket Club all afternoon. You can come too if you like and Grandad said you can have lunch with us.'

'That would be great. Have you told Camelin yet?'

'No, I wanted to see if you were coming first before telling him anything.'

'He'll be fine, he can help Nora with the blackberries.' Elan turned towards Nora, 'I'm going back for lunch with Jack and won't be back till late this afternoon.'

'Lunch!' croaked Camelin excitedly. 'Already?'

'No,' replied Nora, 'it's lunchtime for you when your bowl's full.'

Jack could hear Camelin grumbling under his breath. Both his and Elan's bowls were already full.

'Can you leave them on the kitchen table for me?' said Nora. 'I'll stay a bit longer and help fill the other bowl. Tell your grandad there'll be a pot of blackberry jelly and a pie for him in a couple of days.'

47

After lunch, Jack walked down the back lane with Elan and Grandad. Jack was lost in thought as Elan chatted to Grandad about the goslings. He was cross with himself for forgetting to ask about the Druid's library his Book of Shadows had told him about. He'd presumed it would be in the palace in Annwn but his book might have meant Nora's library. He might get a chance to ask Elan while they were in the pavilion. Crystal magic was something he wanted to know a lot more about. Any hope of talking to Elan disappeared when Jack saw the length of the queue at the Cricket Club.

'Stand back,' said Grandad as he produced the key for the pavilion.

The crowd started to move forward until Grandad turned and held up his hand. 'Doors open in ten minutes, two o' clock, like it says on the notice board.'

A murmur of disappointment ran through the queue. Grandad seemed very excited.

'There's more than last year. It's going to take a while to get through that lot.'

Grandad wasn't wrong. There was barely time for him to show Jack and Elan where to sit and tell them what to do before he went to open the door. Grandad sat at a table near the entrance and collected the registration fees. Elan and Jack were in charge of the forms and information packs. By the time the room had emptied Elan had over thirty team names on her list. Grandad looked at his watch.

'Ten minutes to go. That was quite a turnout. They'll not all be in the race. Some of them just go in for the best looking buggy. You get some strange looking karts. Last year's winner looked like a pirate ship, mast, flag, and all. Can you two manage here while I start bagging this lot up ready for the bank?'

'That's fine,' said Elan, 'I'm sure Jack and I can manage now.'

Grandad picked up the cash box. Jack waited until he'd gone through the door before speaking to Elan.

'I had a dream last night about Velindur, more of a nightmare really.'

'Oooh! Pixie Boy gets nightmares does he?'

Jack swallowed hard. He hadn't seen or heard anyone come in but Max and Tank were now standing in front of the table towering above them. Elan picked up a pen and looked straight at Max.

'Fee first, and then fill in this form please.'

Tank thumped both his hands on the table and glowered at Elan.

'You fill it in.'

'That's not a problem if you can't write,' replied Elan as she held out her hand. 'But I'll need your registration fee first.'

Jack held his breath; he thought Tank was about to explode but Max pushed him out of the way and threw his money onto the table.

'If we don't get a move on we won't get registered, you made us late already.'

Elan offered Max a form and a pen. He ripped the form out of her hand and went over to one of the tables to fill it in. Tank didn't move. He stared at both of them in turn then moved his head closer to Jack's.

'Shame you and your girlfriend aren't entering, we'd show you what a real buggy can do.'

'Oh but we are entering,' replied Elan.

Jack stared at her, wide-eyed. Entering against Max and his gang in a buggy race wasn't something Jack had been planning to do. They didn't even have a team or a name for a buggy.

'Wouldn't bother if I were you, Freckles, we know who's gonna win, don't we Max!'

Tank nodded as he chuckled to himself. Jack did his best to stare back but he knew Tank could see the fear in his eyes. Max brought the form back but instead of handing it to Elan he held it up and let go of it. They all watched it float down to the table. When it landed Jack could see the name of Max's buggy, it wasn't something anyone could miss. Written in big capital letters was the word *TERMINATOR*. Max smoothed his long blond hair back from his face before fixing his eyes on Jack.

'So… what's your buggy called Pixie Boy?'

'The *Comet*,' said Grandad as he came through the door.

Max and Tank turned quickly and without another word left the pavilion. Jack realised he'd been holding his breath. Grandad added Max's fee to his cash box and got out his wallet.

'Just time to register our buggy before it's time to shut up shop.'

'But Grandad, we haven't got a team.'

'I'll help,' said Elan.

'Good lass, and so will I,' replied Grandad. 'But I'm afraid we're stuck with the name *Comet* now.'

'But we still need another team member,' said Jack.

Grandad patted him on the shoulder.

'Don't worry about that, I'm sure one of your friends will want to help when they know you're going to be in the race.'

Jack wasn't so sure. His best friends weren't going to be able to help even if they wanted to and they would have to build the buggy without any magic or it wouldn't be fair. At least Grandad would know what he was doing. Elan gave him a smile.

'It'll be fun.'

Grandad nodded in agreement before closing the door.

'Let's sort these forms out before Don arrives. He's going to give me a lift down to the bank; we don't keep any money here, not since those break-ins a few weeks back. You can come along if you want.'

'If you don't mind, Jack was going to come back to Ewell House; he wanted to look something up in Nora's library.'

'That's fine, and if those boys bother you again, just you let me know.'

Jack tried to give Grandad his best smile but inside he didn't feel too good. As he and Elan left the Cricket Club he realised he hadn't said anything to Elan about the library.

'How did you know I wanted to use Nora's books?'

'Good guess… when you mentioned Velindur I thought you'd have a question you couldn't find the answer to in your Book of Shadows… correct?'

'Correct.'

As they walked the short distance from the Cricket Club to the front door of Ewell House, Jack told Elan about his dream and the strange message he'd received. Elan looked puzzled.

'Hmm! The Druid's library… you won't find what you're looking for in Nora's books or the palace library in Annwn. Your message is referring to a very ancient place.'

'You mean there's another Druid's library!'

'Oh yes, it's where Nora got a lot of the information from for her books. It was traditional for every Druid to write at least one book in order to preserve their knowledge. Once it was finished it would be taken to Falconrock. The library there is much bigger than the one in Annwn and it's unique. Most people think the Druids didn't write things down, they'd get quite a shock if they knew how many books had been written over the years.'

'But I thought Nora was the only Druid left on earth.'

'She is, the librarian at Falconrock isn't a Druid, she's a Sylph, a nymph of the air. Her name is Cloda. She's an archivist, which means she's the guardian of ancient knowledge and a keeper of secrets. She'll be able to tell you how to find out about crystal magic.'

'That's brilliant.'

'Well it is and it isn't.'

'Why?'

'Falconrock is a very special place but it's hidden from the mortal world. No one can enter the library unless they can open the door and to do that you need a golden acorn and a special key.'

Jack's hand went up to the chains around his neck.

'I've got both. Does that mean I can get in?'

'I suppose it does, but it's something you can only do on your own, without any help, and once you enter the library you have to go through a labyrinth to get out again. I think we need to go and talk to Nora about this.'

'Couldn't Camelin come with me?'

'No, only one person at a time is allowed to enter the library and since Camelin doesn't have a Druid's acorn or a special key either you really would be on your own.'

Jack didn't think Camelin would be too happy about that but it was only going to be a quick visit to a library, he wouldn't be gone long. Jack couldn't wait to find out what Nora had to say.

INVESTITURE

Jack and Elan found Nora in the kitchen when they arrived back at Ewell House. The smell of freshly cut mint filled the room.

'I didn't expect you back so soon,' said Nora.

'Jack wants to find out more about crystal magic.'

Nora's eyebrows rose slightly.

'I knew you'd want to visit Falconrock one day but I didn't expect it to be so soon. Is there a special reason?'

'My Book of Shadows told me I need to look in the Druid's library. Elan said it was at Falconrock.'

'It is, but it's hidden, and I'm bound by secrecy not to tell anyone how to get there, not even you.

Falconrock is an ancient place. A long time ago it would have had at least one visitor every day. Druids brought knowledge to the archivist or went to seek answers. There's a rule in the library, known to every Druid. Books with visible titles on their spines are available for anyone to use but books with blank spines are special. They will only reveal their secrets to those who are worthy. Each journey is different and you cannot leave by the door through which you entered. It's a one-way trip and not for the fainthearted, you never know what you might find in the labyrinth. If you make it through to the outer door whatever knowledge you discover inside will be yours to keep forever. If you get lost and need a guide, you'll forfeit anything you may have learnt.'

'Will I be able to open the door with my key?'

'You can open any door, your key just turns the lock, but before you can enter the library you have to find it. There's one last thing you need to know. Once you step onto Falconrock, magic won't help you. You'll need to trust your instincts and make good judgements.'

None of Nora's words had weakened Jack's resolve. He just knew it was something he had to do. He looked pleadingly at Nora.

'When can we go?'

'If you've not got anything else planned, you could go tomorrow. It's not far; you can fly there with Camelin.'

'But I thought you said I'd be on my own?'

'You will be once you get to the rock. Camelin can wait for you by the exit.'

Jack let out a long slow breath. At last he would get some answers. He had no idea what might be inside the labyrinth but having come face to face with Velindur, a fire-breathing dragon, and a fearsome Draygull, he thought he was probably better prepared than most to face whatever it might hold. Jack's thoughts were interrupted by Camelin's arrival through the patio doors. He swerved round Nora and did a figure of eight before landing gracefully on the back of one of the chairs.

'Glad you could join us,' said Nora. 'You know we've got a busy afternoon.'

Camelin humphed.

'You've got plenty of help now Jack and Elan are back.'

Nora shook her head and frowned.

'I need you to take this bucket and find at least twenty grubs. You know the Dorysk has a healthy appetite.'

'Why can't Jack do it?'

Elan laughed.

'You're the best grub collector – Jack wouldn't have a clue where to look.'

'That's true,' said Camelin as he hopped down to the floor and opened his beak for the bucket.

'Thanks,' said Jack when Camelin had gone, 'I really wouldn't know where to look. Why grubs?'

Nora smiled and passed Jack a selection of cutlery so he could help lay the table.

'It's the Dorysk's investiture as an officer of the Night Guard later this afternoon. It would be rude not to have his favourite food on the table.'

Jack wrinkled his nose.

'Will they be… wriggling?'

Elan laughed.

'Just don't eat the little green parcels. It's Nora's special recipe, but grubs wrapped in mint leaves aren't my idea of a feast either.'

'Does that mean I'm invited too?'

'Of course you are,' said Nora. 'I did mention it to your grandad but you'd better go back and remind him you're staying for tea. You can collect your wand and Orin at the same time. Didn't your grandad say anything to you about sleeping here for a couple of nights?'

'No, but it was so busy this afternoon at the Cricket Club we didn't get a chance to say much at all.'

'He's got a really busy week coming up, it's the local flower show next weekend and he's got to help set up the marquee. I suggested you might like to stay for a couple of nights this week and the whole of next weekend.'

'That'll be great, thanks.'

'What'll be great?' asked Camelin as he shuffled in with the bucket.

Nora looked inside before replying.

'Jack's coming to stay for a couple of nights.'

'Aw great! Can we go out flying?'

'You can, in fact you can go tomorrow.'

'On our own, without Elan?' asked Camelin as he winked at Jack.

'Yes, without me. You'll be going over to Falconrock.'

Camelin sighed.

'I had plans.'

'And so does Jack,' said Nora.

Jack shrugged his shoulders and tried to give Camelin an apologetic look.

'I need to visit the library.'

'Whatever for, aren't there enough books here?'

Nora frowned.

'That's enough. If you don't want to show Jack the way to Falconrock Elan can.'

Camelin raised his head and gave Nora his superior look.

'Jack can't transform without me.'

'That means I'll be naked!' groaned Jack. 'Isn't there a spell I can use so I don't have to wander around without any clothes on?'

Nora nodded.

'It's not a spell as such; you have to learn how to visualise.'

'Visualise?' asked Jack.

'I can teach you but it's not easy. It can sometimes take years of practice to get it right but I'm sure you'll get the hang of it.'

'Didn't you know, he's a natural,' muttered Camelin.

Jack ignored him and spoke directly to Nora.

'If you show me how, I'll practise till I get it right.'

Camelin humphed again and grumbled under his breath.

'You can watch if you want to,' said Jack.

Nora picked up the bucket and tipped the grubs out into a dish.

'Off you go to your grandad's and I'll sort out these little delicacies. By the time you get back we should be ready to start.'

'Don't eat anything that's wrapped up,' Camelin warned Jack as he reached the kitchen door, 'you never know what might be inside.'

'I won't,' Jack assured him.

By the time Jack and Elan returned to the kitchen the table was laden with all kinds of food. Jack could see several dishes at one end of the table, each piled high with tiny leaf parcels. In Camelin's place was his favourite bowl, already full of his favourite things.

'Nora said I could choose first if I helped,' explained Camelin when he saw Jack looking at his bowl.

'I didn't mean before everyone arrived,' said Nora.

'I don't have to put it all back do I?'

'Eurgh! No!' replied Elan. 'We don't know where your beak's been.'

Camelin puffed out his chest feathers.

'I'll have you know I keep my beak perfectly clean.'

Jack smiled. He didn't think it was the right time to remind Camelin about the pizza cheese that quite often got stuck on it.

'Any sign of the Dorysk?' asked Nora.

Jack heard a loud buzzing and a tiny voice.

'Did someone mention my name?'

He watched as the Dorysk shape shifted twice in mid-air before his feet touched the floor. His usual prickly form hurried over to Nora. He bowed low to her, then to Elan and finally to Jack.

'What about me? Don't I get a bow?' grumbled Camelin.

The Dorysk ignored him and offered Jack something very small. Jack could barely hold it between his finger and thumb.

'What is it?'

'For the great Jack Brenin, an invitation,' replied the Dorysk as he bowed again.

Camelin frowned and began muttering to himself.

'*The great Jack Brenin*, what about *the magnificent Camelin?*'

'Oh you're not included. I was instructed to give it to Jack.'

Camelin hunched his wings and glowered at the Dorysk. Jack held the paper up to the light and tried to examine it more closely. Nora got out her wand.

'I think we need to make this a bit bigger so you can see what it says, don't you?'

She carefully aimed at Jack's fingers. As she whispered, *Amplio*, the tiny paper began to grow until Jack could see it was a small delicate envelope. The front was covered in strange writing. Camelin flew up onto Jack's shoulder to get a better look.

'Not again, doesn't anyone use proper letters? What was the point of me learning my alphabet when no one else uses it?'

'It's fairy script,' explained Nora. 'If you'd paid more attention over the years you'd have recognised it.'

'Fairies,' grumbled Camelin, 'worse than Timmery for twittering and wittering, usually about nothing.'

'And how would you know that?' asked Nora, 'I didn't know you'd shared food with them.'

Jack smiled as Camelin tried to put on his innocent look. If Camelin had sampled fairy food, it would explain his warning about the small green parcels. He could ask Camelin about it later when they were alone. Right now, Jack was too excited; his heart was racing as he looked at the writing on the front of the envelope.

'I can tell you what it says,' said the Dorysk, 'I'm an expert in all kinds of languages both written and spoken.'

Camelin rolled his eyes but Nora shook her head.

'I think we'll let Jack try to read it first.'

Jack concentrated hard on the letters. As he scrunched his eyes he found he could read the words…

To
The Great
Jack Brenin

'Oh well done Jack,' said Nora.

'Well done Jack, well done Jack, it's always well done Jack,' grumbled Camelin. 'Open it up, oh great one, and read what it says.'

Jack turned the envelope over. It was similar to the one he'd had from Annwn but instead of a letter *A* under the seal, there were two capital letters on either side of a white flower.

'*M M*?' he read before looking at Nora.

'Meadow Mound,' she explained. 'If it was FM it would be Forest Mound, fairies always put the initials of the meeting place on the back. Each mound has its own special symbol too.'

Jack showed it to Nora.

'That's definitely from the fairy mound in the meadow.'

Jack carefully broke the seal. As the flower split in

two a cloud of sparkling dust cascaded to the floor. Jack could see every colour of the rainbow in it as it fell.

'Hmm! Fairies,' grumbled Camelin.

'What's it say Jack?' asked Elan.

He screwed his eyes up and concentrated on the letters.

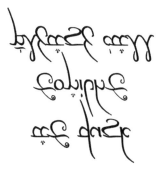

'Please call tonight at dusk.'

'Who taught you how to do that?' asked Camelin.

'No one; if you concentrated hard you'd be able to read it too. It's upside down and back to front!'

Camelin tossed his beak in the air and flew over to the windowsill.

'Why does everyone get excited at the mention of fairies?'

No one answered, but Jack knew Camelin was right, he felt excited at the prospect of being able to see the Fair Folk who lived in the meadow. The Dorysk coughed and bowed low again to Jack.

'I'm invited too and I can be your guide.'

'That would be great, thanks.'

'Urgh! I'm glad they didn't invite me,' mumbled Camelin as he looked over at the pile of little green parcels on the table.

'We've got guests arriving,' said Elan.

They stood and watched as a group of rats, with Motley at the front, marched across the patio. Raggs hobbled along at the rear as he tried to keep up.

'Halt!' ordered Motley.

The rats obediently stood very still.

'All present and correct! Permission to enter?'

'Come in, come in,' said Nora. 'Everything's ready.'

Orin ran over to the patio and waited patiently while Motley dismissed the Night Guard. She went and sat with them, at the far end of the table, on the upturned beakers. Nora had placed a small cushion for the Dorysk to sit on at the head of their small table.

'Where's Timmery?' Jack whispered to Elan.

'He's coming along with the entertainment later, it's a surprise for the Dorysk.'

When everyone was seated, Nora tapped her glass with a spoon. Jack expected her to invite them all to eat but instead she thanked the Dorysk for all his help and listed his many skills. Camelin yawned loudly and looked longingly at his bowl.

'No one said anything about speeches,' he whispered in Jack's ear.

Motley stood up and carried on when Nora had finished and explained what an important asset the Dorysk would be to the Night Guard. When he'd finished, the Dorysk stood and bowed.

'I can't thank you enough for your friendship and kindness. It will be my honour to join the Night Guard, now Raggs has other duties.'

'Hold up your right paw,' ordered Motley. 'Do you swear to do your best at all times, to protect all who live in and around Ewell House, and to obey the rules and regulations of the Night Guard?'

'I do,' replied the Dorysk, solemnly.

A great cheer went up from everyone at the table, especially from Camelin, but Jack thought that was probably because he knew the speeches were now finished and they were going to be able to eat. Jack saw Camelin lower his beak until it was almost touching a large cheese sandwich, which was resting on the top of his pile of food. His beak remained open when Nora stood up again, nodded to Motley and began another speech.

'Thank you to one and all. It is my pleasure to invest Theodore Sniffler, Dorysk of Glasruhen, as a member of the Night Guard.'

Nora sat down and everyone clapped. They continued clapping as four dragonettes, one smaller than the others, burst into the kitchen and began a fiery aerobatic display. The smallest dragon landed between Jack and Camelin.

'Oh isn't this exciting, Nora's transformed me into a dragonette for the night,' Timmery explained. 'Wait till you see the next bit, I've been watching them practise, it's brilliant.'

Camelin humphed as the three dragonettes each flew in tight circles, breathing fire as they revolved. There was more applause as they hovered in front of the Dorysk and bowed their heads.

'Oh bravo, bravo!' he cried. 'I am so honoured.'

'And I'm so hungry,' grumbled Camelin.

'Shall we eat?' said Nora.

Camelin was already halfway down his bowl by the time Jack picked up his first ham sandwich.

'Oh wasn't that wonderful,' said the Dorysk as he and Jack walked down to the bottom of Nora's garden.

'It was,' replied Jack. 'Did you see Camelin's face when Nora told him he'd have to wait until everyone else had finished their meal before he could have a second helping?'

The Dorysk laughed and changed into a large beetle.

'It'll be easier to keep up with you if I fly, and it won't matter if we bump into anyone on the back lane.'

'Is there any way we can get to the meadow without having to go down the lane? There are some boys I really don't want to meet.'

'We could go through the fields if you like.'

'That'd be great. I didn't know you had a real name.'

'All Dorysks do. We keep them secret; names are very powerful things you know. You can still just call me Dorysk, there's only ever one in any area. We get together every so often and swap stories and information. That's how I ended up living next door to the fairies. They've always let us use their mound for our meetings and when I heard the badgers next door had moved out, I moved in. I sort of keep an eye on the place for them when they're not around.'

Jack could see they were nearly at a stile in the hedge. The fairy mound was in the next field. He began to feel a bit nervous. What would he say? There was also the small matter of having to eat something. Nora had given him a bag to deliver with some leftovers from the party, including the rest of the mint parcels. As they neared the mound he swallowed hard.

'What do I do? How am I going to get through the door?'

'Oh, don't worry about that, you'll be told what to do. Wait here.'

There was a quiet popping sound as the Dorysk changed back into his usual form. He shook his prickles before scurrying down the burrow. Jack heard a knock followed by the sound of the tiny fairy door opening and closing. Jack was alone in the meadow; he looked around, just in case they'd been followed, but the fields were empty. He looked up to see if Camelin was around, but he was nowhere to be seen. He lay on the grass, took out his wand and pointed it down the tunnel. Once the tip was glowing he could see the green arched door and the large silver doorknob. Last time he'd been to the mound he had leant forward, so he decided to put his head a bit further in. The doorknob rippled, two pointed ears popped out and a tuft of hair sprang from the top. Two small eyes, a nose, and a wide mouth followed.

'No feast tonight, so sorry. Goodbye.'

'I'm not here for a feast, I've been invited.'

'Name please?'

'Jack Brenin.'

'Ah! Would you be *The Great Jack Brenin*?'

'That's what it said on my invitation.'

'Your food will be delivered shortly. When you've eaten you can enter. Goodbye.'

Jack watched the features on the doorknob disappear. He extinguished the light from his wand, sat up and rested his back against the mound and watched the sun sinking behind Glasruhen Hill. He was beginning to wonder if anything was going to happen when the door creaked. The Dorysk came out of the tunnel carrying a large silver plate with a green leaf parcel on it. Jack gulped, he could see something fat and round had been wrapped up, but worse than that, it was wriggling.

'For you,' announced the Dorysk. 'Eat and enter.'

MEETINGS

The Dorysk came closer with the plate. Jack gripped his wand tightly and stared at the food. He'd been dreading this moment but if he wanted to meet the fairies he'd have to eat what they'd offered him.

'Close your eyes and swallow,' suggested the Dorysk, 'you'll have to eat it if you want to get through the door.'

Jack's throat was dry, he didn't have a drink, and he didn't know how he'd be able to swallow. The parcel moved again, it looked so big. Even picking it up made him shudder. Then a sudden thought struck him: he could shrink the parcel, just as he'd made Camelin's dustbin smaller to fit into his loft. Jack smiled at the Dorysk.

'Would you put the plate on the grass please, and step back.'

Jack took his wand and pointed it at the green package, '*Lunio,*' he commanded.

A faint blue light appeared from the tip and a tiny spark flew towards the plate. The green packet was instantly surrounded by dancing light and began to shrink. When it was the size of a pea, Jack stopped. Swallowing the parcel now wouldn't be so much of a problem. He reached over, picked it up quickly, popped it in his mouth, and swallowed. He immediately felt dizzy. There was a strange fizzing sensation inside him. He dropped his wand as he clutched his stomach.

'You won't be needing this for now,' said the Dorysk as he picked up Jack's wand. 'I'll pop it inside my house for safe keeping.'

Jack was powerless to do anything. He had the feeling the world was getting bigger until he realised he was shrinking. Was this supposed to happen? Had his shrinking spell somehow bounced back at him off the plate?

'Oh good!' exclaimed the Dorysk when he returned. 'Nearly done.'

'But I'm shrinking!'

'Of course you are, all part of the process, not

to worry, you'll be able to get through the door soon.'

Jack was relieved to know it wasn't something he'd done. He wondered just how small he was going to be but when he was the same size as the Dorysk, the shrinking stopped. Thankfully his clothes had shrunk too.

'Ready?' asked the Dorysk as he picked up the empty plate.

'I think so,' replied Jack as he got to his feet and followed the Dorysk towards the tunnel. He had to walk around a huge clump of daisies, which he hadn't even noticed before. Jack suddenly realised he'd been speaking to the Dorysk without having to use his wand.

'What's happening? How can I understand you?'

'From now on you'll be able to talk to any creature without using your wand. It's a special gift the fairies give to those who accept their invitation and eat the food they're offered.'

'Food!' exclaimed Jack, as he looked back at the enormous bag that Nora had asked him to deliver. It was far too big and heavy for him to carry now.

'Don't worry about that. Anything left outside a fairy mound automatically belongs to them, they'll be out soon to empty it.'

Jack hesitated outside the door. The face in the doorknob didn't stir. He knocked and waited.

'They won't be long,' explained the Dorysk. 'They'll be arguing about who's going to open it.'

Jack heard faint voices and footsteps, which got louder and louder. He tried to work out what they were saying but the voices were muffled. He jumped when the door opened suddenly, revealing three young girls, all very much alike. For once, Jack wasn't the smallest; the two taller fairies only came up to the bottom of his chin. Their long frizzy hair cascaded over their shoulders, two were blonde and one was auburn. They all had pale lips, turned-up noses and fair skin. Elan had been right; they did look like the Dryads, only younger and considerably smaller. They grinned at Jack and then looked at each other for a few seconds. Jack wondered if he was supposed to speak first.

'Thank you for inviting me,' he said as he bowed.

Instead of replying the three fairies giggled, huddled their heads together and whispered.

'Don't you know it's very rude to whisper?' commented the Dorysk.

The whispering stopped but the giggling returned until the taller fairy, the one with long auburn hair, stepped forward. She looked like a miniature Elan but without the freckles. Her dress was pink and dark red and she wore a hat made from crimson petals. The Dorysk went and stood by her side.

'This is Rhoda, she is here to represent all the garden fairies. She lives in the rhododendrons in your grandad's garden.'

Rhoda giggled again before speaking.

'Forgive us; we don't get many human visitors.'

Jack held out his hand and shook Rhoda's.

'This is Netty,' continued the Dorysk as the other tall fairy, dressed in green, pushed Rhoda out of the way. She didn't wait for Jack to extend his hand; instead she took it and shook it vigorously.

'I was chosen to come by the fairies who live in the meadows and waysides. I live in the nettles in the back lane.'

'Pleased to meet you,' said Jack.

The smallest fairy peeped around Netty's shoulder. Her pale dress sparkled even though there wasn't any sunlight in the tunnel. Instead of a hat she wore a circular headdress similar to those worn by the Dryads.

'Come out Twinkle, don't be shy,' said the Dorysk.

Netty let go of Jack's hand and stepped aside.

'Please, call me Twink, I live in the eyebright flowers on Glasruhen Hill, I'm here to represent the moors and mountains.'

Jack smiled at Twink as he shook her hand. He instantly liked her.

'You'd better come in,' said Rhoda, 'we've got lots to talk about and there's food on the table.'

'Thank you but I've already eaten.'

The three fairies giggled again.

'That wasn't a grub you ate,' said Netty. 'There wasn't anything inside the parcel, you just thought there was.'

'But I saw it wriggling!'

'An illusion,' explained Rhoda. 'We don't like eating bugs and grubs, not like the Dorysk.'

Jack felt very relieved. The Dorysk put his head on one side and smiled.

'I like my food fresh, not to everyone's liking I know, but each to his own.'

Jack followed Rhoda down a dimly lit, well-made tunnel. Occasionally they had to step over roots that poked through the earthen floor or duck under those that had grown through the roof.

'Nearly there,' Netty told him as they approached a bend.

Jack could see a brighter light ahead and heard many voices. He stepped out of the tunnel into a large chamber. Flames flickered from rush lights that had been placed inside brackets around the room. There were fairies everywhere, too many for Jack to count.

'This is why the Queen asked only three of us to meet you,' explained Netty. 'There's rather a lot of us when we get together.'

'The Queen?' asked Jack.

All three fairies exchanged looks and Rhoda giggled again before speaking.

'The Queen of the Fair Folk.'

'You mean Elan, but I thought she was Queen of Annwn.'

'And of Fairies, Brownies, Elves, Dorysks, even Bogies but they're usually in the *Not So Fair Folk* category,' explained Netty.

'The Bogie Peabody isn't as bad as he used to be,' interrupted Twink.

'Oh Twink!' said Rhoda. 'You've been in Newton Gill again haven't you?'

'He's lonely, I just go to keep him company, and besides, he knows all the gossip.'

The Dorysk coughed politely.

'Shall we go next door?'

'A good idea,' replied Rhoda, 'it won't be as noisy in there.'

Jack was led into a smaller chamber where large cushions had been scattered on the floor. A low table was piled high with all kinds of lovely looking food. The walls sparkled in the flickering candlelight. Netty motioned for Jack to sit down. He noticed the designs on the cushions also twinkled in the light and when he sat on one he found it luxuriously soft.

'Thistle down,' explained the Dorysk when he saw Jack's expression. 'It's softer than feathers. I've got one at home, Twink made it for me, didn't you Twink.'

Jack watched as the smallest fairy blushed.

'Welcome to my room,' she said. 'We each have a room here to use in bad weather but we prefer to be outdoors if we can.'

'Your grandad has a magnificent garden,' said Rhoda.

'And Nora does too,' added Netty.

'Would you like some food?' asked Rhoda.

Jack looked at the Dorysk.

'It's alright, there are only sweet things here.'

'We use a lot of honey, we're good friends with all the bees in Glasruhen,' explained Netty.

Jack thought about the bee that had come to his

and Elan's rescue in the meadow.

'Elan said it was fairies from this mound who came to help us the other day.'

'That was Speedy and some of the buttercup fairies from the meadow,' said Rhoda.

'Well, please give them my thanks.'

'You did that at the time but I'll tell them again. And please remember not to call her Speedy if you ever meet her, she hates it.'

'What should I call her? I wouldn't want to upset anyone.'

'She lives in the speedwell flowers in the meadow but her name is Veronica and she insists we call her that.'

'She's really bad tempered,' explained Twink. 'She spends most of her time as a bee these days. It happens to all of us when we get annoyed but most things make Speedy cross.'

Jack became aware that everyone was eating. He leant over and picked up a small green cube. He resisted the urge to sniff it before popping it into his mouth. The fairies giggled and the Dorysk smiled.

'Nice?' asked Netty.

'Delicious,' replied Jack.

When the table was empty the Dorysk stood up.

'We ought to be going. We don't want Jack's grandad to worry.'

'Please call again,' said Twink. 'It's been lovely to meet you.'

'Will I always be able to see you now?' Jack asked.

'Of course you will,' replied Rhoda. 'We'll be here to help you in whatever way we can, should the need arise. I'll come back to Brenin House with you. It's a fine night and the scent in your grandad's garden on a summer's evening is wonderful.'

As they left the mound they passed a long procession of fairies, each carrying something from the bag Nora had given him. They all smiled at him as they walked by.

The Dorysk scurried around the mound and came back with Jack's wand before bowing low. As soon as Jack touched it he began to grow. A strange rushing sensation travelled though his body as he got bigger. His mind flashed back to Camelin's *bigging* spell and hoped he would stop when he reached the right height. But he needn't have worried, seconds later he was back to his usual self.

'Thanks,' Jack whispered. 'I'd love to come back and see you all again.'

Jack watched as the now tiny Rhoda shut her

eyes and raised her arms. He blinked as a tiny bright light exploded; when he looked again, Rhoda had a pair of beautiful red and black wings. Her body was a lot smaller than before and to anyone else she would have appeared to be a butterfly. Jack looked at her in amazement. They didn't talk as they made their way back to Grandad's house. When they reached the gate, Rhoda fluttered around Jack's head a few times before flying off towards one of the flowerbeds that was full of brightly coloured flowers.

'Is that you Jack?' Grandad called from the pantry, 'I'm just making myself a spot of supper. Do you want some too?'

'No thanks, I'm not hungry; I had a lot to eat earlier. Do you mind if I go upstairs?'

'You carry on, and don't forget to pack some overnight things.'

'I won't,' Jack assured him.

'At the weekend we'll start getting the things together to make that buggy. What d'you say to that?'

'That'd be great but we're still a team member short.'

'I'll ask at the Cricket Club. There's bound to be some young lad who'd be happy to join our team.'

'Thanks Grandad, I'll see you in the morning.'

'Why don't you ask Elan if she'd like to come along to the flower show next weekend? It would be best to come on the Sunday afternoon as there'll be more going on then.'

'Thanks, I'll ask her,' Jack replied before he left the kitchen. He took the stairs two at a time. Jack wished Orin hadn't stayed at Ewell House; he wanted to share his news and see if he really could understand her without his wand. His room was dark but even darker was the familiar shape that sat hunched on his windowsill.

'What are you doing here?' Jack whispered as he let Camelin in.

'Well that's a nice welcome. Can't a raven boy come and visit a fellow raven boy without an interrogation?'

'I just wasn't expecting you.'

'What happened at the mound?'

'Oh it was wonderful,' began Jack, then realised that probably wasn't very tactful. 'But you were right, they do make a lot of noise.'

'Don't say I didn't warn you. Did any of them mention me?'

'No, should they have?'

'Well, a long time ago I sort of ate one of their little green packages. I didn't know it was fairy food at the time, one of them must have dropped it and as every raven knows, if there's food left unattended it belongs to whoever finds it.'

'You mean you ate it.'

Camelin hung his head

'Only realised what it was once I'd swallowed it.'

'Did you shrink?'

'Certainly not! Did you?'

'I did but I was invited and the only way I could get through the door was to shrink.'

Camelin gave Jack a half glower.

'Fairies,' he grumbled.

'They were very nice, especially Twink.'

'Oooh! On first name terms now are we?'

'I was introduced. Can you see them?'

'Yep, and hear them. Don't see anything to get excited about.'

'They gave me a gift...'

'What kind of a gift?'

'A special one, I can hear and understand any creature now.'

'What's so special about that, you could do that already.'

'Without a wand.'

Jack could see Camelin was impressed even though he tried not to show it.

'I'll tell Nora when I get back. You'd better get some sleep, we're going to Falconrock in the morning, just the two of us, so don't go inviting any of your new friends to join us.'

'I won't.'

'Especially not the Dorysk, he's got a nasty habit now of turning up when I least expect it. Since he's joined the Night Guard, I swear he's spying on me.'

Jack smiled. Soon Camelin wouldn't be able to keep any secrets from Nora. A loud knock on the kitchen door interrupted Jack's thoughts. They both listened.

'Nora,' grumbled Camelin as he hopped back onto the windowsill. 'She said she'd come round later with a pie and a pot of blackberry jelly. She'll have heard you were back from the trees.'

'I'll see you tomorrow then.'

'It'll be great, just us two.'

'Nora said I've got to find the library on my own. I'll ask my Book of Shadows; there might be some helpful information in there.'

'You don't need to look in there, you've got me.'

'But Nora said I had to do it on my own.'

'I've been lots of times with her, she's made me promise not to tell you the way but she didn't say I couldn't do any ravenphore.'

'Ravenphore?'

'You know! The signals they do with flags, only I do it with my wings and beak.'

Camelin hopped onto Jack's round table and gave him a demonstration of a technique he'd obviously been working on. First he raised his left wing, then his right. Jack almost laughed when he thrust his head forward and stared into the distance. He pointed his beak down, then up.

'What d'you think?'

'Brilliant.'

'There's more…'

'More!'

'Yep, if you've gone too far I'll do this,' explained Camelin as he pirouetted around and rotated his beak at the same time. 'And if you have to go underground I'll do this.'

Jack bit his lip to stop himself from laughing out loud as Camelin put his head down and pulled his wings back.

'Last one coming up,' said Camelin as he put both his wings over his eyes.

'What's that one?'

'Watch out! I hope I don't have to do that one tomorrow.'

'Me too! See you in the morning.'

Without waiting for a reply Camelin took off. Nora and Grandad were still talking downstairs so Jack got out his Book of Shadows, put his hand on the front and thought carefully before asking his question. He already knew he needed his golden acorn and special key but Nora had implied that finding the library was going to be the hardest part. He wasn't going to be able to take his wand, which meant he'd have to rely on his instincts. Any help his Book might give him would be invaluable. He took a deep breath and let out a long slow sigh before speaking.

'How can I find the library at Falconrock?'

> *To find the door with the special lock*
> *There are things you'll have to do,*
> *Go under, over, along and through.*
> *Find the tower, mount the stair,*
> *The path is clear from the Druid's chair.*
> *Climb the gorge and cross the bridge,*
> *Enter the tunnels under the ridge.*
> *Once you're there you can't turn back*
> *To leave the rock, just follow the track.*

Jack hadn't expected to be given any answers but the riddle hadn't really helped. He decided to learn it by heart, just in case it made sense once he was there. When he was sure he knew the rhyme he asked his book another question.

'What does Falconrock look like?'

Jack stared at the Book on his bed but nothing happened. He was about to put it away when the page opposite the writing rippled. A map began to form. When the drawing was complete he tapped it with his wand. Two rocky outcrops rose from the page, their tops covered in trees. The cliffs were mottled with patches of red and orange and they looked steep and jagged. No wonder he'd have to fly there, it looked very inaccessible. Between the two cliffs was a deep ravine.

The only building Jack could see above the trees was the top of a red tower; this had to be the tower the riddle had mentioned. He wondered what the gorge would be like and if it would be difficult to climb. He tapped the top of Falconrock with his wand and watched as the map sank back into his page. If he found the library and opened the door he would be entirely on his own. If he wanted to find out about crystal magic it was something he was going to have to do.

FALCONROCK

Jack was hot and bothered by the time he reached the bottom of Nora's garden. He'd only packed what he'd needed but his backpack and holdall were bulging at the seams.

'Let me help,' said Elan as she came towards him.

Jack gave Elan the holdall. He expected her to complain about its weight but instead she slung it over her shoulder as if it was empty.

'Nora wants you to have a go at visualisation before you set off for Falconrock. She thinks you'll get the hang of it really quickly; especially now you've been to visit the fairies. They're masters of illusion and some of that will have been transferred to you when you ate what they offered. You did eat it didn't you?'

'I did, but I shrank it first: will that make any difference?'

'Not at all, but let's see how you get on. Nora can put a temporary spell on you if you can't do it.'

'Thanks. I'd feel a lot happier if I was dressed. Where's Camelin?'

'Oh he's busy! He's decided to set up a surveillance team of his own and he's recruiting starlings to be part of a Flying Squad. He wants them to keep a watch on Max and his gang, and report back if they see or hear anything suspicious. He doesn't like being the last to know things.'

'How many starlings are in the squad?'

'Fifteen,' croaked Saige, as she hopped off the patio step before making her way towards the flowerbed.

'He'll be unbearable now,' sighed Elan. 'I don't know if you've noticed but he does like to be in charge.'

Jack laughed. He looked up as a flock of noisy birds flew around the house.

'Is that them?'

'It is.'

Nora stepped onto the patio.

'Take your bags up and go tell Camelin we need him in the herborium so you can practise visualising.'

'I'll bring this one,' said Elan.

'Is it really hard, imagining clothes?' Jack asked her as they dropped his bags on the bed.

'You'll be fine, I'll see you later. You won't want me in the herborium while you're practising.'

Jack blushed. His cheeks still felt hot as he climbed the stairs to the loft. When he reached the bottom of Camelin's stepladder he could hear squawking and chattering coming from above. He called to Camelin but there was no answer. He didn't think he'd been heard above the din. As he poked his head through the trapdoor he smiled. Camelin had his head on one side with one eye shut and the expression closest to a grimace that a bird can have on his face.

'What's up?' shouted Jack.

'It's them,' replied Camelin and turned his beak so it pointed at five starlings that were jostling for position on his windowsill, all speaking at once. Jack decided to test his new skill. He listened carefully. He really could understand what the starlings were saying. They were arguing about who should report to Camelin first.

'STOP!' shouted Jack.

The noise stopped abruptly. All five starlings froze;

it was as if they thought they'd be invisible if they kept still. None of them looked at Jack or Camelin. Jack smiled. They looked quite comical in their different poses.

'That's better. Now, who's in charge?' asked Jack.

All the starlings looked towards Camelin.

'I mean, in charge of the Flying Squad.'

'Who told you I'd got a Flying Squad? A raven can't have any secrets around here, not even when he's trying to help.'

Jack ignored Camelin and looked at each starling in turn. He'd heard a couple of names mentioned as they'd been arguing.

'Who's Crosspatch?'

'Who wants to know,' snapped the darker starling with a slightly orange beak.

Before Jack could answer the other four starlings began squabbling again.

'This won't do,' shouted Jack. 'We need some order.'

'That's what I told them,' interrupted Camelin. 'The one who just spoke to you is Crosspatch, he's supposed to be in charge.'

'Are you that Jack Brenin?' asked Crosspatch, 'The one we're looking out for?'

'That's me.'

'You should have said, we've sworn to spy and snoop and bring back information for you.'

All five starlings nodded, raised their heads, puffed out their chests and stood very still again.

'That's better,' said Jack, 'It would be easier if just one of you reported back at a time.'

'We did. We're each watching one of those boys who don't like you. We didn't come back together. We came because each one of us has got something to report.'

Camelin turned to Jack.

'I've got three shifts and a starling watching each one of the gang so it's round-the-clock surveillance.'

Jack was impressed. Camelin had obviously been very busy.

'Could we have your reports, in turn, and maybe you could introduce yourselves too.'

Crosspatch hopped forward.

'Max is in his garden.'

Jack wasn't sure this was the kind of thing Camelin had in mind until the second starling joined Crosspatch.

'Snaffle, on Tank watch, he's with Max in the garden too.'

'Are all five of them together?' asked Jack.

'They are,' confirmed Snaffle. 'Chortle, Snatch and Grubber came to say the same.'

Camelin groaned.

'So we know where they are but what's more important is what they're talking about.'

Snaffle squawked loudly and the other four joined in until Crosspatch hopped forward again.

'They're plotting, about how to get their own back on Jack and Elan.'

Jack didn't feel too good. He'd anticipated they'd be after him and suspected they might want to pay Elan back too for what happened in the meadow; now his fears had just been confirmed.

'You'd better get back and find out exactly what they're planning,' ordered Camelin.

Snaffle shook his feathers before speaking.

'No need, second shift arrived, they'll report back later.'

'Thanks,' said Jack. Being forewarned would mean the boys wouldn't be able to surprise them. 'You'll have to excuse us, we've got to go now. Camelin and I are needed in the herborium.'

Jack and Camelin watched the starlings take off.

'That was great Jack, I couldn't think how I was going to get rid of them.'

'It wasn't an excuse, we really do need to go down to the herborium. Nora wants to teach me how to visualise.'

Camelin humphed before hopping over to the window.

'You'd better hurry up then or you'll keep everyone waiting.'

Jack didn't rush; he was lost in thought as he went back downstairs. There had to be a way to face up to the gang but five against two, even if Elan was strong, didn't seem very fair.

'Try again,' Nora encouraged Jack, as he and Camelin transformed for the third time.

Jack saw Camelin roll his eyes. They were standing behind a screen at the far end of the herborium and so far Jack had not managed to imagine himself wearing anything. The bright light as they touched their foreheads together was putting him off.

'Just concentrate on one outfit, something simple, something you are familiar with,' said Nora.

Jack lowered his head and made a picture in his mind of his black tracksuit. He squeezed his eyes tightly shut when he and Camelin were almost touching. He tried not to think about the bright light as their foreheads met. Even when he felt himself transforming from a raven into a boy, he kept the image of the dark tracksuit firmly in his mind.

'Wow!' exclaimed Camelin. 'You did it, look!'

Jack opened his eyes and looked down. He had done it; he was fully clothed except for his feet. He came out from behind the screen to show Nora.

'That's very good, Jack. Once more, and try for some shoes this time.'

Camelin sighed.

'When can we go to Falconrock? You promised Jack and I could have whole day together.'

'Ready,' said Jack.

They transformed back into ravens then immediately changed back again. As soon as Jack opened his eyes he knew he'd done it.

'Look!' he cried as he moved the screen so Nora could see.

There was a round of applause, not only from Nora but also from Orin and the whole Night Guard, who were now on Nora's long table.

'Bravo, Jack Brenin,' shouted Motley. 'I knew you'd do it.'

'Thanks,' said Jack, as he admired the pair of black trainers he'd managed to visualise. 'Do you think I'll be able to do it every time now?'

'Oh undoubtedly,' replied Nora, 'you have fairy magic inside you now. Each time you transform it will get easier. I think you're ready to go now.'

'At last!' grumbled Camelin.

'Now don't forget,' continued Nora, 'Camelin will wait for you by the exit. He's not allowed to speak to you so you'll be on your own once you land.'

'Can we go now?' asked Camelin.

'Yes you can, take care.'

'We will,' Jack assured her.

For the umpteenth time that morning Jack and Camelin transformed. Once they were airborne Jack felt the raven in him take over. He loved flying; it made him feel totally free, and without a care in the world. He tried to focus on the task ahead but the excitement of speeding through the air with the wind in his feathers made it hard to think about anything else.

'Nearly there,' Camelin shouted as he circled around Jack.

In the distance was the sheer cliff face he'd seen in his Book of Shadows. The top was densely forested but until Jack got closer he wouldn't be able to tell what kind of trees they were. He knew there wouldn't be any Dryads here, maybe they'd return when the young Hamadryads he and Nora had planted were fully-grown.

'See the cave in the rock face about half way up?' asked Camelin.

Jack scanned the hillside and nodded when he'd located the hole in the orangey-red rock.

'That's where you'll come out so I'll meet you there later.'

To Jack's surprise they didn't fly towards the cliff top, instead Camelin veered right and headed towards an equally high rock. As they got closer Jack could see a deep ravine; on either side a castle had been built into the rock. It wasn't easy to see as its walls had been made from the same red rock as the cliff. He quickly said the rhyme his Book had shown him, this must be where he'd find the tower and the Druid's chair. The trouble was, the castle had more than one tower.

'What you mumbling about?' asked Camelin.

'Nothing, it's just a rhyme.'

Camelin tilted his body and swerved.

'Going down!'

Jack did the same. They flew down and landed in the bottom of the ravine.

'Is this where I've got to start?'

'It is but from now on my beak is sealed. We'd better transform so you can get going.'

Jack concentrated hard as they touched foreheads; he visualised his black tracksuit and trainers. To his relief, when he opened his eyes, he was fully dressed. He turned slowly to have a good look at his surroundings. On one side of the ravine the castle walls and turrets loomed above him, on the other side there was a single tower. Jack could see two arched entrances, one just ahead and one higher up. He looked at Camelin for confirmation.

'I think I'll look inside this tower first.'

Camelin nodded vigorously. Jack smiled as he started off; Camelin's ravenphore had begun. He felt grateful he wasn't going to be alone. As he reached the entrance he looked round but Camelin was nowhere to be seen. There was nothing else he could do now but enter the building. The room was circular, like the towers around the palace in Annwn but with one big difference, there were no windows. Jack shivered, it felt cool and damp and he could hear water dripping. He waited until his eyes were accustomed to the dim light before looking around. There were no stairs. To get to the upper floors he'd have to use the higher doorway. He wondered why Camelin had indicated that this was the way to go. As he turned to leave he noticed a circular piece of wood, about the size of a bicycle wheel, on the floor. He knelt down to get a closer look. There must be something below because it looked like a lid. Jack put his ear to the wood. The only sound he could hear was that of dripping water. His cheek brushed against cold metal. Across the lid was a chain and at the end of the chain was a padlock, both were secured onto a huge metal ring. Jack took the silver chain from around his neck and pointed the tiny key towards the padlock. It immediately began to grow until it fitted perfectly into the lock. Jack hesitated. Should he open the lock or not? If he didn't there didn't seem any point in having come into the room. He turned the key slowly. The padlock sprang open and Jack struggled to lift the lid. He peered into the darkness, and although he couldn't see it, he suspected there was water at the bottom.

'Hello,' Jack shouted.

'...*Hello... hello...*' came the reply as his voice bounced off the wall.

'Who's there? ...*there... there...* ' a deep, grumpy voice replied.

Jack nearly jumped out of his skin. He'd not expected an answer.

'I'm Jack Brenin, and I'm looking for the entrance to the Druid's library... *library... library.*'

'A Brenin, you say! Well you won't find the library down here... *here... here.*'

Jack didn't know what else to say. The conversation seemed to be over. Maybe he ought to put the lid back and be on his way. If a water nymph appeared he wouldn't be able to ask for any help, and besides, he didn't have anything shiny to trade for information. He couldn't part with his key or his golden acorn.

Jack heard water from below begin to bubble; he backed away from the hole. The silence was broken when the voice boomed and bounced off the walls.

'Who sent you... *you... you?*'

Jack thought he ought to give Nora her proper name.

'The Seanchai, Keeper of Secrets and Ancient Rituals, Guardian of the Sacred Grove, Healer, Shape Shifter and Wise Woman.'

'Stay where you are, I'd like to see who the Druid has sent to Falconrock... *rock… rock.*'

A spray of water shot out of the opening. Whoever was down the well was rising rapidly to the top.

Jack had expected to see a water nymph. He was surprised when an old man with pale skin, a long grey beard, and a mass of grey curly hair, appeared. He bowed majestically to Jack. Jack bowed back. He wanted to ask the man what he was but knew that would be rude.

'I haven't got anything to give you in exchange for information and I'm not allowed to have any help.'

The man laughed loudly.

'I am Grannus the gatekeeper, I'm not offering you help or information. It is my permission you need before you can begin your journey.'

Jack's hand went up to his acorn.

'I'm afraid that won't be sufficient. You must confirm your identity.'

Jack watched as Grannus took a pouch from his pocket and proceeded to open it. He produced a large coin and laid it flat on the palm of his hand before extending it towards Jack.

'If you are a Brenin you'll be able to make the mark. Touch the token and let's see who you really are.'

Jack extended the same finger on his right hand that he'd used to touch the stone at the base of Jennet's well. As soon as his fingertip made contact with the cold metal there was a hiss of steam. Both Jack's finger and the token began to glow. As Jack withdrew his hand they both looked at the mark he'd made.

'A true Brenin,' pronounced Grannus as he bowed once more to Jack, 'take this token, keep it safe for you'll need it later. Your destination lies deep within the labyrinth but it's not an easy journey.'

Jack took the token Grannus offered him. The metal was dull and no longer bore his mark. As he put it safely in his pocket he thought about the rhyme from his Book of Shadows.

'How will I know what to do next?'

'You'll work it out. Would you be so kind as to put the lid back on and lock the padlock before you go? I don't want any unexpected visitors.'

Grannus didn't wait for a reply. He disappeared back down the well. Jack peered inside but there was no sign of the gatekeeper any more. He wrestled the wooden lid back over the well, hooked the chain over the padlock and snapped it shut. Once he was back in the sunlight he examined the token. Both sides of the coin were the same; each bore the outline of a large oak tree. Jack shrank his key by putting it into the tiny padlock he kept on the chain before putting it back over his head. Grannus had said he would work out what to do next. There was no sign of Camelin so the answer must be in the rhyme.

'*Find the tower, mount the stair,*' Jack recited as he stepped back and looked up at the second entrance. This had to be it. If there were a staircase inside he'd climb up it. He wondered how he'd be able to tell the difference between a Druid's chair and an ordinary one. Jack took the path that led up to the higher level. It was overgrown and he doubted anyone had been this way for a very long time. This entrance, like the one below, had no door, but instead of the chamber being dark, sunlight filtered in through cross-like slits in the thick walls. At the far end of the empty room was a stone stair. Jack looked up before ascending. He couldn't see the top because the stone steps wound around the tower. On each new floor Jack looked around but each room was completely empty. Up and up he climbed until he had to stop for breath. He looked out of one of the window slits; he was a long way above the ground. For a second Jack felt dizzy. He didn't mind heights when he was flying but as a boy it was different. He hoped he was nearly at the top. As he rounded the next curve the staircase came to an abrupt end. In front of him was an old wooden door with large black hinges. He felt his token to make sure it was safe, just in case he needed it to enter the room. Jack took a deep breath and knocked. There was no answer. He tried the doorknob and needed both hands to turn it. The door creaked loudly as it swung inwards. The room was empty except for one object in the centre. Jack was staring at a large chair. Since he could go no further and it was the only chair in the room, this had to be the one he was looking for. Its arms were carved in the shape of two dragons and its tall back was arched. As Jack walked around it he could see there was no piece of the chair left undecorated. This had to be the Druid's chair. He wondered if the clue he needed was in the carvings but nothing he'd seen seemed to be helping. He decided to sit down and try to think. The great chair was facing the only window slit in the room. As soon as Jack sat down he knew he'd found what he'd been looking for. The view led his gaze across the treetops and down a ravine towards an archway on top of Falconrock. Jack sighed, he had known his task wouldn't be easy but he hadn't realised how far he'd have to travel.

THE DRUID'S LIBRARY

Jack walked over to the window slit and looked out across the ravine. There was no mistaking the pathway he'd need to take; there was only one in sight. Jack closed the heavy wooden door and wound his way down the stone steps. Camelin was waiting for him at the bottom. Jack knew from his expression he'd been waiting a long time.

'It was a long climb to the top,' he explained.

Camelin rolled his eyes and held his right wing out towards the path Jack had seen from the top of the tower.

'See you later then.'

Camelin nodded several times before taking off. He looped-the-loop twice before heading off over the treetops. Jack didn't think this was a new ravenphore message; it was more likely to be Camelin showing off.

As soon as he entered the forest the sunlight disappeared. The path was covered in a layer of pine needles and was soft underfoot. He felt as if he was walking on a cushion. The forest was dense and still, and the only sound Jack could hear was a few birds singing in the distance. He didn't have to choose which way to go, there was only one path. He knew that if he'd been left on his own in the middle of a strange forest a few months ago he would have been a bit apprehensive, but now he felt no fear. He was enjoying the walk until he came to the edge of the trees and saw a sheer rock face ahead. Jack's heart sank. It would be foolish and dangerous to try to scale the rock. There had to be a cave or a crack in the hillside, the path wouldn't have led him to a dead end. To Jack's relief, Camelin appeared above. He glided down and landed a little way to the left. He didn't look at Jack. Instead, he hopped to the rock face, pulled his wings back and thrust his head forward. Jack recognised Camelin's signal, it meant he had to go straight ahead and not up. Jack crossed the short distance to see what Camelin was showing him. There was a narrow crack that hadn't been visible from the path.

'Thanks, I'll try not to be too long.'

Camelin chuckled. Jack wondered what he knew about this next part of his journey. It didn't take long to find out. Once he'd rounded the corner he entered a tunnel; within a few steps he found himself in total darkness. No light came from ahead or behind. He had no choice but to continue. He put his arms out by his sides and found he could touch both sides of the tunnel. The floor was uneven and Jack stubbed his toe more than once even though he was carefully inching his way forwards, one step at a time. The air felt thick, it had been like this in the tunnels inside Silver Hill only this time he was alone.

It was a relief when a shaft of sunlight lit the floor of the tunnel. He didn't need Camelin to show him the way when he stepped out into the light. Before him were giant stone steps that had been cut from the rock. The narrow sides of a steep gulley rose to the top of the stairway. The sides of the rock and all the steps were covered in moss. Jack had never seen anything like this before. It looked unearthly and magical as the sunlight lit the green walls. Ferns grew from crevices and Jack could hear water dripping from above. It looked beautiful but as Jack put his foot on the first step he realised it wasn't going to be easy to get to the top. The moss was slippery and there were no handholds. Jack spread out his arms and pushed his palms flat onto each side of the rock. The moss was wet through but at least he was able to steady himself. By the time he reached the top his hands and shoulders were aching. He sat down to get his breath and to have a look at his surroundings.

The path split three ways. If he turned left or right he'd be heading down and since the arch was on top of Falconrock it would seem logical to take the one that continued upwards. His choice was confirmed when Camelin hopped out onto the path in front of him. They walked together in silence with sunlight beating down on their heads. Jack wished he'd brought his hat and a drink. He felt even more parched when he heard running water.

'I'm really thirsty, is this water safe to drink?' Jack asked as they reached a small waterfall. The clear water cascaded down the rock into a large stone pool. It looked a bit like Jennet's well only much bigger.

Camelin didn't answer; instead he dipped his beak into the water and drank. Jack knelt, cupped his hands and quenched his thirst.

'Who drinks from my well?' boomed a voice from the top of the waterfall.

Jack looked up. He couldn't see anyone and even Camelin had gone.

'Who drinks without permission?' the voice continued.

'Jack Brenin. I'm sorry, I didn't know I had to ask, I was thirsty.'

'Mmm! Jack Brenin you say. That wouldn't be the same Jack Brenin who opened the well in the Red Tower would it?'

'It is.'

'Well drink your fill Jack, I'm glad you've made it this far.'

'Grannus?'

'The very same,' the old man replied as he surfed down the waterfall. 'When you've quenched your thirst you'll be ready to pass through the second gateway.'

Jack looked around. He couldn't see a doorway or anything that looked like a gateway. Grannus glided over to Jack and waited until he'd drunk his fill.

'The gateway you seek is hidden from sight. On the far side is a path, follow it and it will lead you to the bridge, beyond which is the landmark you seek.'

Jack repeated the directions. He wondered why Grannus was helping him or maybe he helped everyone who came to Falconrock.

'You won't get into trouble for telling me which way to go, will you?'

Grannus laughed loudly.

'As the gatekeeper I decide who's worthy to have safe passage. Once you've got what you came for you'll have to enter the labyrinth, it's the only way out. That will be your final test. If you make it to the last gateway, without help, you'll be able to keep all the knowledge you've gained from your visit here. Before you leave the labyrinth you'll be sworn to secrecy.'

'And if I don't pass this test?'

'You'll go home empty handed and forget you ever came here.

'This next part of your journey measures your determination and endurance, the library will test your character, and the labyrinth your worthiness. When you leave the library you'll be completely alone, not even your companion can enter there.'

Jack looked over at the tree Grannus had nodded towards. He could see Camelin hiding in the branches.

The water in the well began to bubble. Grannus laughed loudly before diving into the waterfall. Jack turned slowly in a circle as he looked for the gateway. He walked around the edge of the well to examine the waterfall more closely. Behind the curtain of water was an entrance. Jack stepped into the pool. The last time he'd gone through a waterfall was when they'd escaped from Silver Hill. He took a deep breath before walking through the cascading water.

He shook himself. It was only when he went to wring his sleeve that he realised his clothes weren't wet. He'd forgotten that he'd visualised the black tracksuit and trainers. Jack looked around. He was standing in a short passage that had been cut through the rock. Blinding sunlight streamed in through the opening. He'd nearly reached his destination; he could see the ruined arch with Camelin perched on top. As he stepped out of the passage the bright sun shone straight in his eyes, for a moment he was blinded. He blinked then froze when he saw what lay ahead. Before him was a narrow wooden bridge, only wide enough for one person to cross at a time. It had been made from a single tree trunk with what looked like a small rickety fence on either side. It didn't look safe but if he wanted to reach the arch he knew he'd have to cross it. He could feel beads of sweat running down his back. He knew he shouldn't look down and tried to focus on the arch. He gripped the supports and tried to step forward but his body went rigid. He looked at his foot and willed it to move but nothing happened. Out of the corner of his eye he could see how far above the ground he was. He knew if he wanted to find out about crystal magic he had to get across. He'd come all this way and he couldn't fail now. A sharp peck on his ankle made him jump. Camelin stood looking at him with his head cocked to one side.

'I don't suppose we could transform, could we?'

Camelin shook his head.

'I could fly over this so easily. I don't know if I can walk over. The ground is such a long way down and my legs don't want to move.'

Camelin turned slowly, thrust his head forward, raised his beak in the air and began to shuffle across the bridge.

Just imagine you're flying, Jack told himself.

He took a deep breath, raised his head, extended his arms outwards, and followed Camelin's example. Jack didn't look down or stop until he could feel the grass under his feet. He whooped for joy when he looked back at the bridge. He sat down on the grass and watched while Camelin did his victory dance.

The arch was made from blocks of red and white stone. Jack went and stood in the centre and looked straight ahead. Directly in front of him, a little way off was another arched entrance leading into the rock. This must be the final part of the rhyme his Book had given him. He'd climbed the gorge and crossed the bridge; all he had to do now was to enter the tunnels under the ridge.

'This is it,' he told Camelin, 'I'll see you on the other side.'

Camelin nodded before taking off and flying over the top of the cliff. Jack crossed to the entrance and peered into the darkness. If he'd had his wand, he could have made the tip glow and seen where he was going. Instead, he had to put his hand on the side of the rock and feel his way along the tunnel. Once his eyes grew accustomed to the darkness he was able to see the way ahead. A faint light was coming from somewhere and as he rounded a corner he entered a circular chamber with three round windows. Each had a design outlined in heavy black lead. The middle window was clear but the two on either side were filled with coloured glass. Jack went closer and stood in a pool of coloured light. He stood on tiptoe so he could look through the middle window. He could see for miles. In the distance was

Glasruhen Hill. A muffled sound to his right made him spin around.

'Is anyone there?'

Jack waited and peered into the shadows but nothing moved. The sound came again and Jack realised it was coming from somewhere behind the wall. He walked over and felt the rock with his hands. It didn't feel rough or cold; instead it was smooth and warm. He traced the outline of a wooden door by touch. It wasn't visible but he knew it was there. He took his silver chain off and held the key. He pointed it towards the door in the hope it would grow to the size of the keyhole. The key vibrated between his fingers and not only began to change shape but began to pull his hand towards an invisible keyhole. As soon as the bottom of the key disappeared a large door began to materialise. Jack didn't know whether to knock or just turn the key. Since there seemed to be someone in the room he decided that it would be more polite to knock. He tapped the door three times and waited. A muffled voice, from inside, eventually called to him.

'If you can open the door you can come in.'

Jack turned the key with ease and since there was no doorknob, he withdrew his key and pushed. It creaked noisily as it swung inwards. A figure in a long

117

hooded robe came shuffling towards him.

'I'd heard we had visitors, and what might you be?'

'Jack Brenin, Raven Boy, friend of Eleanor Ewell, Druid of Glasruhen Hill.'

'Are you now?'

As the figure brushed the hood back, Jack could see the librarian was a small woman. She peered over the top of a pair of glasses that were perched on the end of a hooked nose and leant towards Jack. Her piercing eyes held his gaze for a few seconds then flicked from side to side as she examined him. Her lips were pursed and very tightly closed and she didn't look at all friendly. Jack didn't know what to say.

'No noise in here, this is a library and I'll need to see your pass before you can enter.'

Jack fished in his pocket and pulled out the token Grannus had given him.

'No, that's for when you leave, I need to see your identification.'

Jack realised she must mean his golden acorn. He pulled his chain out and let the archivist examine it.

'Forged in Annwn, work of Lloyd the Goldsmith. You're mighty young to be wearing such a valuable object.'

'It was a gift from Coragwenelan.'

The old woman half closed her eyes. She tilted her head sideways and looked at Jack.

'One last question, just to verify that you are who you say you are. What would my name be?'

Jack mentally rehearsed the name Elan had given him before speaking.

'Cloda, Sylph, Archivist, Guardian of Ancient Knowledge and Keeper of Secrets.'

'You missed Shape-shifter.'

'Elan didn't tell me about that.'

'No matter, you got most of it right, you may enter.'

Jack followed Cloda into a vast chamber. One of the walls had circular windows; sunlight streamed in and gave the room a warm glow. The rest of the walls were covered in bookshelves that reached from floor to ceiling. The books were all different shapes and sizes, and handmade, just like the ones in Ewell House. Both the shelves and books looked very dusty. There was a lectern by one of the windows, similar to the one in Nora's library, and next to that was a desk. It was piled high with yellowing papers. An inkpot with a quill was the only other object Jack could see. The quill looked very old and bedraggled. Cloda walked around the back of the desk to the only chair and sat down. She picked up the quill, dipped it in the ink, shook it a few times, and then began to write. Jack could see the yellowing papers were parchment. The nib made a scraping sound as Cloda wrote. She didn't look up and Jack wondered what he was supposed to do. He'd no idea where to start looking or even if he was allowed to get books off the shelves. His throat felt dry and when he spoke his voice came out in a hoarse whisper.

'Excuse me, but could you tell me where I need to look to find out about crystal magic?'

'That's a big subject for such a small boy but if that's what you've come all this way for you'd better follow me.'

Cloda returned the quill to the pot and beckoned Jack to follow. The books were in alphabetical order according to their subject. Solid blocks of stone with letters carved on them separated the different categories. Cloda came to a stop in front of the letter *M*.

'You'll find it here,' she said as she pointed to the bottom shelf.

Jack looked at the books. They all had titles except for a wide book that had been bound in green leather. Cloda pointed to it.

'Touch the spine and if the title appears you'll be allowed to remove it. That's the rule in here. A book won't come out if you're not allowed to read it.'

The book sat between two other books, one about *Magic Carpets ~ their origin and use* and the other *Magic Wands.* Jack watched Cloda return to her desk, he was obviously not going to get any more help. If the title appeared he'd no idea how he'd ever remember everything inside, the book was so thick it would take him a week to read it all. He extended his hand but before it reached the book he felt a tingling sensation travel though his fingertips; it made his whole body shiver. As he touched the book's spine, gold letters appeared… *Magic Crystals ~ and everything you need to know about Crystal Magic.* This was what he'd come for. He pulled the book from the shelf with some difficulty and went over to the lectern. It was a struggle to lift the heavy book onto the stand. He tried to open the cover but it remained firmly shut. Should he go and ask Cloda for help? If he did she'd probably tell him the book didn't want to reveal its secrets. He put his hands on the front, like he did with his Book of Shadows; if he asked the right question it might open. He thought very carefully.

'What do I need to know about crystal magic?'

Nothing happened. Jack tried to lift his hands from the cover, he pulled with all his might but they were stuck fast, he felt cold then hot as he began to panic.

'I'm stuck!' he cried. 'Can you help me?'

THE LABYRINTH

Jack tried to open his eyes. He wasn't sure where he was until he realised he was on a floor, an earthen floor. Everything came rushing back to him; the last thing he remembered was being unable to remove his hands from the heavy book he'd put on the lectern. Jack's head hurt as he tried to look around.

'Up you get,' said Cloda as she put her hand under Jack's arm. 'Nothing to worry about, seen grown men do the same. I should have warned you.'

'About what?' replied Jack as he swayed unsteadily.

'*Book rush*, too much information in too short a time.'

Jack didn't understand; he hadn't even opened the book. He felt dizzy, and when he tried to think his head began to hurt again. Cloda steered Jack towards her chair. He watched as she went over to the lectern and easily lifted the book down from the stand.

'Sit yourself down. I'll put this away, then we'll see how you feel.'

He wanted to tell her to stop; he'd come all this way to find some answers. All he needed to know was how to open the book, but his voice failed him. He watched as Cloda made her way to the far end of the library. Jack began to feel warm as sunlight streamed onto his back from one of the round windows. He opened his eyes wide so he wouldn't fall asleep and concentrated on Cloda as she made her way back to the desk.

'Now, let's have a look at you,' she said, as she put her hand under Jack's chin.

He felt a bit sick as Cloda turned his head sharply to the left, then the right, as she inspected him. The tip of her hooked nose was almost touching Jack's face.

'You'll be fine,' she told him as she let go of his chin.

'What's *book rush*?'

'It can be a bit disconcerting the first time it

happens, in fact, there's many a Druid from the old days who never experienced a book rush. You must be very special to have emptied a whole book.'

'But I wasn't able to open it. I never got to look inside.'

Cloda laughed and tapped the top of Jack's aching head.

'That book was as light as a feather, the only place all that information could have gone is inside your head.'

'Do I have to put the information back?'

'Goodness no, that's yours to keep. The book will refill itself; it'll be ready for the next visitor in no time.'

What Cloda was telling him was difficult to understand but it would explain why she'd been able to carry the large book without any effort.

'I don't feel like I've got a whole book inside my head.'

Cloda peered into Jack's eyes.

'I'd say you've got a headache; it's a side effect of book rush. It'll wear off soon.'

'That's incredible,' said Jack as he looked around. 'Is it possible for just one person to hold all the information inside this room in their head?'

'Of course it is. I absorb every book before it's catalogued. How else would I know which shelf to put it on? A good archivist knows what's inside every book in their charge.'

Jack was impressed. Her knowledge must be vast, and encompass all kinds of different subjects too. He couldn't imagine what it would be like to have all that information inside your head. He'd only got the contents of one book inside his.

'How do I access the information?'

'Ah! When you need to know, you'll just know. It would take years to read and remember everything inside a book that size. This way, you get all the information in a few seconds and it'll stay there forever, providing you can get through the labyrinth. That's the biggest test. Do you want the information badly enough to overcome what lies behind that door?'

Jack swallowed hard. This was the moment he'd not been looking forward to.

'Sign in here before you go,' said Cloda as she looked down at the pile of parchment on her desk. She lifted the quill out of the inkpot and gave it to Jack before placing a small book on the table.

As soon as Jack touched the book, its cover opened and the pages rapidly turned until they reached the right place. Jack had never used a quill pen before. He signed his name at the top, as best he could, complete with a large blot where he'd tried to dot the *i* in Brenin. He watched as his signature disappeared into the page.

'My Book of Shadows does that when I write in it.' Cloda smiled.

'I think you'll find there's a lot more information in here than in your Book. Nora's transferred as much as she could into the Book of Shadows, but there are books in here she's never even had off the shelf yet. In future, if you can't find the answer in your Book you can come back and use the library. Now… since you've got what you came for, I suggest you get going.'

Jack turned and looked towards a small wooden door at the far end of the room.

'Thank you for your help,' he said to Cloda as he stood.

'Goodbye Jack Brenin, I hope we meet again.'

Cloda offered Jack her hand. It was claw like and bony and almost crushed his as he shook it. He set off reluctantly towards the door. The sooner he got through the labyrinth the better.

Jack stepped into a dimly lit cavern. There was light coming from many crystals of irregular shapes and sizes, growing naturally out of the reddish-orange rock. These weren't the same as the ones from the Caves of Eternal Rest. The larger crystals were clear and sparkled while the smaller ones were a dull milky colour. As if from nowhere, a sentence popped into Jack's head… *crystal light takes many forms, not all crystals are magical, some give light, some heat, and some both.* Jack held his hand in front of the nearest cluster. He could feel the gentle warmth from its glow.

The cavern was large and airy, and Jack could see seven rounded openings that seemed to lead into tunnels. They all looked very much the same and he had no idea which one to take. All he needed to do was to get to the exit, where he knew Camelin would be waiting. The sensible thing to do would be to go down the first tunnel to his right. If this was a dead end he could retrace his steps and try the next one. The tunnel walls were the same as those in the cavern except that the light from the crystals looked brighter in the smaller space. After a few steps Jack knew he wasn't walking in a straight line. The walls curved gently to the left. It wasn't long before he entered a large cavern. The wooden library door was opposite him on the other side of the cavern, confirming that it was the same one he'd left just moments before. He'd emerged from the second entrance; he turned and went down the third. This one proved to be a dead end and Jack had to retrace his steps. As soon as he entered the fourth tunnel his body tensed. Something felt different. The tunnel roof was lower and the space inside wasn't as wide. The air felt warmer too. He felt very alone.

Jack quickened his steps; the sooner he got out of the tunnel the better. He lost his concentration and didn't see a rock sticking out of the wall until it was too late. He stubbed his toe and almost twisted his ankle as he tried not to fall. He leant against the side of the tunnel to steady himself. He became aware of a sound in the distance. He wasn't alone; someone, or something else, was also in the labyrinth. Jack strained to hear. The sound was muffled, and although it wasn't coming towards him, it echoed down the tunnel. A chill ran up and down his spine as his dream about Velindur came flooding back to him. Was this where the crystal magic had transported him? Was he about to come face to face with the one person he never wanted to see again? Jack's heart was beating fast. He took several deep breaths and tried to tell himself not to be frightened, but he was, and nothing could change that. He knew he couldn't stay in the tunnel forever. He could go back and try a different one or return to the library door and ask for help, which meant he'd lose the knowledge he'd gained. Jack put his hand up to the golden acorn that hung around his neck and squeezed it tightly. He shut his eyes and wished whatever was in the tunnel would go away. To Jack's relief there was silence but it didn't last long, the sound of a taunting laugh echoed around the tunnels. Jack gritted his teeth. He knew the labyrinth was a test of his courage and he didn't want to fail. Reluctantly he took a step forward and set off towards the unknown.

The laughter stopped abruptly, only to be replaced by the sound of footsteps. Jack stood still until he was sure the footsteps weren't coming towards him. As he made his way down the path he could still hear shuffling and the occasional laugh. It wasn't long before the tunnel widened and Jack stepped out into another chamber. It was similar in size to the one he'd first entered, but this one wasn't empty. Pillars of rock of all shapes and sizes rose from the cavern floor. A loud peal of laughter broke the silence and echoed around the chamber. Jack held his breath. He caught a glimpse of a slight movement from behind one of the pillars. He stood very still and hoped he was hidden from sight. The laughter stopped. Whoever was there stepped out, casting a gigantic shadow on the cavern wall.

'Come out Jack Brenin, I know you're there, I saw you come in.'

The man's voice didn't sound unfriendly, and it definitely didn't belong to Velindur.

'Grannus?' said Jack as he stepped out from behind the pillar.

'The very same. I see you found the right tunnel.

'Come closer,' he continued. 'There's something else you must do before you leave the labyrinth.'

As Jack walked towards Grannus he could see he was standing on a rocky island in a shallow pool. The water was completely still and clear. In the dim light the reflection from the roof above looked like a miniature town in the water. Unlit candles were dotted around the rock where Grannus stood.

'Shall we have a bit more light?'

One by one Grannus lit the candles. The lights flickered and shone into the pool. Below the surface lay a mass of crystals of different sizes, shapes and colours. They sparkled as the light flickered on them. He looked at Grannus for an explanation.

'As gatekeeper and guardian of the labyrinth, I must ask you for your token.'

Jack put his hand in his pocket and brought out the large coin. He offered it to Grannus on his outstretched open palm as he leant across the water. Once Grannus had the token he made a sweeping gesture with his arm.

'You have done well, Jack Brenin, you did not turn back or ask for help, and you overcame your fear. Not only are you worthy to keep the knowledge you have gained from the Druid's library but you are also entitled to exchange this token for a gift. Take any crystal from my pool. Choose wisely for there are many different kinds in there.'

Jack looked into the water. The rock inside the pool was different from the rock of the walls. It had a green tinge and wasn't smooth. There were so many crystals below the water; he didn't know how he was going to choose. He decided to just plunge his hand straight in and see what happened. The icy water made him shiver. A ripple travelled across the surface and he lost sight of the crystals. He ran his fingertips over the bottom of the pool. As he touched each crystal in turn, images and words appeared in his head. He knew instinctively the colour, shape and property of everything he felt. He hesitated and thought about choosing one of the small green crystals but his hand seemed to develop a will of its own. He could feel it being drawn towards a rocky shelf. It was hard to see through the water but it didn't look as if there was anything sparkling in that direction. His fingers went underneath a small overhang and locked onto something warm. As soon as he made contact with the object, Jack felt a jolt travel through his body. The shape of a beautiful octagonal crystal filled his mind. It held every colour of the rainbow in its facets. He knew this was the one he must choose. As he brought out his prize he opened his palm and showed it to Grannus.

'I suspect this crystal chose you, it has very special powers.'

Jack knew, without a doubt, that it contained crystal magic. He watched as it rose and hovered above his open hand. The crystal began to spin. Jack could not draw his eyes away from the flashing colours. There was a bright surge of white light that made Jack blink. When he looked at his palm again, the crystal had gone. He looked down to see if it had landed back in the water.

'Crystal magic,' sighed Grannus. 'It's the oldest and most powerful kind of magic…'

'It cannot be ruled and chooses its own path,' continued Jack.

'I see you've come across this kind of magic before.'

Jack nodded. He felt sad. The crystal had been his for a moment but now it was gone. Grannus had told him to choose carefully.

'Why did it disappear if it chose me?'

'If you search your mind you'll find the answer.'

Jack concentrated hard and thought about the crystal. He closed his eyes and watched as the crystal formed inside his mind, he looked deep into its facets. Words entered his head… *no one has dominion over crystal magic but from this day forth, whenever you are in need, it will come to your aid.* Jack looked at Grannus and watched a broad smile spread across his lips. His deep laugh echoed around the cavern.

'So, Jack Brenin, I see you have the answer. The crystal chose you for a reason. It means there's a storm brewing. Sometime soon you're going to need the kind of help only crystal magic can give. Believe in yourself and have courage, recognise fear but don't ever let it enter your heart.'

Jack thought about Velindur. He would need all the courage he could muster if he ever saw him again. With the help of crystal magic Jack knew he'd be in a stronger position to deal with whatever Velindur might try to do. Jack also thought of Elan and her inner strength. She didn't fear Max or anyone in his gang but he knew crystal magic wouldn't help him sort out his problems with the boys. Finding courage and belief in himself was something he'd have to do if he wasn't going to let them bother him again. Coming to Falconrock had given him more than just knowledge from the Druid's library, he'd found out things about himself. Jack took a deep breath and straightened his back.

'That's good,' said Grannus, 'you've definitely got more now than you came for. Was it worth all the effort?'

'It was. Thank you.'

'Time you were going, call again won't you, anytime, but next time fly straight to the arch, no need to go through all that again.'

Jack smiled. It had been quite an ordeal and he was glad he wouldn't have to do it all over again. Grannus pointed towards the tunnel at the far end of the cavern.

'If you go through there, you'll be out in no time. Remember me to Eleanor, and tell her she's long overdue a visit, it's a while since we had a good chat.'

'Thank you, I won't forget to tell her.'

Jack smiled when he saw daylight at the end of the tunnel. He could see Camelin asleep in the sunshine.

'Sorry I was such a long time.'

Camelin jumped and glowered at Jack.

'At last, you've been ages. You realise we've missed lunch don't you. There's nowhere to get a takeaway around here. You wouldn't believe what it's been like not having anyone to talk to either.'

Jack smiled. There was something very comforting about Camelin's bad temper.

'Thanks for all the help. I couldn't have done it without you, especially at the bridge.'

'Just don't tell Nora.'

'I won't. I promise. Shall we go and find something to eat before we go back to Ewell House?'

'Aw Jack! That's a brilliant idea and if we look

hungry when we get back we'll get another lunch. Ready to transform?'

'Ready.'

Once they were airborne, Jack flew in a wide circle so he could have one last look at Falconrock before following Camelin. He had lots to tell him on the flight back.

THE FLYING SQUAD

The next morning Jack was woken by the sound of birds squabbling. He strained to listen but there were too many voices speaking at once to make out what they were saying. Jack swung his legs out of bed but before his feet touched the floor, Camelin flew in through the open window.

'Please Jack, come and sort them out, they won't listen to me.'

'Sort who out?'

'Starlings, five of them in my loft, wish I'd never started the Flying Squad, more trouble than it's worth.'

'The same five as before?'

'Naw. This is the second watch.'

'It's hard to believe five small birds could make all that noise.'

'You should have heard the din when all fifteen of them were in my loft the first morning. I never expected it to be like this, I thought they'd just come in one at a time to report.'

'Can't you put someone in charge of each squad?'

'I did, but I think I chose the wrong ones… Crosspatch grumbles all the time, Bicker argues and Dazzle, who's leader of the third squad, is too busy admiring himself to take any notice of what's going on around him. Come up and sort them out, please.'

Jack smiled. It wasn't often Camelin asked nicely for anything.

'Let me get dressed first.'

'No, you need to come now, I know they've got something important to say and they'll listen to you.'

Jack sighed. Meeting a squad of starlings in his pyjamas wasn't something he particularly wanted to do but he could hear the urgency in Camelin's voice.

'I'll meet you upstairs.'

'I'll come back in when they're quiet so they won't know I came to get you. Say you've come to talk to me and ask where I am. OK?'

'OK.'

'Thanks Jack… I owe you one.'

Jack put on his slippers and made his way up to the loft. Not only were the five starlings squawking and bickering with each other but there was a lot of tail pecking and beak prodding going on too.

'What's the meaning of this?' Jack shouted loudly. His voice had the same effect as before. All of the starlings froze. Jack pulled himself into the loft and sat looking at the silent squad. 'Bicker, step forward, and give your report.'

Four of the birds gave a sideways glance to one of the group. The starling they were looking at stepped forward.

'Bicker?' asked Jack.

The starling nodded and was about to speak when Camelin flew in through the open window.

'Ah! Sergeant Bicker, you have some news for me?'

Both Jack and Bicker looked at Camelin but neither of them spoke.

'Come on, let's have it then.'

'There's going to be a meeting this morning in Max's garden, they're all going to be there.'

'They are,' the other four starlings agreed.

'Do you know what this meeting's about?'

Another starling stepped forward to join Bicker.

'My watch, Danny, went to call for Techno, that's Twizzle's watch, and Danny told Techno they were going to sort out the final plan... isn't that right Twizzle?'

Jack looked at the starling that was nodding vigorously.

'And...?' grumbled Camelin.

'Well I heard my watch, Tank, telling Digger's watch Benbow, it was going to be about how Max can get his own back on Jack and Elan... didn't I Digger?'

'You did Grudge, you did, I was there, I heard it all.'

Camelin sighed. He fixed each starling in turn with his angry look.

'Sergeant Crosspatch gave me that report yesterday.'

'But Tank said they were going for Elan first,' said Grudge.

Digger nodded in agreement.

'They're sorting out the where, when and how this morning. Our two watches are on their way to see Max now.'

'So are Danny and Techno,' squawked Twizzle.

'Anyone got anything else to add?' asked Camelin as he strutted up and down in front of the five starlings. He waited but none of them spoke.

Jack felt grateful to the starlings. If he could find out what was going to happen he could make his own plan and warn Elan too.

'Do you think Nora would mind if we flew over to Max's house. I think I'd like to listen in on that meeting?'

'Don't see why not. You go and ask her while I debrief the squad.'

By the time Jack was back in his room the squabbling had started all over again. As he dressed he saw Camelin swoop past the window. He must have given up on the debriefing.

Jack and Camelin flew the short distance from Ewell House to one of the estates on the outskirts of Newton Gill. As they circled above the garden of one of the big houses, Jack could see Bicker perched on

142

the top of a summerhouse. He nodded to Jack and Camelin as they landed on the branch of an apple tree that overhung the bottom of Max's garden. It wasn't long before Grudge and Digger joined Bicker. They all watched as Max came down the garden and waited for Tank and Benbow to cross the grass from the back gate. Jack wondered if they'd be able to hear what was being said from their hiding place, especially if the gang decided to go inside. Max signalled for the other two to sit down before pacing up and down in front of them.

'Where are Danny and Techno? We can't start without them.'

'They're on their way,' replied Tank.

'Good, we've got a lot to do before Sunday.'

Camelin hunched his wings.

'What's so special about Sunday?' he whispered.

Jack shook his head for Camelin to be quiet; he didn't want to miss anything Max might say. It wasn't long before Danny and Techno arrived. The pair looked strange together. Danny was tall with long black lanky hair that flopped around his face. Techno was about the same size as Jack and everything about him looked neat and tidy. Max looked excited to see them.

'Sit down so we can get started. You know why

we're meeting. This is top secret. No one is to tell anyone else... understood?'

Max waited for them all to nod before continuing.

'We're going to teach that stupid girl a lesson... we're going to make sure she shows me some respect in future.'

'How we gonna do that Max?' asked Tank.

'That's why we're meeting, so we can work that out.'

Tank sniggered.

'If Benbow and Danny held her I could hit her, she wouldn't like that.'

Max shook his head.

'We've got to think of something better than that, besides, just hitting her isn't going to work, we'd get in trouble and then she'd be smirking again. It needs to be subtle.'

Tank looked puzzled.

'What's subtle?'

'Something clever but not obvious,' explained Techno.

'Precisely,' agreed Max. 'We want her to know it's us but we don't want to be seen... any ideas?'

'We could ambush her and hit her from behind,'

suggested Tank, 'she wouldn't see us then.'

'It's got to be something worse than hitting,' snapped Max.

They looked thoughtful. Max paced up and down until Benbow raised his hand.

'My little brother's got a story book about a rabbit…'

'A rabbit?' shouted Max. 'This had better be good, what's a rabbit got to do with anything?'

Benbow gulped and sat very still.

'Well? I'm waiting.'

Jack thought he could see Benbow's hands trembling. He clasped them together before continuing.

'Well, the rabbit was always annoying a fox who wanted to get his own back so he makes a baby out of tar and the rabbit gets stuck on it. When he finally gets free he rolls in some leaves and they stick to him. I just thought we could do something like that.'

Tank and Danny laughed so much they began to roll around on the ground. Benbow looked uncomfortable again but Max ignored them all. He seemed lost in thought. Tank thumped Benbow on the back.

'That's a good one! A wickle wabbit… ah!'

'Shut up Tank,' snapped Max, 'I'm trying to think.'

Tank abruptly stopped laughing.

'Got your notebook?' Max asked Techno.

The small boy pulled a pad and pencil from his pocket.

'Right,' said Max, 'this is what we're going to do… Danny's going to find the best location on the back lane for an ambush.'

Jack could see Tank smile.

'Benbow, you're going to get enough syrup to fill a bucket.'

Everyone looked at Benbow who began nodding at Max.

'What d'you want me to do Max?' asked Tank.

'You're going to get a pillowcase full of feathers. Think you can do that?'

'Yeah, no problem.'

'And Techno is going to make us a contraption that'll tip syrup all over the stupid girl. She won't see us because we'll be able to control it from the other side of the hedge. Tank, you'll be ready on the opposite side to put the pillowcase over her head. We'll syrup and feather her. She won't know what's hit her and while she's cleaning it all off she'll have plenty of time to think twice about annoying me again.'

There was silence from the gang as Max looked from one to the other. When Techno finished writing he looked up.

'Did you get all that?'

Techno nodded.

'And can you build what we need?'

Again Techno nodded before finally speaking.

'I'll need to go with Danny to find the right place before I start making something.'

'Great, we'll meet on the Back Lane, ready for action on Sunday afternoon. The whole of Glasruhen will be at the Cricket Club and she'll have to come out sometime. That weedy boyfriend of hers will be at the match with his grandad so she's bound to meet him there, only she'll not turn up 'cos she'll be too busy cleaning syrup and feathers off, won't she!'

Max laughed loudly, which seemed to be the cue for the rest of the gang to laugh too. Jack could see Techno and Benbow weren't laughing as hard as Tank and Danny. He wondered if Benbow was regretting mentioning the story about the rabbit. Jack looked across at the five starlings. He was very grateful they'd taken their duties so seriously. Camelin's Flying Squad had been a brilliant idea. Max had been right about the match on Sunday, he was going to be there with his grandad. At least now they knew what was being planned, Elan could avoid the back lane, or stay at Ewell House instead of going to the Cricket Club.

'See you later,' said Danny as he got up to go.

Techno and Benbow got up too and the three of them walked in silence across the grass towards the gate.

'Brilliant plan, Max,' said Tank.

Max didn't say anything but Jack could see he was smirking.

'Better get off too, see ya later.'

Max turned and walked back towards the house. Tank didn't leave; instead he walked over to one of the flowerbeds, bent over, and picked up a few small stones. He came back to the shed and started throwing them at the starlings on the roof. There were shrieks and ear-piercing cries as the five birds took off. One of the stones clipped Twizzle's wing and slightly knocked him off balance. The birds swerved and turned together in mid-air before heading straight back towards Tank. One by one they dive-bombed him. Jack had seen Camelin in action before and the starling's aim was just as good. In no time Tank was splattered. With a loud triumphant shriek the birds flew off to the safety of a nearby tree. Jack laughed. It served Tank right.

That might teach him not to throw stones at birds. A loud buzzing sound made Jack and Tank look towards the trees, a very large bee came into sight. Jack could see this wasn't an ordinary bee, it had the body of a very angry looking fairy and it was heading straight for Tank.

'Come on,' called Camelin. 'Race you back.'

Jack let Camelin go on ahead. By the time he flew into the kitchen, Camelin had already reached the part where the fairy bee was chasing Tank.

'Ah! Veronica!' laughed Nora. 'She can't stand injustice. She'll be watching him closely from now on.'

Elan laughed.

'If he bothers you again Jack, just make a buzzing noise, he'll soon run away!'

Jack tried to imitate Veronica and Camelin joined in.

'That's enough you two,' said Nora, 'we've got things to discuss.'

Jack transformed and tried out his new visualisation skill.

'You've mastered that, haven't you?' said Nora, as Jack stood before her in his black tracksuit and trainers. 'Now, shall we sit down?'

Jack looked at Elan. She didn't look worried. He wondered if Camelin had told her everything they'd overheard.

'Grandad and I can meet you at the gate on Sunday if you like. The gang wouldn't dare do anything with him there.'

'It's not a problem,' Elan reassured him. 'I can take care of myself.'

Nora tapped her wand on the table.

'Shall we begin? We want to hear everything that happened at Falconrock.'

Camelin hopped over to the open door.

'I'll be in my loft if you need me, Jack told me all about it on the way back and I don't need to hear it all again.'

Jack smiled to himself as Camelin flew off before Nora could reply.

Nora nodded thoughtfully once Jack had finished speaking.

'And you say the crystal chose you?'

'My hand was pulled towards it but I wasn't able to keep it.'

'No one can possess or control crystal magic but it will come to your aid if you are ever in need. Let us hope you're never in a position to need that kind of help.'

'What about the knowledge from the book?' asked Elan, 'Can you remember any of it?'

'Not a word but things I couldn't possibly know just pop into my head. When I had my hand in the pool in the labyrinth I just knew the name of every crystal, and I knew what each one could do and what colour it was.'

'From what you say, you absorbed the whole book. You'll keep that knowledge now for the rest of your life and it will be there, like the crystal magic, whenever you might need it.'

Both Nora and Elan smiled.

'You're going to be a great king, Jack Brenin,' said Elan.

Jack blushed. He felt a long way from being *great.*

'You'd better go and get your things together; it's almost time for you to go. Elan says you're going to start collecting parts for the buggy today.'

Jack had forgotten all about the buggy. He'd been far too preoccupied with other things.

Jack felt a bit guilty as he walked through Nora's garden. Elan was chatting away happily and Orin was riding on his shoulder. He knew Camelin was watching them. The buggy was already becoming a problem and Jack didn't want to exclude Camelin but there was no way to include him, not while Grandad was there. It wasn't the only problem on his mind.

'You don't have to come to the cricket match if you'd rather not,' Jack told Elan as they walked through the tunnel to Grandad's garden.

'It'll be fine, you'll see.'

Jack knew they wouldn't be able to discuss the matter any further when he saw Grandad in the garden. He called to them as they came out of the tunnel.

'Hello you two! Come and look at what I've got.'

Jack and Elan stood at the shed door and waited for Grandad to unlock it. On the floor was a pile of wood, pieces of metal, thick rope and two tins of paint.

'We'll need to sort this lot out,' Grandad told them. 'I don't know how much of it will be any good. The plans for the *Comet* are on the bench over there, I dug them out of the loft, so at least we've got something to work from.'

Jack went over and examined the plan. It was old and tatty at the edges. Someone had written, *The Comet*, across the top in thick capital letters. Underneath was a sketch of the finished buggy. It had four small wheels and a tapered body in the shape of a rocket. There were flames attached down both sides. The buggy had been coloured silver and its name had been written in blue capital letters across the front. The rest of the paper was covered in notes, drawings, crossings out and diagrams Jack didn't understand.

'What do you think?' asked Grandad. 'She was a beauty, flew like the wind she did.'

'It looks great,' said Jack with as much conviction as he could muster.

Elan came and stood beside him.

'It's brilliant.'

A broad smile spread across Grandad's face.

'Well, we might as well make a start. I'm going to enjoy this.'

AMBUSH

For the next two days, Jack and Elan helped Grandad sort through the scrap pile in his shed. By late Saturday afternoon the rubbish had been loaded into Grandad's trailer.

'If we get a move on I can make it to the tip with this lot before they close,' he told them.

Jack looked at the inside of the shed. It was very tidy. All the useful bits of wood and metal had been laid out at the far end under the two shelves. Jack had levered off the tops of the paint tins and looked inside. There was plenty of blue, yellow and black paint, but the silver was no longer useable. They'd decided unanimously that the buggy would be blue and they'd use the black to paint the buggy's name along each side.

'Now are you sure you don't want me to bring back a tin of silver?' Grandad asked before he drove off.

'It's fine,' Jack assured him. 'I like blue.'

'So do I,' said Elan.

'Well that's settled then, blue it is.'

Once Grandad's car and trailer had turned onto the road, Camelin swooped down from the tree opposite the open shed door. He swaggered past Jack and Elan and began an inspection of the inside of the shed.

'Can't see what all the fuss is about. Why's it taken you so long to tidy this lot up?'

'Before you say any more,' interrupted Elan, 'we couldn't use magic to help.'

Camelin had a long grumble to himself before flying up onto the table and inspecting the plans.

'Hmm! The *Comet*. I remember all the buggies from the past. Your grandad's used to win all the time. Of course this is all going to be a waste of time, it won't stand a chance this year.'

'Whyever not?' asked Elan.

'Because I know what's going on at Smedley's yard.'

Jack and Elan exchanged looks.

'Aren't you going to ask me what I know?' grumbled Camelin. 'I go to the trouble of setting up a spy network and neither of you seem in the least bit interested.'

Jack tried not to smile.

'So... what's going on at Smedley's yard?'

Camelin puffed out his chest feathers and cleared his throat dramatically before he spoke again.

'You do know who owns Smedley's yard? Frank Smedley's dad, you know, Tank. Well my source...'

'Which one?' interrupted Elan, 'Would that be Grubber, Grudge or Pippa?'

'If you'd let me finish I was about to say... my sources, so it's all three of them, and Crosspatch, Bicker and Dazzle. They all came and told me the same story because Max and Tank have been over at Smedley's yard since this morning.'

'And?' prompted Elan.

'That's where their new buggy is.'

'You mean they've finished it already?' asked Jack.

'It's finished but the boys haven't built it... it's been made for them by two of the workmen at the yard.'

Jack frowned.

'But that's cheating.'

'Maybe they'll be disqualified,' added Elan.

'Oh no they won't, Dazzle heard them laughing about it; seems Max's uncle is one of the judges.'

'That's why they were so confident when they came to register,' groaned Jack. 'We really don't stand a chance.'

'We're not giving in,' said Elan.

'I agree,' replied Jack, with more confidence than he felt.

'Any news on the ambush?' asked Elan.

'Oh plenty, they're all set for tomorrow afternoon. Snaffle saw Benbow carrying two big tins of syrup yesterday and Digger says he's been down to the shops and got two more this morning. That's four tins of syrup. It won't be enough to fill the bucket though.'

'How do you know?' interrupted Jack.

'Saige said it would take nine tins and she's always right.'

Elan laughed. Jack would normally have laughed too but this wasn't funny.

'Please don't come to the match tomorrow, not unless you walk down with us. Grandad won't mind.'

'It's alright, Jack, honestly, there's nothing to worry about.'

'But there'll be five of them.'

The rumble of Grandad's car cut their conversation

short. Camelin hopped down from the table and shuffled out of the shed before the car turned into the drive. Jack gave Elan one last pleading look.

'Honestly Jack, it will be fine.'

Jack was woken early the next morning by something tickling his nose. He couldn't hear any buzzing but he didn't scratch it just in case it was the Dorysk. He didn't feel good. Not only was he worried about Elan's ambush, and his own problems with the gang, but he'd also had his bad dream again. Velindur was another problem he hadn't fully resolved and no matter how much assurance Nora or Elan might give him, he couldn't shake off his fear. His nose tickled again and he thought he heard someone whispering his name. He forced his eyelids apart and tried to focus on the end of his nose. A small white butterfly fluttered around his head, and he could see it was no ordinary butterfly.

'Twink?'

'Good morning Jack Brenin, please forgive my uninvited intrusion.'

Jack sat up; he was really pleased to see the little fairy.

'You're welcome anytime.'

'The others sent me; they're in the back lane watching two of those boys we chased from the meadow the other day. They've got rope around one of the branches of the beech tree with a bucket on the end of it. They were talking about you and Elan. We thought you ought to know.'

'Thanks Twink, we already know what they're up to but I can't persuade Elan to keep out of their way.'

'We'll keep a watch on them, I'll send the Dorysk if we need you.'

Jack didn't know what help he'd be but if Elan did get into trouble at least he could raise the alarm.

'Thanks Twink, will one of you let Elan know?'

'There's never any need to take news to Ewell House, not if the trees are involved, Nora will already have been informed. I'd better get back; I don't want to miss anything.'

Jack felt a bit better now he knew the fairies would be there to help. They wouldn't be able to stop themselves turning into bees if they thought the gang were doing something wrong. Most of them had run from the bees before and Tank seemed to have a big problem with them. Jack got out of bed and opened his curtains. He could see Camelin watching the house from the tree opposite. He opened the window wide so he could fly in.

'You're awake early, thought I'd be sat there a while yet.'

Jack was about to tell him about Twink's visit but thought better of it. Camelin had obviously got some news of his own to tell and if it was the same news he'd be annoyed if he thought Jack already knew.

'Has something happened?'

'Aw Jack, you should have seen him, talk about laugh, I nearly fell out of the tree.'

'Seen what?'

'Tank, with the feathers!'

'Feathers?'

'You know, you can't have forgotten, Max told Tank to get a pillowcase full of feathers. Grubber came with his report this morning and he'd laughed so much he'd got hiccups, so I had to go and see for myself. You should have seen him. He had two cushions on the grass and a pillowcase. Grubber said when he ripped open the first cushion the feathers exploded out, and went everywhere. He's been chasing them round the lawn trying to catch them all. I arrived just as he picked up the other cushion… and guess what? Poof! He did it again. You'd think he'd learn from the first one. If he doesn't want anyone to find out what he's done he'd better hope there's a strong wind before his family wake up. Their lawn's not green anymore, he'll never pick them all up, there's just too many of them.'

Camelin bobbed up and down as he chuckled to himself.

'Does Elan know?'

'She will by now, there's not much goes on in Glasruhen they don't know about at Ewell House.'

'They didn't know about the gang's buggy.'

'That's not surprising; you'd know why if you'd seen Smedley's yard. There's not a living thing inside their fence. Chopped everything down they did, cleared the land, covered it with concrete, and then piled it high with old cars, motorbikes and other stuff. You don't even get weeds growing there.'

It didn't sound like the kind of place Jack would want to visit.

'I'm worried about the buggy race.'

'You worry about everything, it's the boy in you. Try to listen to the raven part and you'll worry a lot less.'

Jack knew Camelin was right; when he transformed he really did feel different.

'I'll try to remember that, thanks.'

'It sounds like your grandad's up, I'll see you later. I'll be sitting in that blabbermouth of an old ash tree this afternoon, you know the one I mean, don't you? I can keep an eye on the back lane and the cricket match from there.'

Camelin was gone before Jack could say another word.

There was a lot to do at the Cricket Club in preparation for the match. The visiting club were only travelling a few miles, which meant there'd be, what Grandad called, *a good turn out.* As Jack went back and forth with chairs from the pavilion to the grassy area, he scoured the trees for any sign of Camelin. He even took the rubbish out to the dustbins in the hope of finding him there but he was nowhere to be seen. Every time a small insect buzzed around Jack's face he peered hard to see if it was wearing a pair of glasses. He hoped Elan would change her mind and not leave Ewell House but she had seemed determined to come to the match.

At lunchtime, Jack wasn't hungry, the worry was gnawing at his stomach and the plate of sandwiches he was given didn't interest him at all. He asked to be excused and took his plate outside with his glass of juice. He leant his back against one of the trees. He didn't have long to wait. Camelin landed on a branch above where Jack was sitting.

'Aw Jack! Are they to share?'

'Come and help yourself but don't let anyone see you.'

Camelin dropped down behind the trunk and Jack passed a sandwich round.

'Do you know what's going on? Has Elan changed her mind?'

Jack had to wait until he'd heard Camelin gulp before he got his answer.

'Elan's coming over later; she's going to make the gang wait for as long as she can. I've been and had a look, they're all set up. Max, Danny, Techno and Benbow are in the field behind the hedge under the trees. Tank's on the other side of the back lane with his pillowcase full of feathers, he's hiding behind the widest tree trunk. You should have heard Max shouting at Benbow when he brought out the tins of syrup. They had a big problem prising the lids off. Max said he should have bought the ones in the squeezy bottles, not tins, but they got the lids off in the end and got most of it in the bucket. There's loads of syrup all over the grass and they've just left the empty tins in the hedge.'

'Oh dear!' sighed Jack.

'Are you eating that other sandwich?'

'Not really but I've had a bite out of it.'

'Not a problem, pass it round.'

Jack heard the familiar gulp that told him the sandwich was gone.

'Do you want the cake too?'

'Cake! I didn't see any cake!'

Jack reached into his pocket and brought out an individually wrapped chocolate roll. Camelin's head peeked from around the tree trunk.

'Ah Jack, you saved me one.'

Jack smiled.

'I know, I won't tell Nora.'

'I'd better go, I need to get myself a grandstand view, it looks like the other team are arriving.'

Jack watched a coach turn off Forest Road and drive past the pavilion towards the car park. He took his plate back to the kitchen.

'The team are here,' he told Grandad.

'Do you want to come and do the scoreboard with me or would you rather watch the match?'

'If you don't mind I'd like to watch the game.'

'See you later then, if you need anything you know where I'll be.'

Jack went over to the trees at the other side of the pitch. From here he could see over the small hedge into the football field. He wasn't sure he could vault the hedge but he knew he could squeeze under it if he needed to.

It was hard to concentrate on the match. The only good thing was that he was in the shade. Jack hoped the frequent clapping wouldn't prevent him from hearing anything that might be happening in the back lane. There was a loud crack as the opposing team's batsman hit a six. Jack strained to listen; he thought he'd heard a scream. What should he do? A loud buzzing in his ear distracted him.

'It's started,' shouted the Dorysk.

Jack didn't need to think, his whole body shook, not with fear but with anger. He dropped to the floor and wriggled under the hedge. He was halfway through when he heard the gang running towards him. He knew they'd see him but he didn't care. He'd face them and tell them what he thought of them for being so horrid to Elan. The boys were shouting as they reached the bottom of the field. They yelled as they scrambled over the fence. Jack couldn't believe his eyes as Max, Benbow, Danny and Techno all ran past him and vaulted over the hedge into the cricket field. They'd nothing on except their underpants. Close behind them was a swarm of bees. He watched as they fled over the pitch. The crowd stood, some shouted, others pointed but most of them were laughing. One of the police on duty began to chase after the gang. Jack was about to go and find Elan when Tank also burst over the fence. He had one very large bee chasing him. Jack had never met Veronica but he knew this had to be her. He couldn't imagine any of the fairies he'd met so far looking so angry. Tank ignored Jack and leapt over the cricket club hedge. As he ran after the gang Jack could see his back was streaked with bird droppings. Camelin swooped down to the verge.

'Did you see that?'

'I did but where's Elan? Is she alright?'

'Did you see his back?'

'I did, but never mind his back, where's Elan?'

Jack heard Elan laugh as she turned the corner of the back lane.

'I'm here, did you see them?'

Jack frowned at them both.

'I've been worried sick for days and you two think it's funny.'

'Oh Jack, I told you not to worry. I was planning on teaching them a lesson. I thought I'd make sure the bucket tipped back on them instead of on me.'

'But I thought we couldn't use magic.'

'You can't but there's nothing to stop me from defending myself; I'm not from this world and the same rules don't apply. Anyway… I didn't have to do anything. Their own stupidity sorted them out.'

'What do you mean?'

'Let's go and sit under the tree in the shade and Camelin can start. He saw all of it and I'll fill in the bits I know.'

Jack and Elan squeezed under the hedge and sat in the shade of the tree.

'Well?' said Jack. 'Don't leave me in suspense.'

Elan laughed again as Camelin gave a couple of coughs before beginning.

'You should have seen them. I told you they had trouble opening the tins. Well they'd managed to get syrup everywhere. It was on the grass, on the trees, on their clothes and just as Elan was about to come through the garden gate, one of them shouted *ants*. Then the other three shouted too and started screaming. That's when they started tearing their clothes off. They started swatting the ants on their bodies and stamping on the ones on the grass, which was a big mistake.'

'Twink came to find me,' interrupted Elan. 'I don't know how any of the ants survived but they did, and by then the fairies were really annoyed. The boys were mistreating the ants and weren't going to stop. They instantly transformed into bees, just like they did in the field when Max tried to squash the spider.'

'Did you ploop on them?' Jack asked Camelin.

'Didn't have to, got my own Flying Squad. Think they got a bit carried away though. I hope they taught Tank a lesson.'

'He still had his clothes on when he passed me,' added Jack.

'I think I can explain what happened there,' said the Dorysk as he flew over the hedge. 'When the gang started shouting, Tank leapt out from the hedge with the pillowcase. When he saw Elan wasn't there he went back behind the tree. Max shouted for him to leave the feathers and help. That's when he bumped into Veronica. He flung his arms about and tried to hit her, which was enough to make her very annoyed. She'll not give up chasing him now till he gets indoors with the windows shut. It's going to take her days to calm down after this.'

Jack looked over to the pitch where play had resumed. He couldn't see any of the gang; they'd already disappeared into the next field. The police officer had given up chasing them and was on his way back to the pavilion. Jack finally laughed as he replayed the scene in his head. Elan, Camelin and the Dorysk laughed too. Jack wiped the tears from his eyes, his chest hurt and when he finally managed to calm down he lay on his back and smiled.

'So you were never in any real danger?'

'I told you it would be alright didn't I?'

'They're going to be even more angry now, aren't they?'

Elan laughed.

'But we're going to deal with it aren't we?'

'We are,' came a chorus from a group of starlings who were perched next to Camelin in the tree.

'Thanks everyone,' said Jack. It was good not to feel alone even though his friends weren't the usual kind.

THROUGH THE PORTAL

For the next few days Jack and Elan helped Grandad in the shed. The new *Comet* was taking shape and beginning to look more and more like a buggy. Occasionally Jack caught sight of Camelin sitting in one of the trees. He knew he wasn't happy about being left out but there wasn't anything Jack could do or say that would make him feel better about the situation. Grandad wanted to get as much of the buggy finished as possible before the Flower Show. Work would have to stop anyway when Jack went to stay at Ewell House.

Every so often Jack would have a little chuckle to himself when he thought about the gang being chased across the cricket pitch in their underpants. There'd been a report in the local paper about the incident but it didn't refer to the failed ambush. The gang were described as *inconsiderate youths* and their run through the match was seen as a *deliberate attempt to disrupt the game*. Since the incident, the Flying Squad hadn't seen much of the boys. They hadn't met together or been into town. Jack was relieved. Maybe they would leave him alone now, he certainly hoped so. Jack was trying to take Camelin's advice and think like a raven but it wasn't really helping. It only made him miss Camelin's company. They'd only been able to send brief messages to each other over the past few days.

By late Wednesday afternoon the pile of wood, wheels and metal had been transformed into something resembling a rocket. The buggy looked almost identical to the picture in the plan except that they'd decided to leave the hardboard flames off. Even without the paint it looked good. After Elan had said goodbye, and gone through the hedge at the bottom of the garden, Jack was exhausted. Grandad put two wooden crates in the doorway before going back to the house. Jack did a final tidy up and when Grandad returned with a cup of tea for them both, they sat on the crates and admired their work.

'We've done well,' said Grandad. 'A lick of paint,

a few tweaks here and there and she'll be ready for a test run next week.'

'Test run?'

'We'll need to test her to see how she performs. The course goes around Monument Hill. Whoever's driving won't be allowed out of the driving seat. On the uphill stretches the one riding on the tailgate can get off and help push.'

'Aren't we both allowed to push?'

'Not a chance, that's what makes it even more of a challenge. That's why we need a third member for the team; their job is to help push the buggy up the steepest part at the end. The driver's on his own for the last downhill stretch. The other two have to run down the slope to the finish. The clock only stops when all the team members are across the line.'

Jack wished he'd read the rules before he'd agreed to enter the race. It had all sounded exciting when Grandad had told him about the races he'd been in but now Jack was involved he'd didn't feel quite the same. He knew he wasn't strong enough to push the buggy uphill on his own and using magic would be out of the question.

'Will you or Elan be driving?'

'I don't know. It's not something we've discussed.

'We used to have a rule, whoever was the strongest pushed and the lightest would be the driver.'

'Elan's a lot stronger than me.'

'Really! She looks such a delicate little thing.'

Jack smiled. He'd never really thought of Elan as *delicate*.

'I'll talk to her about it over the weekend.'

'Best thing to do is for you both to have a go. Driving isn't for everyone. Those buggies pick up a lot of speed on the downhill and whoever's riding the tailgate needs to be a good runner too. We'll all go over to Monument Hill next week so you can get a feel for the route. We'll have time to make any adjustments and give her a second coat of paint before the race.'

'Were you ever the driver?'

'Oh yes, I was a slip of a lad like you when I was young, I didn't weigh much in those days. The lighter the driver, the easier it was for the others to push, not so much weight to get up to the top of the hill.'

Both Jack and Grandad sat in silence for a while and admired the *Comet*. Eventually Grandad stood up and handed Jack his mug before taking the wedge out from under one of the doors.

'I think it's time we went in, don't you?'

Jack had almost finished packing when he heard a gentle tapping on the window. As he looked round he could see Orin was already at the windowpane. He could tell from the way her tail curled at the end that it was someone she was happy to see.

'Come in Motley,' said Jack as he opened the window.

'Don't mind if I do, don't mind if I do.'

Orin greeted her brother and when Motley stood to attention she ran up Jack's arm and settled down on his shoulder.

'Is this an official visit or did you want to see Orin?'

'Oh official, but it's not something I've discussed with Camelin so I'd appreciate your discretion.'

'Is there a problem?'

'Not so much of a problem, more of an annoyance. Camelin's set up this raggle taggle band of starlings, calling themselves the Flying Squad. An undisciplined rabble if you ask me.'

Jack smiled, Motley's description was very accurate but the squad had taken their duties seriously.

'Is there something you'd like me to do?'

'Oh yes! I hear they listen to you, Camelin's got no power of command, likes to be in charge but no natural ability for it. There's going to be a meeting before you go to Annwn tomorrow night. While you're away Nora's putting me in charge. I just want you to make sure the so-called Flying Squad understand it's me they need to report to when Camelin's not here.'

'Are you sure you want them to report to you? They're a noisy lot.'

'I'll soon have them in shape once they know it's me they have to answer to. Can't have enough eyes and ears watching, and reporting, but the air forces must have the same kind of discipline as those on the ground. As long as you tell them they need to report to me, I'll make sure they're sorted out. We'll have three efficient, well-disciplined squads by the time you get back.'

'I'll have a word with them.'

'Thank you kindly, knew I could rely on you. Better be off, got things to do, don't you know.'

'Before you go, is there any news about the gang?'

'They're all together at this very minute behind closed doors. The Dorysk has infiltrated their headquarters and will report back later. Something's brewing. I can feel it in my whiskers. Well, can't stand here talking all night.'

'Thanks,' said Jack as Motley scurried through the open window onto the ivy. 'I can feel it too Orin, it's been too quiet and I don't think they're going to give up that easily.'

'Now are you sure you don't mind staying at Ewell House till Sunday?' Grandad asked Jack, as he was ready to leave.

'I'll be fine; there'll be lots to do.'

'I'm not going to be home till late but you've got your key if you've forgotten anything, just remember to lock up if you do come back.'

'I'm sure I've got everything, I'll see you at the show.'

'That's fine. Nora knows which marquee we're in. I'm hoping my dahlias are going to do well this year, be nice to add a rosette to my collection.'

Jack smiled. Grandad had quite a collection of cups and rosettes from various shows but this seemed to be the most important one of the year.

'I hope you win.'

'Thanks. There'll be a lot of competition, keep your fingers crossed for me.'

Jack showed Grandad his crossed fingers before he went out of the back door. As soon as he entered the tunnel he took Orin out of his pocket. She'd asked if she could run on ahead. It wasn't often she got the chance to have a long run and Jack could see her enjoyment as she scurried down the path. It wasn't long before she was out of sight. Jack didn't rush; he wanted time to think before he reached the bottom of Nora's garden. He was hours away from returning to Annwn and he was feeling a mixture of excitement and apprehension. It would be great to see everyone again but this wasn't just a visit to see friends. He'd been summoned and was due to stand before Coragwenelan and the Blessed Council. Somehow they expected him to prove to them that he was their rightful king. Elan had said it was only a formality but he'd no idea what he was going to say. He didn't feel he had the right to be a king, if he'd been born a prince he'd probably feel differently but he was just a boy. He still found it strange to think of Elan as anything other than Elan. Tonight she'd transform into the Queen of Annwn but it was only yesterday that they'd both been covered in dust and grease working together in his grandad's shed. A rustling in the hedge made Jack look up. He could just see Camelin's beak sticking through the leaves.

'Come on slowcoach, I've been waiting for days for you to arrive and now you're dawdling... fancy a flight this afternoon?'

There was nothing Jack wanted more.

'Did you have anywhere in mind?' he asked Camelin.

'No, why? Is there somewhere you'd like to go?'

'Monument Hill.'

'What you want to go there for? Oh! Don't tell me, it's for the buggy race.'

'Well it is but I thought if we looked at the route together we could see where you could perch during the race without being seen.'

'You mean I can be there for the race.'

'Of course you can. I'm sorry you've not been able to help during the last few days, I've missed you.'

'Oh! I've been busy, not had time to miss you at all. You will hurry up, won't you? I'll see you in the loft.'

Hurry was one thing Jack was not able to do with a full backpack and heavy holdall.

'See you in a bit,' he called as Camelin took off.

Jack felt good with the sunshine on his back and the wind in his feathers as he and Camelin flew towards Monument Hill. He'd expected Nora to say they couldn't go but instead she'd told them to enjoy themselves. Everything was ready for their visit to Annwn. She wanted them back by late afternoon and ready to make their way to Glasruhen Gate before sunset. Jack wasn't sure that Nora's idea of enjoyment was the same as Camelin's and he suspected that at some point, while they were out there would be a search for food.

Jack had never flown in this direction before. Below him lay fields, and in the distance ahead was a steep-sided hill. Camelin swooped past.

'That's Monument Hill, it's not far.'

'What's on the top?'

Camelin chuckled and flew in a huge circle.

'Aw Jack! You make me laugh! It's a monument.'

'Of what?'

'Some man or other. It wasn't always there. A long time ago there used to be a standing stone on the top with lots of little ones around it, you could see the big stone for miles. Had a hole in it just like the one on Glasruhen Hill, you know, the one Cory put her hand in when we went to collect the cauldron plates.'

'What happened to it?'

'Don't know, it used to be called Liller's Hill but that was a very long time ago… ready to have a look around?'

'Ready.'

'We'll start over there, that's the Cricket Club.'

They landed on the pavilion roof. A large field lay at the foot of the hill.

'The buggy race starts over there,' Camelin said, using his ravenphore signal for Jack to look to the right. 'They don't all start at once… it's a long way round the course and the final push up that hill takes forever, but once you get to top, there's a long downhill stretch.'

Jack looked over to Monument Hill. He could see what Camelin meant; the path that led to the top of the hill was very steep.

'There's nowhere for you to sit here, or anywhere on the top, everyone would see you.'

'What about that tree over there?'

Jack tried not to laugh as Camelin made an exaggerated gesture with his other wing.

'That looks perfect.'

'Can we fly over the whole bridleway now?'

'Follow me,' said Camelin as he took off and flew low up the steep path that led to the top of the monument.

Jack had to use all his flying skills as he followed Camelin. They flew close to the ground and sped around the course. Eventually Camelin soared and flew over a long stretch of trees. Occasionally Jack could see the pale path below. The route looked long and challenging. It was going to be a bumpy ride. There wouldn't be any problem for Camelin, he'd be able to follow the race and find plenty of places to perch. When they reached the top of Monument Hill Camelin landed on the ground.

'See over there?' he said, as he unfolded his wing slowly and pointed beyond the pavilion.

'It's Glasruhen Hill!'

'Well don't sound so surprised, you've been up there often enough.'

'I know, but there's just so much to see from up here, it's hard to know what you're looking at.'

'We'd better be getting back. I know where we might get a burger if we're lucky.'

Jack didn't argue. It was hungry work being a raven.

Nora and Elan were waiting for them in the kitchen. The cauldron was on the table and Jack could see it was full of jars of blackberry jelly. Balanced on top was a large pie. Camelin hopped over and inspected it. Nora gave him a disapproving look.

'That's for later. Go and get yourselves ready, we'll be setting off soon. Oh and Jack, don't forget your acorn, invitation, wand and Book of Shadows.'

'He doesn't need that wand these days,' grumbled Camelin.

'He'll need it in Annwn,' said Elan. 'It needs to be verified.'

'Verified?' asked Jack.

'Only a formality,' explained Nora. 'Your wand will prove you are who you say you are. It's not something you could have just picked up off the ground, only a Hamadryad could have given it to you.'

'The Blessed Council will give you a task to perform, but it won't be too difficult. It's written in the Book of Law so they have to follow the rules, there are no exceptions,' explained Elan.

'It's most important that they know exactly who

you are if they're going to crown you king,' Nora added. 'Now, off you go, be back here in ten minutes.'

'Race you,' Camelin called to Jack when he was halfway through the patio doors. Jack flew after him.

Once he'd transformed and was back in his room he checked the contents of his backpack. When he was sure he had everything he went back down to the kitchen. Elan was on her own.

'Are you alright?' she asked.

'A bit nervous.'

'You'll be fine, just be yourself. There'll be a better welcome for you this time, we're expected.'

Jack's mind went back to their unexpected visit through the Caves of Eternal Rest. At least this time they'd be going into Annwn through Glasruhen Gate. He didn't want to think about the last time they'd been through the portal either… that visit had ended with a trial. He hoped his visit to the Council Chamber wouldn't be as gruelling this time.

'Ready?' called Nora from the garden.

'Ready,' they replied.

'Camelin's flown on ahead. The portal is hidden in the clearing near the standing stones. He'll wait for us there.'

Jack wanted to ask Elan some questions but Nora

chatted all the way about the arrangements she'd made at the meeting earlier. Jack suddenly remembered he was supposed to tell the Flying Squad they were to report to Motley.

'Should I have come to the meeting?' he asked Nora.

'No need, it was only to make sure everyone knew what to do while we were away.'

'I promised Motley I'd speak to the starlings and I didn't.'

'I did,' said Elan, 'Orin told me what Motley had said and I called them all over while you were out.'

'Thanks, I completely forgot.'

Elan giggled.

'Camelin won't recognise them when he gets back, Motley will have them trained up into an efficient squad in no time.'

Jack thought Motley really would have his work cut out. The starlings didn't seem to have very good memories. They'd probably forget everything in a couple of days.

It was a short climb to the edge of the bushes that surrounded the standing stones. Three Dryads were waiting for them. Jack recognised Cory but he didn't know the other two.

'Is all well?' asked Nora.

'All is well,' replied Cory, as she touched one of the leaves on the nearest bush. 'We knew you were on your way and thought we'd come to meet you.'

The bushes parted and Jack could see the ring of stones in the centre of the clearing. Camelin was just outside the circle.

'This way,' called Nora.

Jack turned round to say goodbye to Cory but the bushes had already closed and all three Dryads were gone. He followed Nora up to the top of the meadow.

'Would you like to open the portal?' Nora asked Jack as she gave him her Book of Shadows.

Jack looked at the page and read aloud.

> *To open up a Portal wide,*
> *Into Annwn's fair countryside,*
> *Hold the Treasure from the shrine,*
> *Then let the golden acorn shine.*

The words were slightly different. Last time Elan had laid branches and Nora had performed a ritual before the two sentinel oaks.

'Hold your acorn in one hand and your wand in the other,' Nora told Jack as she and Elan held up the cauldron.

Jack took his chain off and laid his golden acorn on his palm before picking up his wand. A blaze of golden light burst from the acorn. As the beam of light extended in the direction of the cauldron, two gnarled oak trees began to appear.

'Now, point your wand between the trees, keep a steady light,' said Nora.

Last time Jack had aimed his wand between the sentinel oaks his hand had trembled. This time was different; he felt in command of both his wand and emotions. He closed his eyes before the blinding flash appeared. He felt the explosion of light through his eyelids. When he opened his eyes the tall arched doorway had materialised. The golden leaves and acorns on the green door shone in the light from his acorn.

The door fascinated Jack. It was incredible to think something so big could be hidden from sight.

'Shall we go through?' asked Elan.

'About time,' grumbled Camelin, as he shuffled towards the closed door. 'If you hadn't hidden it I could have been through half an hour ago.'

Nora frowned at him.

'Tonight Jack must go through first, he's the one with the invitation, you're just here as a guest, as I am.'

Camelin looked annoyed but he stood away from

the door. Jack took one step forward and extended his hand. He was about to push when a low rumbling noise began. The two halves of the door parted before he touched the wood. A glowing green light shone beyond the portal. Jack took a deep breath and stepped into Annwn.

THE COUNCIL MEETING

With each step Jack took, the glowing green light faded. He screwed up his eyes in anticipation of bright sunlight but Annwn was in darkness. As his eyes became accustomed to the dark, he turned and watched Elan and Nora step through the portal followed by a disgruntled looking Camelin. Nora reached into the cauldron and brought out her wand. She held it above her head and sent a blaze of golden light high into the night sky. It exploded into a shower of tiny sparks that cascaded to the ground. As the first landed on the grass in front of Jack's foot a low sound began. It filled Jack's head, and seemed to echo around the hills. Another sound, slightly higher than the first joined in, followed by two more. Four columns of golden light from different locations rose into the night sky, before each exploded into showers of red, blue, green and silver. As the last faded, the sound stopped. Jack turned to Nora; he knew she was smiling.

'Your welcome has begun. This is how expected visitors used to be received. The old ways have returned once more to Annwn.'

'What happens next?' asked Jack.

'We'll make our way to the top of the hill that overlooks the citadel. By the time we get there we won't have long to wait.'

Jack could see Camelin was swaying impatiently from side to side but he couldn't see Elan.

'She'll be back soon,' explained Nora. 'She's gone on ahead. As Queen of Annwn she has to welcome us officially to her land. I'm afraid you'll have to help me with the cauldron now she's gone.'

Jack gripped the large metal ring. Try as he might he could not lift his side of the cauldron off the ground. Camelin tutted loudly.

'I think we need a little bit of assistance, don't you?' said Nora, as she pointed her wand at the contents of the cauldron and whispered, '*redigo.*'

Jack found he was now able to lift the cauldron easily.

'Better?' asked Nora.

'A lot better, thanks.'

'Can we go now?' Camelin whined.

'You may fly on ahead but only to the brow of the hill.'

Camelin was airborne in a flash. He looped-the-loop twice before flying off towards the hill. Jack was surprised when he saw Camelin flying back.

'Is there a problem?' asked Nora.

'Two problems!' croaked Camelin. 'Part of the welcoming party is already on its way. The raven part.'

Jack was glad Camelin couldn't see him smile. He'd wondered if Winver and Hesta would be waiting for them. This was one of the times he felt glad he was a boy.

'I'll walk with you two, or I could sit in the cauldron now it isn't heavy any more.'

'You'll walk,' replied Nora.

It didn't take long to get to the top of the hill. Jack gasped when he saw the sight below him. Three torch-lit processions were making their way towards them, each advancing from a different direction. It was fascinating to watch the lights as they wound their way towards a small group that stood by the foot of the hill.

When they converged, an ear-splitting sound filled the night as all four notes began again. The larger group began to ascend the hill. Jack could hear giggling, of the raven kind, coming from somewhere close by.

'We're safe for a bit,' Camelin whispered, 'I don't think they can talk to us until we've been officially welcomed; we'll try to keep out of their way, if you don't mind.'

Jack nodded. He didn't want to speak. He was spellbound by the sight before him. As the group approached he could see the first four men were blowing into strange instruments, each was made from one long tube which extended upward, and ended in an animal head. From their silhouettes, Jack could see each one was different but it was hard to make out exactly what they were. He knew, without a doubt, that the sound was coming from the gaping mouths of the horns. Without warning the droning stopped. The men parted and a group of hooded figures, each with a lighted rush torch, filed though the gap. They walked slowly, in pairs, until they reached Jack, bowed their heads, turned sideways, and took three steps away from each other. The figures formed a lighted passageway down which Coragwenelan began to make her way; another group of hooded figures followed behind. Jack recognised Gwillam's staff and presumed the others were the members of the Blessed Council. Coragwenelan's flowing white robes made her look as if she was floating towards him rather than walking. The silver knotwork designs on her cape glinted in the torchlight. Jack could feel his heart thumping in his chest, not from fear but from anticipation. When Coragwenelan stopped she raised her arms slowly until they were above her waist. Winver and Hesta flew onto her shoulders. Jack bowed his head and kept it lowered until the Queen spoke.

'Jack Brenin, you are most welcome here. Annwn will forever be grateful to you for your help. On behalf of myself, the Blessed Council, and the people of Annwn I bestow on you the right to enter this land at any time. From this day forth you shall have free passage throughout Annwn.'

'I am honoured,' replied Jack as he bowed low.

'What about me?' whispered Camelin. 'Don't I get everything free too?'

Jack could see the glimmer of a smile on Coragwenelan's lips.

'Camelin, you too are most welcome. The freedom of Annwn will also be yours whenever you are allowed to visit.'

Camelin bowed too. Then he made a strange face at Jack.

'Does that mean you get to come when you want but I've got to ask permission?' he whispered.

'It does,' Nora whispered back.

'Humph!' Camelin grumbled.

'We'll discuss this later,' replied Nora. 'Now is not the time.'

'Eleanor, Seanchai, Keeper of Secrets and Ancient Rituals, Guardian of the Sacred Grove, Healer, Shape Shifter and Wise Woman, you, as always are welcome.'

Nora tilted her head to one side and lowered it slightly before replying.

'We are all thankful to be here and appreciate the welcome you have given us.'

'Shall we proceed to the palace?' Coragwenelan replied. 'A banquet awaits us.'

As the Queen turned, Winver and Hesta winked at Jack and Camelin. Each slightly shook their feathers before facing in the direction the Queen was heading. Nora and Jack picked up the cauldron and followed. The hooded figures with the lights stepped towards each other and followed too. When Jack reached Gwillam he signalled for two young boys to carry the cauldron and then extended his arm for Camelin. They set off towards the Glass Palace. No one spoke, it would have been impossible to hear what anyone was saying anyway because the four animal headed trumpets began to drone again.

'That was some feast,' Camelin said to Jack, as they made their way to the room they shared in Gwillam's house. 'Why have you got to go back to the palace later?'

'Elan said it was just a formality. I've got to prove that I am who I say I am.'

'That's stupid, of course you're you, who else would you be?'

'An impostor.'

'Why would anyone try to be you?'

'I suppose if I'm to be crowned king they want to make sure I'm worthy.'

''Course you're worthy; you're the best, Jack. If they let me come too I could tell them that.'

'I'm sorry. It's something I've got to do on my own.'

'I thought we were friends; you're always off doing things without me these days. I liked it better when it was just us two.'

'You don't stop being friends with someone just because you're not with them.'

'It's not the same when you're not there. It's fun when we're together.'

'Once the buggy race is over we'll have the rest of the summer to do things before I go back to school.'

Camelin hopped around Jack and started his shuffle dance then stopped abruptly.

'Ouch! I think I need to lie down, that was one big meal, even for a hungry raven.'

Jack opened the door to their room. Someone had laid clothes out for him on his bed. A long tunic, leggings, a sash and a cape, were neatly folded on the sheet.

'I'll get changed while you sleep your dinner off.'

By the time Jack was dressed, Camelin was laid on his back with his feet in the air snoring loudly. Jack closed the door quietly and made his way back to the kitchen.

'Are you ready?' asked Nora, as she turned Jack around and inspected him. 'You'll do. Now, just be yourself, do what's asked of you, and don't look so frightened.'

'I'm not frightened.'

'Try to smile then.'

Jack smiled weakly. His stomach was churning and although he felt honoured he still wondered if they'd got the right person. How could he be king? He wasn't a man, he didn't have much experience of the world and he wasn't big or strong. His thoughts were interrupted by Gwillam's arrival.

'It's time Jack. We need to be going, we don't want to be late for the Council Meeting.'

As Jack stood up Nora passed him his wand and invitation. Gwillam also passed him something.

'It goes on your belt. You can use the pouch for the invitation and you'll find your wand fits into the loops at the side.'

Jack let Nora put the pouch on him. When everything was safely stowed away he checked the chain around his neck to make sure he'd not forgotten his acorn. That was one thing he wouldn't have to verify, his acorn had been a gift from the Queen, made by the master goldsmith of Annwn. He took a deep breath and followed Gwillam out of the kitchen and into the darkness beyond.

'Wait here,' Gwillam told Jack as they approached a bench outside the council chamber. 'Someone will call for you soon. When they do, enter. The Blessed Council will be waiting to greet you.'

Jack sat on the hard wooden bench. He was in a corridor that was lit by rush lights. As the lights flickered he tried to see if there was anyone on the other side of the circular window beyond where he sat. After what seemed like an eternity the door opened again. A tall Druid banged his staff three times and announced loudly, 'Jack Brenin.'

Jack stood and walked into the dimly lit chamber. All the curtains had been drawn. This was to be a private meeting. Gwillam stood up. He didn't speak until the Druid who had admitted Jack was seated.

'We have invited you here, Jack Brenin, to verify your right to the kingship of Annwn. All rise for the Queen.'

There was a scraping of chairs as the other twelve members of the Blessed Council stood. Jack turned around so he was facing the door through which Coragwenelan would emerge. He'd been in the room beyond before, as a prisoner. His mind flashed back to the events of his trial. If Velindur knew he was standing here before the council as their prospective future king, he would be furious. The door at the far end of the room swung open soundlessly and out stepped Coragwenelan. Not only was she wearing her pearl encrusted crown but she also carried a silver staff. The long blue mantle, draped over her shoulders, trailed behind her as she slowly walked to her throne.

'I bid you welcome,' she said, as she sat.

Gwillam walked to Jack's side and bowed.

'Your Majesty, before you stands Jack Brenin, the one we believe to be the true heir to throne of Annwn. The one who is worthy to sit by your side and rule this fair land.'

Gwillam gave Jack a nudge in the back. He stepped forward and bowed.

'And what says the Book of Law?' asked the Queen.

From the corner of his eye, Jack could see one of the members of the Blessed Council walk to a lectern, upon which lay an ancient book. He used two hands to open the cover then carefully turned the pages to the place he needed. He coughed twice before reading aloud in a great booming voice that filled the chamber.

'One day, the heir to the throne of Annwn will stand before the Queen and Blessed Council. He shall have all the qualities of kingship, be compassionate and just, courageous and strong, and a friend to all, a true Brenin. He will be charged with a quest, to prove beyond doubt his worthiness to rule over this Fair Land and its people.'

Coragwenelan nodded her thanks to the Druid. She turned and smiled encouragingly at Jack.

'Who verifies this boy's ancestry?' asked Gwillam.

'I do,' replied the Queen. 'There is one who lives on Earth at Ewell House. She has lived next to the old king's ancestral home from the beginning and watched each generation come and go. This boy, who stands before you, is the true heir of the king who was never crowned. The heir of the one who lies in The Mound, whose reign was measured only by the length of each feast, and no more. He who was unable to be crowned, and who never had the opportunity to recover the torc of kingship before mortality overtook him. I swear to you all, this boy is his direct descendant.'

Gwillam nodded to the smallest Druid standing at the far end of the curved table. He sat, picked up a quill pen and wrote onto a piece of parchment. Gwillam turned and addressed the rest of the council.

'Please be seated, it is time for Jack Brenin to verify his identity.'

Jack swallowed hard. He suddenly felt very small and insignificant. Nora had told him to show the council his wand and his acorn. He pulled his wand from the side of the pouch and offered it to Gwillam, who examined it, before passing it to the first Druid at the table. Jack watched as each Druid examined his wand. Finally, Gwillam passed it back to him.

'Are we agreed this wand came from a Hamadryad Oak?' asked Gwillam.

'Aye,' the members of the council replied.

'Are we agreed this wand could only have been given to Jack Brenin by Arrana, last of the great oaks on Earth?'

'Aye,' the council agreed again.

'And are we agreed, if the wand answers to the boy's call, he is the true owner of the wand?'

There was a resounding *aye* from every Druid in the room. Gwillam smiled and turned to Jack.

'You must show the Queen and the Blessed Council your power by summoning the Stone of Destiny.'

Jack's mind went blank. Had he been told about this? He didn't think so. How would he summon the stone? He knew it was one of the four treasures of

Annwn and opened the Eastern Portal but he'd no idea where it was kept or how he could bring it to the council chamber. He took his wand in his right hand. Immediately it became smooth. Jack looked at the Druids; all had leant forward to get a better look. He closed his eyes and concentrated. He visualised the stone. He drew its shape in his mind and thought about its smoothness and its greeny-blue colouring. Without speaking he opened his left hand and extended his flat palm towards Gwillam. He raised his wand and willed the Stone of Destiny to appear. He willed and willed with all his might. He felt a sudden weight in his palm. He opened his eyes a fraction and there, in his outstretched hand sat the stone.

'This is proof,' shouted Gwillam so he could be heard above the noise the council members were making. 'Now call Lloyd the Goldsmith.'

The Druid who had admitted Jack to the chamber went to the door. When Lloyd entered, the council members stopped talking.

'You have been summoned here for two reasons. The first is to verify the workmanship of a golden acorn in the possession of this boy who stands before us,' announced Gwillam.

Jack slipped the chain from his neck and offered

his golden acorn to Lloyd.

'This is my workmanship; this is the acorn Coragwenelan commissioned me to make for Jack Brenin.'

'Thank you,' replied Gwillam. 'Have you your drawing book and pen?'

'I have.'

'Are you ready to draw what we are about to see?'

'I am.'

Gwillam turned and bowed to the Queen then addressed Jack.

'You must hold the Stone of Destiny in both hands. Clear your mind and it will show us all what is to be.'

Jack returned his wand to the loops on the side of his pouch and cupped his right and left hands together so the stone sat inside both his palms. He tried to clear his thoughts. At first, Jack didn't think anything was happening and then the lights in the room began to flicker. One by one the flames reduced to almost nothing. Without warning, a greeny-blue light erupted from the stone. It rose to the ceiling in a column of swirling colours before turning into a shimmering dome that filled the top half of the chamber. A picture began to form. Jack could see Coragwenelan sitting on a silver throne. On her head was a crown Jack had never seen before of silver flowers and leaves. Next to her was an empty golden throne. She stood and extended her arm.

Jack realised that everyone else in the room could see the images too. They gasped as an arm, from beyond the light, reached forward and took the Queen's hand. The Blessed Council rose from their chairs as Jack, wearing a golden crown, came into view. Without looking, Jack could hear Lloyd the Goldsmith furiously sketching the oak leaf and acorn crown.

'Hold the stone still,' Gwillam commanded. 'Do you have the details of the crown now Lloyd?'

'I do,' replied the goldsmith.

'You may cover the stone now.'

Jack put his right hand over the top of the stone. The image on the ceiling instantly disappeared and the lights glowed brighter again.

Coragwenelan stood.

'You have done well, Jack Brenin. There is no doubt as to your claim to the throne of Annwn. Are we all agreed?'

A unanimous *aye* filled the chamber. Jack felt his cheeks reddening.

'You will make the crown,' the Queen told Lloyd.

'In time for Samhain.'

'Yes, Your Majesty,' replied Lloyd as he bowed so low that his head almost touched the floor.

'Tomorrow night at the First Fruits Festival, before all the people of Annwn, you will be given your quest. Until then I bid you farewell.'

Jack bowed again as the Queen left the room. As he stood up, he looked at the beautiful heavy stone in his hand. There was an image inside it. He froze in horror as he realised he'd seen it before. There in the centre of the stone was Velindur with his arm raised in a gesture of defiance. In his hand was a book.

'Gwillam, look,' whispered Jack.

THE LOST TREASURE

'Wake up Jack,' called Camelin as he bounced up and down on Jack's bed. 'We can't have breakfast till you get up and I'm hungry.'

Jack woke from a deep sleep. He'd not dreamt, or not that he could recall but as soon as he opened his eyes he remembered what he'd seen in the Stone of Destiny.

'Don't you want to know what happened last night?'

'Naw, I just want my breakfast. See you in the kitchen.'

Jack sighed and swung his feet out of bed. Hopefully a cold wash would shake all thoughts of

Velindur from his mind. Besides, they were in Annwn and there were far more exciting things to think about. At sunset they'd be going to the First Fruits Feast. He wondered what Nora had planned for the rest of the day.

Jack could smell freshly baked bread as he got nearer to the kitchen. When he opened the door he could see the table had already been laid. Camelin had positioned himself directly in front of one of the jars of blackberry jelly they'd brought with them into Annwn.

'Did you sleep well?' asked Nora.

'I did, thank you.'

'Gwillam's gone to the palace library and he won't be back for a while.'

Camelin groaned.

'We haven't got to wait for him too have we? I'm feeling very faint; I really do need my breakfast.'

'You may eat now Jack's here but don't you dare put your beak in that jar.'

Jack quickly spooned some of the blackberry jelly onto Camelin's plate.

Breakfast didn't take long. Jack and Nora had just finished clearing the table when Elan stepped through the open door.

'Are you two coming to help?'

'Of course,' replied Jack.

'You don't even know what you're volunteering for, you should always ask *why* or *what for* before you say yes,' interrupted Camelin.

Both Elan and Nora frowned at Camelin.

'We need to use the equipment we bought in Newton Gill,' replied Elan and winked at Jack.

'What kind of equipment?' asked Camelin.

'Oh, just a few scrubbing brushes, dusters and some varnish,' said Elan.

'Well you can count me out. I've got important things to do today.'

'You're welcome to help,' said Jack.

'Naw, cleaning's not for ravens, see you later.'

'He'll be back,' said Nora. 'He won't be far away and his curiosity will get the better of him.'

'Shall we go and groom Ember?' Elan asked Jack.

'I can't wait. Where is she?'

'She's meeting us by the lake.'

'Are you coming too?' Jack asked Nora.

'Not just yet. Unlike Camelin, I really do have important things to do!'

It was only a short distance from the Druid's village to the lake. They'd almost reached the water's edge when Elan stopped. She fished in her pocket and pulled out a small silver whistle. Jack saw her blow it but he didn't hear a sound.

'Ember won't be long,' she explained, 'she has incredible hearing and if I need her I use this.'

Elan passed Jack the whistle. It was beautiful. As he turned it around he could see the likeness of Ember had been etched into the silver.

'Lloyd made it for me,' she said.

The sound of beating wings made Jack turn. Ember in flight was a magnificent sight. As she got nearer she roared and circled around the lake before landing. The draught from her wings nearly knocked Jack and Elan off their feet. They clung onto the signpost until Ember had folded her wings.

'Come and say hello properly.'

Elan went over and stroked Ember's lowered head.

'We're going to make you look really magnificent for tonight,' she explained. 'We'll scrub and polish you and then varnish your nails silver.'

Ember nodded and bent her head towards Jack so he could stroke it too.

'We'll need you to get into the lake first so we can scrub your nails and scales.'

Jack watched as Ember stood by the water's edge. She put one foot in the water but quickly brought it out again. Without warning the great dragon opened her mouth and breathed a huge flame directly into the water. Ember closed her heavy jaws and tested the water again before plunging into the lake. A great wave of water erupted and drenched Jack and Elan.

'We might as well get in too,' laughed Elan.

The water was lovely and warm and for the next half hour, Jack and Elan scrubbed Ember's scales.

'We'll paint your nails on the shore when you're dry,' Elan shouted.

Ember nodded and moved her tail towards them.

'Climb on,' she said.

When both Jack and Elan were ready, Ember set off at speed around the lake. It was difficult holding onto her spines but it was such a thrill to skim the water on her tail. They both whooped and squealed as Ember circled the lake. A crowd had gathered by the oak trees where the stalls were being erected in readiness for the feast. Each time they passed the crowd cheered and waved. Jack could see Camelin watching from the battlements of the Glass Palace. He couldn't complain about being left out this time since he'd been invited. When Jack didn't think he could laugh any more Ember finally slowed and landed near the signpost. They basked for a while in the sunshine until they'd all got their breath back.

It was a long hard job polishing Ember but it was worth it. When they'd finished with the beeswax her red scales glinted in the sunlight.

'We'll paint your nails now,' Elan shouted. 'Don't touch anything until they're dry.'

Ember nodded and moved her right foot towards them. There was just enough silver nail varnish in each bottle to paint one of Ember's claws. By the time they'd finished the last one, Jack felt a bit giddy from the pungent smell of the varnish. He lay back on the shore and looked up.

'Shouldn't we polish her horn too?' he asked.

'I've got that covered,' replied Elan as she turned and waved both arms towards the Palace.

Jack smiled as Winver and Hesta glided down towards them. They took the cloth Elan offered them and flew onto Ember's snout. They each held one end of the cloth in their claws and began to pull it back and forth around Ember's horn. Winver flew down and Elan put polish onto another cloth. When the two white ravens had finished, Ember's horn shone. They dropped the cloths at Elan's feet and flew into a nearby tree.

'You really do look magnificent,' Jack told her.

Ember stood and walked down to the water's edge. She peered at her reflection in the water.

'Thank you, I feel magnificent.'

'I'll call you when it's time for you to light the barbecue,' said Elan.

Ember turned and ran a short distance away from them. She opened her wings and began to beat them. Jack knew he'd never tire of watching Ember fly and now she'd been scrubbed and polished, she looked even more impressive than she had before. Winver and Hesta flew over to them and landed on Elan's shoulders.

'Have you seen Camelin?' asked Elan.

'He said he wouldn't help,' said Winver. 'He wouldn't even stop to talk to us.'

Jack looked up at the battlements. Camelin was

nowhere to be seen.

'Do you know where's he gone?'

'He said he was off to find Gwillam in the library,' answered Hesta.

'He will be able to sit with us at the feast, won't he?' Winver asked.

'I think he should sit between the two of you, don't you?' replied Elan.

Both ravens giggled and tittered before flying back to the palace.

'Time to go,' said Elan as she gathered up the empty nail varnish bottles. 'Could you take these back to Gwillam's house for me, I really should be getting back to the palace. There's a lot to do before tonight's feast and I shouldn't leave it all to Cora and Gwen.'

'That's fine, I'll see you later.'

Jack didn't go back to the Druid's village straight away; instead he lay on his back in a patch of tall grass and watched the clouds. This really was the most wonderful place to be; especially now Velindur was gone. Jack sat up abruptly. He hadn't intended to let any bad thoughts spoil his day, but like Max and his gang, Velindur was ever present. He knew deep down he'd have to face them all sooner or later. It was time he got back. He wondered if Camelin was still in the library or whether he'd only used that as an excuse to get away from Winver and Hesta. Jack picked everything up and made his way back to Gwillam's house.

'Psst, Jack,' came a hoarse whisper as Jack entered Gwillam's kitchen, 'follow me.'

He followed Camelin to the top of a flight of steps. A row of unlit candles lay on a shelf. Jack lit one before following Camelin down the steps. The air felt cool as they descended.

'Where are we?' asked Jack.

'In Gwillam's cellar, we can't be overheard here and there are no trees to snitch on us.'

Jack could see from Camelin's expression that he had something important to tell him, something he didn't want Nora to know about.

'What's wrong?'

'Lots.'

'Like what?'

'Like they aren't going to tell you.'

'Tell me what?'

'About a lost treasure!'

'What kind of treasure?'

'If you stop asking questions I'll tell you. I went to the library. Winver and Hesta were pestering me and trying to get me to come down to the lake and help, so I said I had to go find Gwillam. I was really going to go for a nap. You know how quiet it is in a library.'

'So what did you hear?'

'I'm coming to that. I found myself a secluded little alcove and was just nodding off when I heard Gwillam talking to the librarian. I couldn't hear what they were saying at first but they got closer and eventually sat down together near where I was perched. Gwillam sounded concerned and so did the librarian. They were talking about a missing book but the librarian assured Gwillam no one had taken any books from the library.'

Jack thought back to Falconrock, they obviously had the same rule in Annwn as on Earth.

'I don't think anyone's allowed to take any books out of a Druid's library,' said Jack.

'They're not, but Gwillam thought one might have been taken without permission... sort of stolen rather than lost.'

'Velindur was holding a book in my dream and in

the Stone of Destiny.'

'Stone of Destiny?'

'Last night, when I'd shown the Blessed Council my destiny I saw Velindur in the stone. I showed it to Gwillam and he saw him too.'

'No wonder Gwillam was worried.'

'Why?'

'Because the stone can only show what is to be.'

'So Velindur has a book. It could be any book, it could be one that belongs to him.'

'Not a chance. Gwillam says it was definitely from Annwn. He just needs to know which book it is and where he got it from.'

'Could it be one from the throne room?'

'The librarian asked Gwillam that too, but he said he'd checked there first. None of those books are missing. Gwillam's really concerned; he won't rest until he finds out. He told the librarian he'd rather there had been a book missing from the library. He said, *What if Velindur has got hold of one of the treasures?*'

'But none of the four treasures are books.'

'I know, it doesn't make sense. I wondered if you might know something.'

'Not a thing. I could ask my Book of Shadows.'

'Someone might hear and they'd see us if we went

to get it. Can't you just ask?'

Jack remembered the crystal from Falconrock. Grannus had told him its magic would work for him if he were in need. If he needed to know something about Velindur, maybe he could summon the crystal and it would somehow tell them what they wanted to know. Jack opened his hand, stared at his palm, and concentrated hard.

'Tell me about the treasures of Annwn,' he said in the most commanding voice he could muster.

When nothing happened he repeated the question. A blinding flash filled the small cellar. For a few moments Jack was unable to see. As his vision returned he could see the crystal suspended above his palm. It was spinning slowly.

'Tell me about the treasures of Annwn,' Jack said again.

The crystal slowed to a halt. Jack thought it was about to disappear as the light from most of its facets dimmed and then without warning four beams shone brightly onto the cellar walls. The image of the Stone of Destiny was to Jack's left, ahead was the spear, to his right was the cauldron and as he turned his head he could see the sword on the wall behind him.

'Aw Jack, you're just incredible. Ask if there are

any more treasures.'

Before Jack could speak the images changed, then rapidly changed again.

'Did you see them all?' asked Jack.

'No, did you?'

'There was Coragwenelan's blue cape, her staff, and a helmet.'

'I saw the helmet, an old chest, and a two-wheeled chariot, but the rest went too quickly; ask it again only say to go a bit slower this time.'

Jack looked at the dimly glowing crystal and was about to repeat his question when it faded and disappeared. Jack shook his hand, held his palm flat and tried again but the crystal would not reappear.

'That's it I'm afraid; Grannus did say it had a mind of its own.'

'Did you see a book?'

'No. Did you?'

Camelin shook his head.

'The only thing we do know is that there are more than four treasures and Gwillam seems to think one of them is a book.'

'Maybe we'll find out more tonight. I'm going to be given my quest before the feast.'

'Oh no! Not a quest. That means you'll be off on

your own again.'

'I don't see why.'

'It's that worthy thing again… you'll have to go and find something and prove you're the rightful king and I bet you have to do it on your own.'

Jack didn't answer. He'd had an awful thought. What if he had to find the book Velindur had in his hand? Jack remembered the look on Gwillam's face when he'd shown him the stone. If it only showed what was to be, even if Velindur didn't have the book yet, he would have it at some point and it must be important if Gwillam was worried.

'We'd better be getting back or they'll start wondering where we are.'

'I'll go first, so we're not seen together.'

Jack held the candle up so Camelin could see the stairs. He slowly counted to sixty and then made his way out of the cellar.

A great crowd had gathered around the Monolith. A platform had been raised in front of it and as Jack and Gwillam approached, the outer ring of people parted to let them through. A great cheer went up. Jack saw the four animal headed horns above the heads of the people. As they reached the steps an ear-splitting sound from the instruments drowned the cheers and cries of the crowd. Jack followed Gwillam onto the platform. He watched as Coragwenelan and the other twelve members of the Blessed Council mounted the steps at the back. When they were all on the platform Coragwenelan raised her arms. The sound stopped and the people bowed their heads.

'People of Annwn, we are gathered here tonight to give our thanks to the one who stands before you. Without him you would no longer have a Queen. Without him, death would have invaded our land. He saved the lives of Eleanor, Seanchai, Keeper of Secrets and Ancient Rituals, Guardian of the Sacred Grove, Healer, Shape Shifter and Wise Woman. He breathed Arrana's life force into the acorns from the Mother Oak and ensured there will always be Hamadryads to watch over the forests of Earth. He is known to you as Jack Brenin, Raven Boy, and Friend to All. He has been granted the freedom of our land. He may enter and leave as he chooses and none may hinder his passage.'

Coragwenelan waited until the cheers from the

crowd subsided.

'Is there any here who dispute this title?'

No one made a sound. Jack felt awkward. He wasn't used to having so many people looking at him. Coragwenelan stepped to one side and Gwillam went and stood next to Jack. He banged his staff on the platform three times before speaking.

'The Druids of Annwn wish to thank Jack Brenin for his help.'

Another great cheer rose from the crowd. Gwillam banged his staff again.

'The Queen and Blessed Council are pleased to inform you all that Jack Brenin, the one who stands before you, is the true heir to the throne of Annwn. He is hereby charged with the quest to find the lost treasure of Annwn and return it to us at Samhain.'

Another roar from the crowd gave Jack chance to look for Camelin. He was on Nora's shoulder. They exchanged a look. Jack felt apprehensive as Gwillam spoke again.

'He must locate the three parts of the King's torc, for without it there will be no coronation. Should he fail, he will only ever be crowned King of the Festival, as was his ancestor before him, until the day he can recover the torc.'

Gwillam reached into his pouch and produced a curved and twisted piece of gold. He turned and held it aloft for the crowd to see. Jack expected the crowd to cheer again but a hush fell.

'Your quest, Jack Brenin, is to find the other two pieces of this torc. Only he who is worthy to be King will be able to find and remake the lost treasure. This is the first piece, the second can be found in Elidon, the Land of Shadow, and the third is on Earth, hidden in the Land of the Living.'

Jack swallowed hard. He didn't know if he was supposed to say anything. Gwillam passed him the piece of gold. As soon as it was in his trembling hand the horns blared and the crowd began cheering again. Gwillam patted Jack on the shoulder and Coragwenelan shook his hand. One by one the members of the Blessed Council filed past him and each smiled before bowing their head. Jack hoped someone was going to tell him where to begin.

Coragwenelan stepped forward and raised her arms.

'Let us make our way to the amphitheatre, it is time for the Feast to begin.'

Jack watched as the Queen blew into a small silver whistle. The two of them looked towards the mountains. Jack strained his eyes until he saw Ember's silhouette appear in the sky. It wouldn't be long before the crowd saw how truly magnificent she looked. Every face turned upwards as she flew over. Jack smiled when he saw her land on top of the middle hillside where the amphitheatre was. She stretched out her wings, lowered her head, breathed a great flame, and lit the barbecue. Jack bowed to the Queen as she left the platform. He remained to watch the procession as it moved from the Monolith towards the amphitheatre.

'Come on,' Camelin called from the bottom of the platform, 'if we don't get a move on we'll miss the start of the festival.'

Jack reluctantly climbed down the stairs. When he reached the bottom Nora gave him a hug.

'I know it's a lot to take in but you'll be fine. Camelin is right, it's time to go.'

Jack nodded. He knew it was useless to try to speak. He blinked back the tears that were welling up in his eyes. In his heart he knew Camelin was right about something else too, he knew he'd be expected to complete his quest alone.

SABOTAGE

The First Fruits Feast itself was almost the same as the one Jack had attended at Midsummer. There was plenty of food, entertainers and storytellers, but this time Jack's thoughts were elsewhere and he wasn't able to enjoy himself. He wished the Blessed Council had given him his quest after the feast and not before. The enormity of the task that lay ahead had overwhelmed him. Doubt, concern and worry filled his mind. Camelin was oblivious to Jack's problem; he'd eaten his fill, laughed at the jugglers and listened intently to the stories. As it grew late Camelin hopped over to Jack.

'Can I have first choice of story to tell everyone when we get back?'

'You can tell them all, I'm not sure I'd remember any of them well enough.'

'That's great! I can't wait to tell the dragonettes the one about the Hag cave. My favourite was the *Case of the Missing Broomstick*, I bet the Dorysk will love it too. Which one did you like best?'

Jack began to answer but was interrupted by loud clapping coming from a group to their left. Jack couldn't see what they were looking at until two brightly coloured hummingbirds darted towards their table. The crowd seemed to think some more entertainment was about to begin but Jack wasn't so sure, he thought he recognised the two tiny birds.

'Timmery? Charkle?'

'Oh Jack, something awful's happened,' squeaked Timmery as he hovered in front of Jack's face. 'We had to come and find you. None of us knows what to do.'

'What's wrong?' asked Nora.

'There's been a break-in at Brenin House,' replied Charkle. 'Motley and the rest of the Night Guard are keeping watch but there's no one to help. Jack's grandad hasn't come home yet.'

'Is the house in a mess?' asked Nora.

'It's not the house, it's the shed,' said Timmery, as he darted back and forth. 'It's terrible. Your buggy's been smashed to pieces and there's paint everywhere. Twink knows what happened, she was there. She's really upset. The Dorysk heard crying and went to investigate. When he saw the mess he thought we'd better come and tell you.'

'Is Twink alright?' asked Jack.

'The Dorysk and Rhoda are with her, they've gone back to the fairy mound,' answered Charkle. 'Norris and Snook are guarding the meadow.'

Nora signalled to Gwillam and Coragwenelan to join them.

'We've got a problem; I'm afraid Jack and I are going to have to get back to Glasruhen as soon as possible. Charkle and Timmery will explain. Jack and I need to be there when his grandad gets home. Maybe Elan and Camelin can come back as soon as the feast is over.'

The Queen nodded Gwillam stood and signalled for Charkle and Timmery to follow him.

'I'd rather come back with you now,' said Camelin, looking meaningfully at Winver and Hesta.

They quickly said their goodbyes and set off at speed for the Western Portal.

'This wasn't quite how I expected our visit to end,' said Nora as they reached the two sentinel oaks, 'I'm sorry if it's spoilt your fun but I really think we should be there for when your grandad gets back.'

'It's fine,' both Jack and Camelin replied.

Jack was worried about lots of things but leaving Annwn wasn't one of them. He felt the pouch Gwillam had given him. Inside was the first piece of the torc. He checked his wand; it was safely in the loops. His golden acorn and silver key hung safely around his neck. At least he'd got everything with him, well almost everything.

'My clothes! They're at Gwillam's house,' cried Jack.

Camelin sniggered.

'Can you remember what you were wearing?' asked Nora.

Jack nodded.

'If you visualise your clothes I'll transform them when they appear, they'll be as real as the others; just remember to wear them when we come back again. As soon as you step into Annwn they'll instantly revert back to these robes and shoes.'

Jack concentrated hard. His soft shoes transformed into his trainers. He could see the robes changing shape until he stood in the clothes he'd worn the day before, when they'd entered Annwn. Nora took her wand and closed her eyes.

'*Muto*,' she commanded.

Jack felt his clothes get heavier as they transformed, they felt solid. Unlike the clothes he'd visualised, these were just like his real ones. Nora nodded her approval.

'Now, I think we'd better get back.'

When they arrived at Ewell House, Nora sent Camelin to find Motley to let him know they were on their way before she went to the herborium to put her cauldron away. Jack went up to his bedroom to get his house key.

'What are we going to say to Grandad?' Jack asked Nora as they walked through the tunnel to the garden of Brenin House.

'I think we're going to have to tell him we heard a commotion and came to investigate, otherwise, it's going to be difficult to explain how we knew about the break-in.'

As they approached the shed, Motley bounded over to meet them. His whiskers twitched rapidly and he looked very upset.

'Terrible mess inside, terrible, the police need to be informed. Those boys need arresting for what they've done.'

Jack's heart sank. He thought he knew who *those boys* might be. Nora held up her wand and shone the lighted tip towards the shed. The door had been left open. When they peeped inside Jack saw that Motley had not exaggerated. There was a terrible mess inside. The buggy had been smashed and lay in bits. The wheels were bent, the wood was broken and all of the metal parts were missing. There was paint all over the floor and the remains of the buggy. A trail of blue footprints led away from the shed towards the back lane.

'Two sets of prints, child size, don't you know,' said Motley. 'Fergus and Berry tracked them as far as they could but they fade away to nothing halfway across the field. Do you want me to send for Twink? She was here and saw what happened, knows who's responsible for this… too upset to be questioned earlier.'

'It would be helpful if she's feeling up to coming over, but if not we'll see her later. Do you know where Sam Brenin is?'

'Having supper at the Fox and Duck in Newton Gill with some of his friends from the Gardening Club.

Lester and Podge are keeping watch. Camelin's gone to let them know you're back. As soon as Sam Brenin's on his way home, Lester has orders to take the short cut and report to me. Lester is the swiftest runner we have and always knows the best route to take, he'll be back well before Sam Brenin.'

Jack had listened to Motley but he'd not been able to take his eyes away from the mess. Why would anyone be so mean as to wreck their buggy? It had to be Max, and probably Tank. This must be their way of getting their own back.

Nora put her arm around his shoulders.

'Try not to worry. We could clear it all up in a couple of minutes but I don't think we ought to use magic. Your grandad needs to know about it and I think Motley's right, we need to inform P.C. Stone. We mustn't touch anything. Do you want to wait in the house?'

'No I'd rather wait out here in case Twink comes over. You don't think they've damaged Grandad's garden, do you?'

'Flowers, fruit and vegetables all undisturbed,' said Motley. 'Morris and Midge had a good look round. They couldn't get into the greenhouse but nothing seems to have been touched. It looks as if the intruders

230

were only interested in the shed.'

A loud buzzing noise stopped the conversation. They turned and watched as a swarm of bees approached the shed. At the head was a different insect. It looked like an overgrown wasp. As it got nearer Jack could see it was wearing a pair of glasses. On its back sat Twink. The swarm circled around the top of the shed and the Dorysk landed next to Motley. As Twink stepped onto the grass Jack could see she had been crying. He bent down and offered her his hand to climb onto.

'Thank you, I'm so sorry I couldn't do anything to stop them.'

Jack held his hand higher so Nora could see her.

'Are you hurt?'

Twink shook her head.

'She's had a shock,' said the Dorysk as he transformed into his usual prickly form. 'Too upset to fly. We've got more than enough help now in case there's any trouble, the rest of the fairies from the mound are so cross it'll take them all night to calm down. If the lads come back they'll find a swarm of very angry bees waiting for them.'

'I don't think they'll be back,' said Nora, 'they've done what they came to do.'

'Did you see who did this?' Jack asked Twink.

'There were two of them, nasty boys. I was on my way to see Rhoda when I heard them climb over the fence. They were arguing. I heard their names, the one with the long blond hair was called Max and he called the big one Tank.'

Jack nodded, Twink had confirmed his suspicions but they'd never be able to prove it. P.C. Stone would think they were mad if they told him a fairy had witnessed the whole event.

'Can you tell us exactly what happened,' asked Nora.

'The one called Max said he knew there wasn't anyone in and no one would hear them. When they got to the shed they kicked the door, pulled it open and shone a torch around. Max told Tank to smash the buggy up *good and proper*. He tried jumping on it and kicking it but nothing happened, then they found your grandad's big hammer. The one he uses when he puts the posts in. That worked. They laughed as they took it in turns to smash the buggy. Tank had a bag and he bent over and started putting all the metal bits in it. As he stood up his head hit the shelf. A tin of paint bounced off and spilt. It went all over the blond one's head and all over the floor.'

'We still can't prove it was them,' said Nora.

'They could say they'd got paint on their clothes from anywhere.'

'No fingerprints,' interrupted Motley, 'must have worn gloves.'

'The blond one used some very bad language and pushed the bigger boy. He was furious he was covered in paint.'

'Serves him right,' said Nora. 'He'll have a hard job explaining that one away at home.'

Jack could imagine how cross Max would have been. He seemed very proud of his hair.

'Thanks Twink, I'm sorry they upset you,' Jack said as he lowered her to the ground.

'Make way, make way,' shouted Motley as a brown rat, with a distinctive black splodge on his back, bounded into the garden.

They all waited expectantly as Lester tried to speak. Jack could see his chest heaving as he fought to get his breath back.

'Sam Brenin, on his way,' he eventually managed to blurt out.

'Good job, estimated time of arrival?'

'Ten minutes,' panted Lester.

'Back to the mound,' the Dorysk called to the swarm of bees that were still buzzing madly around the shed. 'Give me a second Twink and you can hop on.'

There was a loud popping sound as the Dorysk shape-shifted back into a very large wasp. Twink climbed onto his back and away they flew.

'Great member of the Night Guard, invaluable in a tight spot, could come in handy if he knows how to use that sting too. Hornets are feared by most. We'll see how that big boy reacts. If he's afraid of bees he's not going to like an overgrown wasp.'

'You'd better get back to Ewell House before Sam arrives,' Nora told Motley.

There was a long low whistle followed by rustling and the sound of small feet making their way through the undergrowth. When Jack turned round to thank Motley and Lester, they'd already gone.

'Shall we go and meet your grandad by the gate? We can explain what's happened before he sees it.'

Jack nodded. He knew Grandad would be very upset. He'd been so excited when they were making the buggy.

When Jack's grandad saw them he waved and quickened his pace.

'What's wrong?'

'I'm afraid the shed's been broken into and there's rather a mess,' said Nora.

'Who could have done such a thing?'

'I think it might have been two of those boys who don't like me,' explained Jack.

'Have they done any damage? Is the buggy alright?'

Jack swallowed hard and tried to speak but the words just wouldn't come out. As he looked up at his grandad, tears streamed down his face.

'There, there, nothing to cry about, come here.'

Grandad opened his arms and Jack let himself be hugged. He buried his head deep into Grandad's chest. He sobbed and sobbed, for himself, for Grandad's disappointment and for his mum. He didn't care who saw him or what they thought.

When the tears eventually stopped he closed his eyes. He felt safe in his grandad's strong arms. No one had spoken and when he felt able to open his eyes again he was alone with Grandad.

'Let's get you inside, Nora's gone to the police station. What do you say to a nice cup of cocoa? It'll make you feel a lot better, and while you have your drink and settle yourself down I'll go and have a look at the damage.'

'They've ruined the buggy, it's all smashed up.'

'We'll start again. We're not going to let a little thing like this upset us, are we?'

Jack tried to smile but his lips started to tremble again. Grandad took him by the hand and led him inside.

'Up you pop, you can sleep in your own bed tonight, I'll bring you a drink up in a few minutes, and don't you worry, we'll sort it out.'

It wasn't long before Jack heard his grandad climbing the stairs. He came into Jack's room with two mugs of steaming cocoa and put them down on Jack's bedside table. Jack climbed into bed and shuffled over a bit so Grandad could sit on the edge.

'Feeling a bit better?'

'A bit.'

'Nora's suggested we rebuild the buggy in her shed. What do you say? Shall we give it another go?'

Jack nodded.

'That's the right attitude. We're not going to let a small setback like this stop us, are we?'

While they sipped their cocoa Grandad chatted

about the Flower Show but Jack wasn't really listening. There were lots of thoughts going round in his head. He wondered how he was going to fit everything in. The buggy was going to take up a lot of his time and he had to start looking for the torc. His life had unexpectedly become quite complicated.

'Have you finished?' asked Grandad as he stood up and held his hand out for Jack's mug.

Jack drained the last of the now lukewarm cocoa.

'That's a good lad, now you sleep tight, and in the morning you can make a start on the new buggy with Elan.'

Grandad closed Jack's bedroom door and went back downstairs. When the back door opened, Jack went over to the window and peeped from behind the curtain. He watched Grandad walk across the grass with his big flashlight. He went and joined Nora and a tall policeman by the shed. He could see them peering inside but no one went through the doors. They were too far away for him to hear what they were saying. He looked over to Ewell House; it was in darkness, which probably meant Elan wasn't back yet. He knew she'd want to rebuild the buggy; she wasn't afraid of any of the gang. He resolved to be stronger and not let them bother him. Maybe then they'd leave him alone.

He got back into bed and lay on his back. He wondered when he'd be able to look for the missing pieces of the torc. In all the confusion, he'd not been able to ask anyone about Elidon, and he didn't have his Book of Shadows to consult. He yawned deeply. He was too drowsy to think any more, it was all going to have to wait until the morning. He let his head sink deeper into his pillow and his eyelids close over his tired eyes.

AN UNEXPECTED VISITOR

Jack struggled to open his eyes. He could hear Grandad talking to someone in the kitchen but he'd no idea who it was. He tried to make out what was being said but couldn't. When the voices stopped he could feel himself drifting back to sleep. The sudden memory of the night before jolted him awake. He swung his legs out of bed, pushed his feet into his slippers and made his way to the kitchen in his pyjamas. He put his ear to the kitchen door. The only sound he could hear was Grandad setting the table. He opened the door a fraction and hesitated.

'Grandad…'

'Come on in, P.C. Stone's gone. Nothing's been

taken except a few bits of metal from the framework, but I'm afraid we're not going to be able to salvage much. They did a pretty good job of smashing it up. P.C. Stone's got a good idea who's responsible and he's going to be paying them a visit this morning.'

Jack groaned inwardly. He didn't think a visit from the police would stop Max wanting to get his own back, if anything it would probably make things worse.

'Will we have time to rebuild the buggy?'

'It'll be tight, and unfortunately the plans are covered in paint. Finding wheels might be our biggest problem but we'll give it our best shot, won't we?'

Jack nodded.

'Get yourself ready and we'll have breakfast. I've got to be in the judge's tent soon but you and Elan can make a start by taking anything we can reuse to Nora's and I'll see you all later this afternoon at the show.'

As Jack stood up there was a knock on the front door.

'Who could that be at this time in the morning?' said Grandad as he went to investigate.

Jack raced upstairs and quickly got dressed; whoever it was he didn't want to be seen in his pyjamas. He raced back downstairs when Grandad called him.

He'd half expected to see Nora or Elan in the kitchen so it was a complete surprise to find the smallest member of Max's gang talking to Grandad.

'I've come to apologise,' said Techno, before Jack could say anything.

'For what?' asked Jack.

'For your racer being trashed.'

Grandad patted Techno on the shoulder.

'He heard about what happened to the buggy.'

'It wasn't me… I didn't have anything to do with it and I don't want to have anything to do with Max or his gang any more either.'

'So it was Max and Tank?' asked Jack.

Techno bit his lip.

'What's done is done,' said Grandad. 'We mustn't let a couple of ruffians stop us. I think you need to listen to what this young man has to say. It took a lot of courage for him to come here this morning.'

Jack smiled weakly at Techno. They were about the same size but unlike Jack, everything about Techno was neat and sleek, including his jet-black hair. Techno took off his glasses and polished them on the bottom of his shirt before replacing them and speaking again.

'I'd like to help you repair the damage.'

'Why?' asked Jack a bit too abruptly.

'I've got a plan, a good plan. The gang didn't want it. Max and Tank didn't want to make anything themselves. The men who work for Tank's dad have made a racing car for them at the scrapyard. I didn't know your buggy was going to get smashed up. I'm really sorry about it and I'd like to help, if you'll have me.'

'See?' said Grandad. 'I told you it'd be fine; looks like we've got ourselves another team member.'

'We ought to ask Elan first,' said Jack.

'Ask Elan what?' she said, as she appeared in the doorway.

When Grandad had explained, Techno fished in his back pocket.

'I've got the plans here if you want to have a look.'

Jack watched as Grandad and Elan helped Techno to anchor the four corners of his plan down with the jar of marmalade, a jug, and the salt and pepper pots. Grandad eagerly examined the plans.

'This is good, very good, much better than the ones we had for the *Comet*. Did you draw these out on your own?'

Techno nodded. Jack looked at the diagram on the table. It didn't mean much to him but he could see this buggy didn't look anything like Grandad's *Comet*. It was designed around the frames of two bicycles only there were two big wheels at the back and two smaller ones at the front. The rest of the technical information was a mystery to Jack. Grandad patted Techno on the back.

'I say we welcome this young man to the team. Are we agreed?'

Elan nodded. They all looked at Jack.

'It's fine with me, thanks for coming round.'

Techno grinned at them all.

'We need to get started as soon as possible.'

'You'd better come and see if we've got anything you need,' said Grandad, as he showed Techno to the shed.

'Are you alright?' asked Elan, when they were alone.

'Yes and no,' replied Jack honestly. 'I'm worried about finding the torc. How do I get into Elidon? No one's told me anything.'

'We would have if you hadn't had to leave so soon. I'll tell you all about it later, when Techno's gone.'

'Shall I meet you at Ewell House? I haven't had my breakfast yet.'

'That'll be fine. Techno and I can start taking what we need to Ewell House. Nora's already cleared a space… with a little bit of help!'

Jack smiled as Elan waved an imaginary wand around before turning and making her way to the shed.

As Jack got his breakfast he realised that he'd have to visit Camelin later and let him know that Techno was going to be the fourth member of the buggy team so would no longer need to be watched by the Flying Squad. He also realised that Camelin would be annoyed because now he would be excluded every time Techno or Grandad visited Ewell House. Jack sighed; pleasing others wasn't always easy.

'You took your time,' grumbled Camelin, as Jack climbed up the loft ladder.

'I'm sorry; there was a lot to do,' said Jack, before explaining about Techno.

'Why did you say Techno could join in?'

'He asked and said he was sorry about our buggy. Besides, even if I'd said *no*, it would have been two against one, both Grandad and Elan were really happy about it and we did need a fourth member for the team.'

'Well I'm not happy.'

'You don't think Max has sent him to spy on us do you?'

'Naw, Crosspatch told me Max and Techno had a big row this morning and your new team member told Max he wanted nothing more to do with him. Max grabbed Techno by the collar so Crosspatch did a flyover and left a huge deposit on Max's hat. Max soon let go of him. Snatch saw the whole thing too and gave me the same report. And, Max has got blue hair this morning!'

'No!'

'Crosspatch said he watched his mum trying to wash it out but it's stuck good and proper. He's got to have his head shaved.' Camelin laughed loudly.

'He'll be even more annoyed now,' said Jack.

'Naw, he's got gang problems. Techno's walked away from him and Chortle said he'd had a big row with Danny too.'

'Does he know what that was about?'

'Max wants the rest of the gang to have their heads shaved too but Danny refused. He told Max he wasn't cutting his long hair off for no one. Max shouted at him and said he'd have to leave the gang. Danny said good and walked off.'

'What about Tank, has he got blue hair too?'

'Naw, but he did agree to have his head shaved. He said his mum would do it. She does his older brother's hair all the time. They've arranged to have it done together tomorrow afternoon at Tank's house. We can go and watch if you like.'

'I've got to go now. We're meeting Grandad in the judging tent at the Flower Show.'

'I suppose you'll be going back to Brenin House after the show.'

'Grandad's helping me to carry my bags back when it's over.'

'You'll come and see me tomorrow though won't you?'

''Course I will.'

By the time Jack and Grandad got back to Brenin House they were both feeling tired. They'd eaten at the show so they didn't need to make dinner.

'I think I'm going to have forty winks,' Grandad told Jack as he flopped down in his favourite chair.

Jack went into the kitchen and poured out two glasses of squash. By the time he got back to the front room Grandad was already snoring. He left one of the glasses on the table and went upstairs with the other one to unpack. He didn't have to sort Orin out as she'd decided to stay at Ewell House until after the race was over. He took out his Book of Shadows but decided he ought to put his clothes away before he opened his book and started asking questions. The only sound Jack could hear in the house was the loud ticking from the hall clock and Grandad's snores. He'd be asleep for at least a couple of hours, maybe more.

When the holdall and backpack were empty Jack picked up his book and lay down on his stomach on the bed. He closed his eyes so he could concentrate on the right way to ask his question about Elidon. A loud creak from outside the window broke his concentration. He opened one eye and squinted at the window. Nothing was on the windowsill but a second creak made him go and investigate. He opened the window and was about to look down when a single black feather came into sight, followed by an old battered hat and then Peabody's face.

'What are you doing here?'

'Oh great wizard, I had to come and see you, I don't know what to do. You're the only one who can help me.'

Jack knew it must be important if Peabody had risked being seen to visit Jack in daylight.

'You'd better come in.'

Peabody nimbly swung himself into Jack's room.

'Oh thank you, Your Wizardness.'

'What's wrong?'

'Everything! He's here somewhere in Glasruhen, he grabbed me in the forest, I couldn't see him but I knew it was him, I could feel his hands digging into my arm, and I felt his hot breath when he whispered in my ear. Thought I was my brother, he did, didn't know I wasn't Pyecroft. Wants help. I don't know what to do. He scares me.'

'Who? I don't know what you're talking about.'

'It was him, I know it was… you know… the Big One.'

'Velindur! Here in Glasruhen?'

'Yes, him, thought I was Pyecroft, obviously doesn't know my brother's more like a pig than a Bogie these days.'

'How do you know it was Velindur if you didn't see him?'

'Told me what he wanted. Only one person, apart from yourself who'd want what he's after.'

'And what would that be?'

'The torc of kingship. It's a long time since I've heard that mentioned. The old King of the Forest never came back to claim it as his own but the Big One thinks it belongs to him.'

Jack didn't know how far to trust Peabody; this could be a trick to get information from him, after all, Bogies specialised in collecting information. He decided to admit nothing and try to find out what Peabody knew.

'Why did he think you'd know where it was?'

'He didn't. He wants me to find out where it is. He knows that whoever finds the torc will be crowned at Samhain. He said because I was his servant I had to help him. Oh that dreadful brother of mine, he's always getting me into trouble. I don't want anything to do with any of this. Make the Big One leave me alone.'

'Are you sure it was Velindur?'

Instead of answering straightaway, Peabody dropped to his knees, clasped both his hands together and hung his head. When he spoke Jack could barely hear him.

'It was him. He was there but not there. Invisible. Please help me. Can't you give me a spell to make him go away or put some kind of protection around me? I don't ever want him to grab me again.'

'I'll get you some help but you'll have to be patient, it might take a while.'

'Oh thank you, thank you; from the tip of my nose to the top of my toe I thank you.'

Jack got Peabody a cushion to sit on before opening his Book of Shadows. He picked up his wand and wrote to Nora. He waited for an answer but none came. Peabody's legs were trembling and Jack was sure he was genuinely scared. He tapped the open page in the hope his answer would come but no writing appeared. A loud buzzing made them both turn towards the open window. Jack smiled as a large beetle wearing a tiny pair of spectacles flew into the room and landed on his bed.

'I think help has arrived.'

The Dorysk transformed into a small bird and then a large rat before his prickles finally appeared. Jack wondered if he was showing off for Peabody's benefit.

'I have a message from Nora. The Bogie is to follow me back to Ewell House. Nora wants to hear for herself exactly what happened, and when and where the encounter took place.'

Peabody looked pleadingly at Jack.

'You'll be fine, just tell the truth and I'm sure Nora will help you.'

'Are you ready?' the Dorysk asked Peabody, as he transformed back into a large rat, identical to Motley except for the glasses.

Peabody stood and followed the Dorysk onto the windowsill but before he climbed down the ivy he turned and bowed low to Jack.

'You truly are a friend to all.'

When they'd gone Jack wrote down the information he'd gained from Peabody. Velindur was obviously looking for the torc but he didn't seem to know it was in pieces, not if what Peabody had said was true. He hoped Nora would send him a message later, but while he was waiting he settled down to ask his Book of Shadows about Elidon.

ELIDON

Jack was already in bed when Grandad came in to say goodnight. He turned his bedside light off and lay on his back thinking about the events of the last few days. He tried to pick out the information he might need for the quest that lay ahead. He desperately wanted to talk things over with Elan and Nora but he knew he'd have to wait until the morning. His book had answered a few of his questions and he'd read a whole chapter about the Lost Treasure of Annwn. He now knew what the King's torc looked like, how heavy it was and who'd made it but he'd not had any of his questions answered to his satisfaction. He'd read a lot but learnt nothing at the same time. When he tried a direct question his book had slammed shut. Either it didn't know the locations of the two missing pieces of the torc or, as he had suspected, this was something he'd have to find out for himself. No matter what he'd tried, his book wouldn't open again. Elidon was still a mystery. He'd not learnt anything new about the strange land he had to enter. He'd only been told what he knew already by heart...

Elidon, Land of Shadow, where secrets are hid.

Was this where Velindur had been transported to? If so, it meant crystal magic was involved.

It's in the here and now but nowhere to be seen.

Peabody had said he couldn't see Velindur, but he'd been spoken to and grabbed. This would confirm there was a land no one could see. But how could Velindur see Peabody? The more Jack thought about it the less sense it made. He repeated the last piece of information he knew.

Knowledge is needed from the Druid's Library and the Labyrinth beyond before Elidon can be found.

Only those with the key may open the door,
and once inside, there is no turning back.

He'd used his key, he'd been into the library and
the labyrinth, and Elidon certainly wasn't there. The
only knowledge he'd managed to bring out of the
Druid's library was the complete book about crystal
magic. He knew it was stored inside his head but he
didn't know how to access the information. Jack was
drifting off to sleep when another thought struck him.
He'd brought something else away from Falconrock,
the magic crystal he'd found in the pool. What if the
key his book had mentioned wasn't the one that hung
round his neck? What if the words were referring to
the crystal? If he could summon it he might be able
to enter Elidon. There was a lot he needed to discuss
with Nora and Elan. There was one thing that reassured
him: one of the missing pieces of the torc was hidden in
the here and now so surely that wouldn't be too hard to
find. Jack closed his eyes and visualised the crystal he'd
pulled from the pool. As the crystal spun and shone in
Jack's mind he fell asleep.

Jack yawned. He still felt sleepy. He half opened one eye then shut it again. He couldn't see any daylight so with any luck he'd get a few more hours of sleep. A draught made him shudder. He must have left the window open. He reached for the covers but they weren't there. He rolled over and groped around with his hands but instead of the soft mattress Jack felt grass. He rolled back again; there was grass on the other side too. He must be dreaming; where had his bed gone? He reluctantly opened his eyes. He was still in his pyjamas lying on his back in a meadow near a tall tree. This wasn't just any meadow, he could see the fairy mound close by and he was next to the old thorn tree. There wasn't total darkness but there wasn't any light in the sky either. He rubbed his eyes. Was he dreaming or had he been sleepwalking? It wasn't something he'd ever done before but there was always a first time for everything. He reached out and touched the bark of the tree. It felt solid enough. He looked at his bare feet and wriggled his toes. If it was a dream why wasn't he dressed? He wasn't in the habit of going outside in his pyjamas but dreams weren't always predictable. He tried to visualise himself in his black tracksuit and trainers. In an instant his bare feet were shod and his pyjamas gone. This still didn't prove anything, he could still be dreaming. The last thing Jack had seen before he'd fallen asleep was the spinning crystal. He stood up, opened his hand and willed the crystal to appear. The dimness around him grew brighter as the crystal hovered above his palm. It rotated slowly at first but soon it was spinning so fast it became a ball of dazzling light. There was a flash. Jack blinked. When he could see again, the crystal was still. One single beam of light shone directly onto a knot in the bark of the thorn tree. As he watched, the light spread until the bark in front of him disappeared. He couldn't take his eyes away from the light as it expanded. When it finally stopped, an arched opening of shimmering light appeared within the trunk. He felt compelled to step into it. With each step forward the light dimmed. As he stepped out of the trunk on the other side he was once again in the half-light. He tried to make sense of what had just happened. The crystal and the light had gone. He was still in the meadow. He turned around to look at the archway, but that too had vanished.

'Welcome to Elidon,' a breathless voice whispered.

Jack turned around slowly. A moment before there'd been no one in the meadow, but someone, or something, had spoken. Jack nearly jumped out of his skin when he felt something touch his leg.

'Don't be afraid,' the voice hissed. 'No one is going to hurt you. Open your eyes and the veil of disbelief will fall. Let yourself believe and you will see me.'

Jack didn't know what the voice meant. His eyes were already open. Or were they? Maybe he was just dreaming he was awake? He made a conscious effort to open his eyelids wide. When he saw what blocked his path he hoped he wasn't awake. An enormous snake lay on the ground before him. On its head were two twisted horns. Jack caught a glimpse of two sharp fangs inside the snake's partially open mouth. He shut his eyes quickly and stood very still. When nothing happened he opened his eyes a fraction. The snake was still there, swaying from side to side. Jack felt very alone. He wished Camelin were with him. Jack swallowed hard and tried to work out what he could do. If this wasn't a dream and the snake was real he was in big trouble.

A muffled sound reached Jack's ears. It sounded a long way off but he knew it was the call of the raven owl. He instinctively looked up. The very indistinct outline of a raven flew above him. It circled around and around, hooting as it flew. Jack knew it was Camelin but he couldn't see him clearly. Jack caught a sudden movement out of the corner of his eye as the snake began to slither towards him.

'Run,' Camelin screeched, as the snake reared.

Jack's heart pounded. His feet wouldn't move. He felt transfixed by the snake. Camelin flew towards them at speed with his extended claws aimed at the snake. There was a rush of air. The snake moved easily to one side and avoided Camelin's attack. A loud moan came from the ditch. Jack ran over to the stream where his friend had crash-landed. He was surprised to see a boy rather than a raven rise from the water.

'Camelin?'

'What's happening?'

'I think I'm dreaming. This can't be real.'

'I assure you it is,' hissed the snake as it slithered towards them. 'You are both in Elidon but only one of you was invited.'

'I'm naked,' wailed Camelin. 'If this is a dream can't you think me some clothes.'

Jack tried but nothing happened.

'Don't bother, I'll do it myself,' he grumbled as he closed his eyes.

Within seconds Camelin was dressed in a bright yellow jumper, green trousers and blue shoes. Jack pulled a face.

'They're a bit bright aren't they?'

'I like them… they're not bad for a first attempt.

I was listening and watching when Nora gave you the visualisation lessons but I never thought I'd get to have a go.'

'You have shown great courage raven boy,' the snake said as it reared before Jack.

Camelin jumped in front of Jack and extended his right arm. As he opened his hand an umbrella materialised, which he brandished at the approaching snake.

'Keep away,' he yelled.

'I wish you no harm. I can see the bond of friendship is strong between you. When you thought your friend was in danger you were able to break through the veil between the here and now into the Land of Shadow. It takes great courage and determination to do what you've done.'

Camelin didn't lower the umbrella.

'Is this really Elidon?' asked Jack.

'It is, and I was sent to welcome you. There is one who would speak with you. He alone can help with your quest. It was something you were supposed to do alone but your friend has proven his worth and maybe he will be allowed to accompany you. Follow me, Kerne wishes to speak with you.'

'Not Kerne, the Horned One,' gasped Camelin as

259

the umbrella shook slightly, 'Lord of Elidon, Protector of the Wildwood?'

As Camelin spoke the snake lowered its head, Jack could see clearly the two curled horns. He still wasn't convinced he was awake.

'My Lord and Master awaits us, come this way.'

Camelin lowered the umbrella and turned to Jack.

'I don't think this is a dream. If he's the servant of Kerne his name is Permeris, and I think we ought to do what he says.'

'Ah! You know my name raven boy, we have known about you for a very long time. My master is impressed by your friend, the Brenin boy. He has done well to come so far in such a short time. We have watched your progress, for in Elidon we can see your world while only those with a key may gain access to the Land of Shadow. Your entry was most unusual, but not unheard of; your friend must have great power to be able to summon you.'

Camelin looked at the key that hung around Jack's neck.

'I'm afraid that kind of magic is useless here, there is something far older and more powerful in Elidon.'

'Crystal magic,' whispered Jack, as words formed

in his mind. '*The oldest and most powerful kind of magic throughout all the lands. It cannot be ruled and chooses its own path.*'

'Many underestimate crystal magic, it chooses who it will serve but none have been its master. You are wise for one so young,'

'He swallowed a book,' explained Camelin.

Jack frowned.

'I didn't swallow it, and I still don't know what's in it. Words just pop into my head.'

Permeris stopped and looked intently at Jack. He slithered around them slowly. His body was so long it surrounded them completely. Jack felt uncomfortable as he watched the snake's body ripple and slither through the grass. Permeris had said no harm would come to them but he still wasn't sure he trusted the snake.

'I feel your doubts,' Permeris hissed, 'but I assure you, while you are here in Elidon you are in control. When you want to return to your world just wish yourself back and in the blink of an eye you'll be there.'

Camelin closed his eyes and screwed up his face. He grumbled loudly when he opened them again.

'Well that didn't work.'

'Jack is the master of your fate here, raven boy;

you bound yourself to him when you answered his call and broke through the veil between the two worlds. I'm afraid wherever Jack goes you must go too.'

Jack could see Camelin was disgruntled but he didn't openly complain any more. It was strange seeing Camelin as a boy again. When he'd chosen to be a raven in Annwn Jack thought he'd be like that forever.

'This is Elidon,' Permeris whispered, 'here your friend will be his true self. No one can hide who they are from my eyes.'

'Is Velindur here?'

'I may see the truth but I am not bound to answer your questions. Kerne will tell you all you need to know.'

'Do we have far to go?' asked Jack.

'We must enter the forest and make our way to the old well. My master will be waiting for us there.'

Jack watched as Permeris slithered on ahead before waiting for Camelin to catch up.

'We're going to an old well in Newton Gill forest.'

'That'll be the hazel well. Nora got her wand from that old hazel tree. It used to be the tree where Cory lived a long time ago, before Allana died. I don't have to explain what happens when a forest hasn't got a Hamadryad do I?'

'We've put all that right now. The young Hamadryads

are growing rapidly into strong healthy trees.'

'You have, but it will be a long time before Newton Gill will live again.'

Jack knew Camelin was right. He looked around at the trees. He hadn't been into Newton Gill forest by this path before but the rest of the landscape was familiar. Jack tried not to laugh when he glanced back at Camelin. He looked very bright in his choice of clothes.

'Why the umbrella?'

'Nora always says you should never go anywhere without an umbrella. It was the first thing that came into my head. It worked didn't it? That creepy snake didn't attack us, did he?'

'Shhh! I don't want him to overhear us. I think he can read minds, at least he seems to know what I'm thinking.'

'You know this isn't a dream don't you? You dragged me from my warm raven basket. The last thing I'd expected was to be walking through Elidon tonight. You're going to have to say it was your fault if Nora finds out.'

'She'll know all about it by morning.'

'I don't see how, the trees from this place can't tell her anything.'

'No, but I can, and will. She needs to know.'

'I'll be in trouble.'

'Why? When Nora finds out what you did, she'll be impressed.'

'She grounded me earlier, told me I wasn't to leave the house unless she knew where I was going.'

'Need I ask what you did?'

Camelin sighed.

'She found out I'd been for a second supper.'

'You won't be in trouble for helping me out, I promise.'

Jack could see Permeris not far ahead. He waited for them to catch up with him. Together they walked in silence through a meadow. They'd almost reached the edge of the field when a man came towards them, walking a dog. Both Jack and Camelin stopped but Permeris slithered into the undergrowth. The dog stopped and sniffed Camelin's foot. The man turned round. Jack was sure he was going to speak to them but he whistled his dog back and they both carried on.

'Couldn't he see us?' asked Jack, when the snake reappeared.

'No, you are in the shadows here. You are able to see your world through the veil. It might look a bit fuzzy around the edges but from the other side it's almost impossible to see into Elidon. Animals and fairies can usually see both worlds quite clearly, that's why I hid, I didn't want to scare the dog. Shall we proceed?'

When they reached the edge of the meadow Jack's heart sank. The sight of the lifeless trees in Newton Gill forest made him feel sad. He looked for faces in the trunks but he couldn't even see any Gnarles. This part of the forest was completely dead.

'There used to be a grove of Silver Birch trees here,' said Permeris, 'sadly they are no more.'

Jack looked at the pale peeling bark and the brittle branches. The forest floor was littered with broken twigs that crunched underfoot as they made their way deeper into the gloom. Permeris stopped and turned to Jack and Camelin.

'I must leave you for a while. You'll find the hazel well in the clearing ahead. My master will join you shortly.'

'Come on Jack, I know where it is, I'll show you the way,' said Camelin as he pulled Jack's arm.

Jack turned to thank Permeris but the snake had

vanished. He let himself be led through the trees until they came to the edge of a clearing. Large boulders, covered in moss, surrounded an old well. It looked like Jennet's except that the tree beside it wasn't alive. It didn't seem as gloomy in the clearing. As he looked around he could see why: a thin shaft of moonlight was doing its best to break through the veil between the two worlds.

'Who's Kerne?' Jack whispered in Camelin's ear.

Instead of answering Camelin pointed towards the light. Between the trees and moss-covered stones, the silhouette of a great stag appeared. It stretched its neck, tipped its head back and bellowed loudly. Jack had never been so close to a stag before. The noise was deafening and it made Jack's heart race. The stag's magnificent velvet covered antlers looked like a pair of gigantic hands. Jack held his breath and didn't dare move. He could see Camelin was very still too. Should they bow or say something? He wished Permeris hadn't gone. If the snake were here, he'd have been able to introduce them.

'You need no introductions,' the stag said as it took a step towards them. Its voice was deep and soft and although the creature towered above them, Jack felt no fear.

The stag carefully chose a path between the rocks and as it got closer, Jack could see it was completely white. It also appeared to be getting smaller as it approached. With each step the stag changed. First its antlers shrank, and then its body changed from that of a stag to a man. Jack and Camelin exchanged a glance when the transformation seemed to be complete. A young man with two antlers moved nimbly over to one of the mossy rocks beside the well and sat down. He crossed his legs then held out his left hand. Permeris slithered towards him. When the snake reached the young man he reared before bowing his horned head.

'Master, your guest has arrived and one who is worthy accompanies him.'

Camelin moved close to Jack and whispered in his ear.

'That's Kerne, Lord of Elidon, Protector of the Wildwood known by some as the Horned One, and the worthy one is me?'

'That's right raven boy,' said Kerne, 'if you were not worthy you would not be standing before me.'

Jack bowed and nudged Camelin to do the same.

'Come and sit with me,' said Kerne. 'We have a lot to discuss.'

As Jack and Camelin made their way towards the

well he wondered why Kerne looked familiar. Part way through his transformation, when he'd been half man and half stag, Jack had been reminded of a story his mother had once told him but now the transformation was complete he knew he'd seen the Lord of Elidon somewhere before. As he sat before the horned man a memory came flooding back. He was standing behind the Prefects' office in Viroconium; in his hand was a bronze cauldron plate, and on it was a picture of a young man sitting cross-legged holding a snake. Jack concentrated hard until he could see the plate in his mind. The seated figure had antlers and was wearing a torc around his neck, in his left hand was a horned snake, and in his right, another torc. Camelin nudged Jack as Kerne opened his arms wide. Permeris moved closer to his master. Kerne reached out and closed his hand around the snake's body. Permeris instantly changed. His body shrank and became a rigid staff. Jack looked expectantly at Kerne's right hand but it remained empty. The Lord of Elidon lifted his head as the shaft of moonlight shone directly onto him. Something glinted. As Jack looked closer, he could see a heavy golden torc around Kerne's neck.

KERNE

'Welcome to Elidon,' Kerne said as he slowly gestured towards the forest with his right hand. 'You seek the lost treasure of your ancestor, I believe?'

Jack waited expectantly to be presented with the piece of torc he'd come for. When it wasn't forthcoming he realised Kerne was waiting for an answer.

'I seek knowledge from Elidon so that I might find the two missing pieces of my ancestor's torc. I have one part already, given to me in Annwn by Gwillam, leader of the Blessed Council.'

'You have the freedom to go wherever you wish in my land but you may only enter three times before Samhain.'

Jack bowed his head and nudged Camelin to do the same.

'Can you tell me where the piece of torc is hidden?'

'Alas no, it is not that easy. I do not have the knowledge you seek. You must find Sabrina, for only she can help you. What I do know is that you must find the torc, for without it there can be no coronation. Only the rightful heir has the power to remake it, so if someone else finds the pieces, they would be of no use.'

'Easy peasy,' said Camelin. 'Gwillam said it was only a formality. Once we've got the pieces, and you've remade it we can...'

Camelin stopped in mid-sentence when Kerne banged his staff against one of the rocks. He sighed deeply before speaking again.

'Finding the pieces of the torc will not be easy but the most dangerous part of your quest will be keeping them safe until the coronation, for whoever enters Annwn at Samhain, and presents the Queen with the Lost Treasure will be crowned. I can see into your heart Jack Brenin, and I know kingship was the furthest thought from your mind the day you found the golden acorn. However, there is one who desires to be king and will stop at nothing to regain the position he believes belongs to him. You know of whom I speak?'

'Velindur,' said Jack and Camelin together.

At the mention of his name, Jack's heart beat quicker. He remembered his nightmare. Velindur was the one person he never wanted to meet again. Without thinking, he blurted out the same question he'd asked Permeris.

'Is he here in Elidon?'

'And what does your heart tell you?'

'That he is here and that he somehow knows I've got to come here too.'

'Velindur did not arrive by choice; he was transported to Elidon by crystal magic. You will find many creatures here, some are fair folk and some not so fair but all have chosen this realm as their home. Beware, however, any men you may encounter for they are here against their will. All were banished from their homes for past crimes. If they should repent and prove they are sorry they will find peace and maybe return to the life they once knew. The fate of the unrepentant is sealed and they are condemned to remain in the shadows forever.'

'I can't see Velindur ever saying sorry,' said Camelin. 'From what little I know of him he always thinks he's right.'

271

'That may be so,' replied Kerne, 'but Permeris tells me he's been trying to enlist help from some of the immortals who dwell on Earth. I advise caution. He is not to be trusted.'

At the mention of Permeris, Jack had glanced at the staff in Kerne's hand. The snake had assured him he could be trusted but how could Jack be certain. He still felt afraid of the snake, even when it wasn't moving.

'You need not worry about Permeris,' laughed Kerne. 'He is my trusted companion, a bit like yours.'

Camelin frowned at Jack but was prevented from saying anything when Kerne continued.

'You'll not find another ram-horned snake in any land. Permeris abides with me in Elidon and is my faithful friend. He sees all, can read men's thoughts and sees into their hearts. That is why you have nothing to fear from him, he knows you are honest and true.'

Jack felt happier knowing the snake liked him and meant him no harm. It was one less thing to worry about. However, even though he'd entered Elidon he was still no wiser about the task that lay ahead of him. The Blessed Council and the Queen had complete faith in his ability; they didn't understand how daunted he felt by the quest. It wasn't something he'd ever done before, and having been told he couldn't use magic he felt very vulnerable in this strange land. If he were not alone it might help. Jack became aware Kerne was waiting for him to speak.

'Permeris said Camelin might be able to accompany me. Would that be possible?'

'True friendship is a rare gift. Camelin has proved his loyalty and concern for you beyond doubt. He may stay at your side and help in any way he can.'

Jack could see Camelin out of the corner of his eye. He didn't know if he was smiling or smirking but whichever it was, Camelin looked pleased with himself.

Kerne smiled encouragingly at Jack.

'The torc is the symbol of kingship, and if the Blessed Council were in any doubt as to your worthiness or ability to locate the missing pieces, you would not have been given this task.'

'I don't know what to do or where to begin.'

'This is where you start, right here, which is why you were brought to this place. When you've drunk from the well and eaten the nuts from this tree you will be empowered with the knowledge you need to find Sabrina. She alone can tell you what happened to the torc after it was broken.'

'Who's Sabrina?' asked Jack.

'Don't you know anything,' grumbled Camelin before Kerne could answer. 'She's the nymph of the Gelston River, the most knowledgeable of all water nymphs, and she can shape-shift, unlike the nymphs who live in wells and lakes.'

'That is true,' agreed Kerne, 'but she can also cross through the veil which separates our worlds for the river flows through both. However, on Earth, she can only appear as a great fish. Over the centuries many men have tried to catch her. None have succeeded for she is the river too, and can shape-shift into water in an instant.'

As Jack listened to Kerne's description he looked at the tree that stood next to the well. It was dead wood. Even on Earth it would not be alive. How was he going to be able to eat hazelnuts from a dead tree?

'The answer to your question lies within you,' explained Kerne.

Camelin gave Jack a puzzled look.

'The tree is dead. I don't know the answer.'

'If I'm not mistaken, Arrana empowered you before she faded away. You have the gift of life to give this tree, if only for a short time. For you it will bear its fruit.'

'How? What do I have to do?'

'Step up to the tree and do exactly what you did when you transferred each Hamadryad spirit into the acorns from Annwn.'

Jack approached the hazel tree. He placed one hand on the rough bark and held his golden acorn in the other. As he breathed gently onto the dead wood he felt warmth travel from his acorn, through his body and out through the hand that touched the bark. There was a slight movement within the tree. He kept his hand firmly pressed against the bark, and watched in amazement as small buds appeared, followed quickly by long pale catkins. From every branch leaves burst from the buds, rapidly followed by small clusters of green nuts, which quickly turned a yellowish brown. Within seconds, ripe nuts began falling to the ground, some fell into the well from the nut-laden branches that overhung the water but most were strewn around Jack's feet.

'You can stop now,' said Kerne softly, as he put his hand on Jack's shoulder.

As soon as Jack removed his hand the green leaves began to turn yellow and drop from the tree. The nuts on the ground were covered with autumnal leaves before they crumpled and disappeared completely.

'The hazelnuts have gone!' exclaimed Camelin. 'It's as if it never happened.'

'Not all the hazelnuts,' replied Kerne as he lowered his hand into the well and scooped several out of the water. 'You did well, Jack Brenin, we have just the right amount here, you'll need to crack all nine nuts open, eat them and then drink from the well.'

Jack laid the hazelnuts on top of a flat rock and found a stone. He proceeded to crack open each shell. When all nine were in his hand, he began to eat. He was glad he was able to scoop water from the well because the nuts were dry and difficult to swallow. When he'd finished eating, Jack felt dizzy. The whole world appeared to be spinning. He closed his eyes but it made him feel worse. He'd felt like this in the library at Falconrock after his *book rush* experience.

'Don't worry,' said Kerne. 'Sit down for a moment, the feeling will pass.'

'What's wrong with him,' asked Camelin.

'Your friend is adjusting to a surge of wisdom, it won't take long.'

'I'm fine,' announced Jack as he stood.

'Are you sure? You don't look too good,' said Camelin.

'Positive, and I know exactly where we've got to go

and how to get there. I must speak with Sabrina before sunrise, for she is only a nymph at night.'

Jack felt sure he was right but he'd no idea how he knew about Sabrina. The hazelnuts and water from the well, must have worked. He could see in his mind the place where Sabrina lived and he knew they'd find her on an island in the middle of the Gelston River. He was still trying to make sense of this new skill when Kerne began speaking.

'Before you go I must warn you. This land is inhabited by those who find it difficult to live on Earth. Unfortunately there is a mean-spirited Hag between here and the river.'

'We don't have to disguise ourselves, or use that vile shampoo again, do we?' grumbled Camelin.

'There'll be no need for a disguise; I have a gift for you both, hold out your hands.'

Kerne laid his staff on the floor, closed his eyes, and clapped his hands together twice.

Something heavy landed on Jack's open palm. When he examined the object he found it was a stone with a hole through its middle. A very long leather thong had been looped through the hole. Jack could see Camelin had one too.

'Wear these hag stones whenever you enter

Elidon,' said Kerne.

'What's a hag stone?' asked Jack.

Camelin sighed.

'Hag stones are almost impossible to find. We could have done with some when we went into Silver Hill. They make you invisible to Hags.'

Kerne nodded slowly.

'That's true, but they don't hide your smell and you can still be felt even if you can't be seen.'

'I'm not frightened of any Hag,' said Camelin.

'This isn't just *any Hag*, this one is a lot more vicious and cantankerous than the ones you meet on Earth, that's why she's here. Keep upwind of her and mind your ankles, this Hag bites.'

'Thank you,' said Jack as put the hag stone around his neck. He nudged Camelin to do the same.

'Yes, thank you,' he mumbled.

'May good fortune be with you on your quest, Jack Brenin. Be mindful, take heed of your instincts and be careful what you wish for. You have the power of crystal magic within you, use that power wisely. I hope we meet again soon.'

Jack bowed his head. When he looked up again Kerne had begun to transform. Already his legs had changed, and instead of two, he now had four cloven-hoofed feet. As he shook his hair a mane appeared and his antlers grew longer. In seconds the transformation was complete. A great white stag stood before them. It stamped its right foot and bellowed loudly. The discarded staff began to transform too. It wasn't long before Permeris slithered at their feet. He reared and slightly bowed his head.

'Farewell, until we meet again,' he hissed softly. 'And remember, when you want to go home, wish it and it will be so.'

'Thank you,' replied Jack. 'We ought to be going.'

Without warning the great stag turned and galloped off into the forest. Jack held his breath as he watched the stag weave in and out of the trees until he disappeared from sight. When he looked around, Permeris was gone too. He and Camelin were alone.

The quest had begun.

'So… what now?' asked Camelin.

'We need to find Sabrina. Have you ever met her?'

'Nope. I don't like the Gelston River, it's a dangerous place and this raven doesn't swim.'

'You're not a raven now.'

Camelin shrugged his shoulders and stuck out his bottom lip.

'How are we going to get there before sunrise? It's a long way to the river and we can't fly there.'

'I can use the crystal, I know it will work.'

'Let me change first.'

'Change?'

'It won't take a minute.'

Jack watched as Camelin screwed up his eyes and concentrated hard. His shoes changed into wellingtons, a bright yellow sou'wester appeared on his head, and a waterproof cape covered his clothes.

'Is all that really necessary?'

'I'm being practical.'

'Well at least you won't need the umbrella.'

From underneath his cape Camelin produced the brolly.

'Nora always says you should take an umbrella with you wherever you go…'

'I know… it might come in handy.'

'Well it might.'

'Are you ready now?'

'Ready.'

Jack opened his hand and visualised the crystal. He closed his eyes and formed its shape in his mind.

'You did it Jack, look it's spinning over your palm.'

Jack opened his eyes. He felt a rush of excitement. Should he ask the crystal out loud or just visualise the place he wanted to go to? He decided to use his mind to show the crystal where they needed to go. He held out his free hand to Camelin.

'You'd better hold my hand.'

Camelin wrinkled his nose and held out the pointed end of his umbrella.

'I'd rather you held this.'

Jack didn't have time to disagree. He grabbed the end and showed the crystal the place where he knew Sabrina lived. In an instant the landscape changed. They hadn't moved or flown through the air, it was as if the Gelston River had come to them. They were standing on a grassy bank. Before them a wide river flowed swiftly. It looked deep, and the dark swirling water felt menacing. In the middle of the river was a small island.

'Wow Jack! That was amazing, you really are a natural.'

'Thanks, shall we go and see if the Lady of the River will speak with us?'

'How do you know her proper name?'

'I don't know, I just do. The same way that I know Sabrina lives on that island over there.'

'It's those hazelnuts you ate. I suppose you're going to be a know-it-all now.'

'I can't help what I know.'

'So how are we going to get across, you'd better tell your crystal to take us over.'

Jack tried to summon the crystal but nothing happened.

'I think we might have to get ourselves over to the island.'

'We need a boat, can't you wish for a boat?'

Jack took a deep breath before he spoke.

'We need a boat to get across to the island.'

From nowhere, a small round boat appeared on the bank behind Camelin.

'We have a boat,' announced Jack and nodded for Camelin to turn round.

'Boat! Call that a boat. It looks like someone's done my bigging spell on a basket!'

'It's a coracle.'

'A what?'

'A boat the fishermen have used for generations on the Gelston River, it's…'

'Stop, please! It was bad enough when you swallowed the book, now you're the fount of all knowledge.'

'I just know what it is.'

'Well get it changed, it looks unstable and I don't want to get wet.'

Jack tried to visualise Nora's rowing boat but the coracle stayed the same.

'I think this is what we're meant to use. Are you coming?'

Camelin grumbled to himself as he helped Jack take the small boat to the water's edge. He held it still while Jack climbed in. The boat wobbled violently from side to side as Jack leant over to pick up the paddle.

'Are you coming?' Jack asked again.

Reluctantly Camelin got into the boat and gripped the sides. When the boat steadied he looked down at Jack's wet feet.

'You should have got yourself a pair of wellingtons.'

Jack didn't answer. He was trying to concentrate. He instinctively knew how to use the paddle but he didn't have the strength in his arms to make it go where he wanted. After three failed attempts Camelin sighed loudly.

'Give me the oar. We'll be here for hours if you're going to paddle like that.'

Jack didn't complain. Camelin was much stronger. It wasn't long before the coracle was heading across the river towards the island where Sabrina lived.

SABRINA

'Are you sure this is the right island?' said Camelin, as they got out of the coracle.

'It feels right; we're going to have to trust in crystal magic because without it I wouldn't have a clue where to begin.'

'There's only a clump of trees, a few bushes and lots of grass. Who'd want to live here?'

'Maybe that's the point. If it looks uninhabited you won't get people calling on you.'

Camelin sighed loudly when they'd heaved the coracle onto the grass.

'Where do you want to look?'

'Follow me.'

Jack could see Camelin was reluctant to go any further. At first glance there didn't appear to be anywhere for Sabrina to live, but Jack wasn't about to give up so easily.

He led the way towards the clump of trees. As they got closer, Jack could see they formed a circle. He knew they were in the right place when he saw the pool in the middle.

'This is it, look, over there, a perfect place to find a water nymph.'

'And what have you brought with you to exchange for information. You did think about that didn't you?'

Jack swallowed hard. He could feel a rush of panic flood through his body. He had nothing to offer Sabrina.

'You forgot, didn't you?'

'I didn't know we'd be visiting a water nymph.'

'There's no excuse for bad planning, you should always be prepared for every eventuality.'

'I'll try to ask the crystal.'

'No need.'

'Why? Did you bring something?'

'I did.'

Jack's jaw dropped. He was amazed Camelin had

thought that far ahead.

'How?'

'When I changed my outfit I also visualised a few things from my collection of shiny bits, you know, just in case you hadn't thought about it.'

'But they won't be real.'

'They look and feel solid to me.'

Jack watched as Camelin half opened his umbrella, turned it upside down, and gave it a shake. Onto the grass fell a small sparkly stone, a large sea-green marble, and an ordinary looking shell.

'Did you mean to bring the shell?' asked Jack.

'Pick it up and turn it over, you'll see.'

Jack turned the dull looking shell over. The inside was completely different; it was smooth and colourful. As Jack moved it around he could see the colours change, even in the dim light of Elidon. The deep blues, greens and purples fascinated him, as they shimmered and shone.

'This is beautiful, I think I'd love this if I were a water nymph, we'll offer her this.'

'See, I told you an umbrella always comes in handy.'

Jack didn't reply. The objects could have been carried, just as easily, in Camelin's pocket. He handed the stone and marble back and watched as Camelin dropped them safely into the umbrella before closing it again.

'I'd better try calling her,' said Jack, as he knelt by the edge of the pool. He put his lips to the water and spoke as clearly as he could. 'Sabrina, Wise One, Lady of the River.'

Jack remained kneeling. He scanned the water for any sign of movement. He'd just decided to try to call Sabrina again when a ripple began spreading out from the middle. By the time it lapped the water's edge Jack could see a dark shape below the surface swimming towards him. He'd seen several water nymphs before and was prepared for a green-skinned woman to appear. It was quite a surprise when a pale-faced nymph with luminous skin broke the surface. Her hair was silvery and looked like silk. Unlike Jennet's hair, Sabrina's was well looked after. Although she looked very different there was no mistaking what she was. Jack thought she looked sad. He bowed his head and immediately held out the multicoloured shell towards her.

'You need my help I see.'

Sabrina spoke softly, in a voice unlike the harsh, sharp tones of some other water nymphs he'd met. Jack also heard sadness in her voice.

'I need some information. Could I exchange it for this please?'

Sabrina took the shell from Jack and examined it carefully. A faint smile crossed her lips before she spoke.

'You'll be wanting to know where to find the missing torc pieces, I presume?'

'I do. My quest is to find the Lost Treasure of Annwn. If I can find the pieces and remake the torc, I'll be crowned king at Samhain.'

'I will gladly tell you all I know in exchange for this beautiful shell, but alas, a long time has passed since the torc was broken. One part of the golden band was kept for safety in the darkest cave at the foot of the hill you call Glasruhen, but that was before a Hag arrived in Elidon. As I'm sure you know, Hags seek out the dark places in which to make their homes. This Hag did just that. She found the piece of torc in her cave and mistook it for a hair band, which she now wears to keep her long hair out of her eyes. It's safe where it is and would probably be the last place anyone would think of looking but it will be a hard task to persuade her to part with what must be her greatest treasure.'

Jack's heart sank. He had hoped Sabrina's information would help him to find the torc without too many problems.

'Do you know anything about the other piece? The one I have to look for on Earth.'

'Again, it is so long ago. I live in both worlds but choose to spend most of my time here in Elidon. The world of men is not the place it once was and I grow weary of change.'

'I'd be grateful for any information you might have.'

Sabrina didn't speak. She had a faraway look in her pale green eyes. Jack took Camelin's umbrella, opened it a fraction and pulled out the marble.

'I have another gift. I don't know who else I can ask. I was told you would have the information I need.'

Camelin frowned and pulled his umbrella back from Jack. Sabrina extended one of her long arms and stroked the marble in Jack's hand.

'You mistook my silence; I was not awaiting another gift. I have a very long memory for I have seen many things. The reason the torc was broken was to keep it safe. Your world has had a tempestuous history but not all the secrets of ancient times have been forgotten. The knowledge was given to the Hamadryad and myself. Alas, Arrana is no more.'

'Before she died, Arrana gave me her power. Do you think she gave me the knowledge to find the missing torc too?'

'You have the power of the Hamadryad within you?'

'He can make trees grow,' explained Camelin.

'Green magic is a precious gift. It is rare for a mortal to have such power.'

Jack could see Sabrina was impressed. He could also see she liked the marble. Camelin might not be pleased if Jack gave it to her but he liked the nymph and he felt sorry she was so sad.

'Please take the gift. I'd like you to have it.'

'You have a kind heart, Jack Brenin. When you return to Earth you must visit the King's stone. Look through the eye and you'll see where you need to go. When you have journeyed to the destination you'll find a similar standing stone. Read the inscription, and it will lead you to the place where the torc was hidden for safekeeping. Arrana would have been able to tell you more had she still been with us.'

'Thank you,' said Jack, as he bowed his head. 'We are very grateful for all your help.'

Camelin also bowed. Jack passed the marble to Sabrina. Her whole expression changed as she held it tightly in her long fingers.

'I shall treasure this. You and your companion will always be welcome. There will never be any need for gifts again. If I can ever help you I will. I bid you good fortune in your quest.'

They watched Sabrina as she sank gracefully into the pool. A large ripple travelled across the surface once she'd disappeared completely.

'Well,' said Camelin, 'it's a good job we've got these Hag stones, looks like we're going to be needing them.'

'I'm sorry about your marble but it seemed the right thing to do.'

'Aw! It's fine. I've got plenty in my loft. Be nice if Jennet was as sociable.'

'Sabrina wasn't what I expected. She was calm, and very beautiful, in an unusual way.'

'Unlike the other water nymphs we know!'

Camelin laughed loudly. Jack thought Nora would probably have given him a disapproving look.

'We'd better get back to the coracle,' said Jack.

'Yeh, we can have some fun now that's over with.'

'I think we'd better get home; look, the sun's about to rise,' replied Jack as he pointed to the horizon.

'That's not fair. I get my body back and as soon as there's a chance to have a bit of fun it's time to go home.'

Jack ignored Camelin's moan. They both knew they'd have to go.

'Do you think we need to hold hands when I wish us back?'

'No! You can hold the end of the umbrella, and don't forget to make sure Nora knows it wasn't my fault I was here.'

'I promise. Ready?'

'Ready.'

Jack held onto the end of the umbrella, closed his eyes and wished they were each back home. He waited for a rushing sensation but nothing happened. When he opened his eyes he was in his bed at Brenin House. It was as if nothing had happened. Had it been a dream? He instinctively put his hand to his neck. The thong was there. He ran his hand down the leather until he felt the hag stone at the end. His quest really had begun but he'd only got two more visits to Elidon in which to find the missing piece of torc. Jack leapt out of bed. He washed and dressed quickly; there wasn't a moment to lose. The sooner he got to Ewell House and spoke to Elan and Nora about the King's stone the better. He could start looking for the next piece of torc as soon as he knew where to find the standing stone.

'Hello,' Jack called as he reached the open patio doors. He bent over and put his hands on his knees as he fought to get his breath back. Maybe running all the way to Ewell House hadn't been a good idea. 'Hello, is anyone up?'

'Of course they're up,' grumbled a familiar voice. 'But too busy to bother about me, I've had to get my own breakfast.'

As Jack stepped into the kitchen, Camelin shuffled out of the pantry.

'Does Nora know you've helped yourself?'

'Had to, she won't be back for ages, they've got a visitor. It's that new friend of yours. They're all in the shed.'

'Techno?'

'Yes, him.'

Jack sighed loudly.

'Humph! Thought you liked him?'

'It's not that; I wanted to talk to Nora about last night. Did you tell her what happened?'

'You promised you'd tell her so she'd know it wasn't my fault. She knows something's up… said she'd speak to me later. I bet one of the trees told her.'

'I will sort it out, but I'm not going to be able to say anything while Techno's here and Grandad will be here to help soon.'

'Why'd you have to get involved with all this buggy making in the first place?'

'It just sort of happened.'

'I'll be glad when it's finished. Do something useful and give me a hand upstairs with this lot, I'm starving after all that excitement last night.'

Jack watched as Camelin used his beak to drag a canvas bag through the pantry door.

'Won't Nora miss all that?'

'Naw, the trick is to just take a bit from everything. Trouble is, there's nothing interesting in Nora's pantry… it's all healthy stuff.'

Camelin stopped pulling once he'd reached Jack's feet.'

'Bring this lot up to the loft for me. It'll save me having to find places to stash it all.'

Before Jack could protest, Camelin was already

heading for the open patio door.

As Jack struggled up to the loft with Camelin's bag of supplies he tried to think of a way to get Nora on her own so he could tell her about the visit to Elidon. Surely she'd know about the King's stone or maybe have a book about it. He'd tried to ask his Book of Shadows but he'd not got any answers. He was sure he'd be given the information if he asked the right questions.

'You took your time,' grumbled Camelin, as he looked through the trap door.

Jack didn't answer. He managed to get the bag up the ladder and push it towards Camelin's emergency ration dustbin.

'Ah thanks Jack! I can take it from here.'

'See you later.'

'You will. I can't wait to go back to Elidon.'

Jack tried to share Camelin's enthusiasm but in his heart he felt apprehensive. He didn't want to go back until he'd learnt as much as he could. The next time he crossed into the shadows he wanted to be prepared, especially now he knew Velindur was there.

Jack realised the conversation was over when Camelin started sorting through the bag. He made his way back down to the kitchen and over to the shed. It was going to be a long day.

Jack was surprised to see Nora's shed had been filled with wheels, frames, wood and an enormous toolbox. Elan and Techno were busy assembling a frame out of two bicycles. One looked old and battered but the other looked brand new. Nora seemed to be in charge of the various tools and passed what she was asked for.

'Hi, can I help?'

'Of course you can,' said Nora, 'come and hold this steady for Elan while she tightens it up.'

Jack held onto the new bicycle frame and watched as Elan copied everything Techno did. Neither of them offered him a go with the spanner.

'Where did you get the bikes from?' asked Jack.

'This one's my old one, it's too small for me now,' explained Techno, 'and the one you're holding was my birthday present from my dad.'

'It looks brand new!'

'It is, but we needed two bikes to make the buggy.'

'But what about your bike…'

'I can dismantle the buggy and remake my bike when the race is over.'

'It might get scratched.'

'I'll repaint it.'

Jack watched Techno as he worked. He couldn't believe someone would sacrifice their new bike and take it to pieces. It would never be the same again.

'Are you sure this is alright? What will your dad say when he finds out?'

'Techno's dad was here first thing this morning, and most of what you see here came out of his trailer, including the new bicycle,' explained Nora.

'When I told Dad what happened to your buggy and said I wanted to help, he said it was OK. I've been working on these plans for ages. Your grandad offered me his bike but it wasn't the right size.'

'Thanks,' said Jack. He knew it didn't sound much but he felt close to tears and didn't want any of them to see him cry.

A crunching sound on the gravel made everyone turn. Grandad rounded the corner carrying his own toolbox and a canvas bag.

'How's it going?'

'Really well Mr Brenin,' said Techno, 'Everything's going to plan.'

Jack watched as his grandad inspected the bits and pieces that littered the shed floor. It looked like a pile of scrap to Jack but his grandad seemed to be impressed.

'It's looking good; if we crack on we might get back on target and have it ready for a test run by the weekend.'

Nora let Grandad take the frame she'd been holding and stepped out of the way.

'I'll be in the herborium if anyone needs me. I'll bring you all a drink in a while and maybe when it gets closer to lunchtime one of you might like to give me a hand with some sandwiches.'

'I'll help you,' Jack volunteered. He felt like a spare part in the shed and helping Nora would give him a chance to explain about Elidon and ask her some questions. Time dragged for Jack. Grandad, Techno and Elan were totally engrossed in the buggy making. They chatted away discussing how best to do things and what should go where. He felt useless now Techno was involved. Jack wondered if they'd get on quicker without him. They kept having to explain what the tools looked like each time they needed something. It was a relief when Nora shouted for him to help with lunch. He raced from the shed to the kitchen.

'You butter and I'll fill,' Nora said, as she nodded for Jack to sit next to her at the table.

Now Jack was able to speak to Nora he didn't know where to start.

'Something happened last night…'

'I know,' she replied. 'I had a report this morning, it seems Camelin went out for a night flight.'

'It wasn't his fault, it was mine.'

Nora smiled then laughed.

'I have one nervous raven upstairs who thinks he's in trouble. I know what happened; don't forget, fairies can see both worlds. Twink told me how you used crystal magic to enter Elidon and how Camelin broke through the veil between the two worlds. I presume you called for him.'

'I was frightened and wished he was there, and there he was. It was all very strange but it was real, look.'

Jack pulled out the hag stone and showed it to Nora.

'Camelin has one too; Kerne gave them to us. He said there was a mean Hag in Elidon. I'm only allowed to go back twice before Samhain to find that missing piece of torc. I've got to go to the King's stone to find the piece that was hidden on Earth. Do you know anything that might help? I know I've got to do this on my own but the more information I can get the better.'

'Start at the beginning and tell me everything and then I'll know if I can point you in the right direction.'

While they made lunch for everyone Jack told Nora everything that had happened during the night. When he'd finished Nora nodded thoughtfully.

'Go and tell them lunch is ready, and later, when everyone's gone I think we need to pay a visit to Cory, she'll be able to answer any questions you may have about the King's stone.'

'Thanks,' said Jack. 'I don't want to fail.'

'You won't. We are all very proud of you. At Samhain you will be crowned, the Stone of Destiny is never wrong. Now, off you go and fetch the others. I'll take Camelin his lunch and let him know he's not in trouble.'

Jack hoped Camelin had moved his stash somewhere safe, if not, there was a strong possibility he would be in trouble after all.

PROBLEMS

Work resumed on the buggy after lunch. The only break they had during the afternoon was when Nora brought lemonade and biscuits. Jack caught a glimpse of Camelin flying towards Glasruhen as they sat in the sunshine with their drinks. Jack had plenty of time to think while the others discussed the progress of the buggy. He needed to plan the two remaining visits to Elidon carefully. The best place to start would be the Hag's cave. Maybe Camelin had gone to find out where it used to be. He was certain there weren't any Hags living in Glasruhen now. He was glad Camelin would be with him in Elidon.

For the rest of the afternoon, Techno and Elan worked on the framework and Grandad made the seat.

302

All Jack was required to do was pass screwdrivers and spanners from the toolboxes. He would rather have been flying with Camelin but helping with the buggy was something he couldn't get out of. He listened to Elan and Techno chatting happily together. They were both excited and engrossed; he knew how Camelin felt now when he was left out. Grandad looked happy, too. Jack hoped he might be allowed to help paint the buggy when it was finished. He looked over at the shelf where the paint was kept. As he scanned the neat row of tins he saw the one that had been spilt. The outside was covered in blue. Jack smiled; Max and Tank were having their hair shaved off today.

'I think it's time to stop,' announced Grandad. 'That's a good day's work; she should be finished by the weekend. Shall we see if we can get her over to Monument Hill on Sunday afternoon and give her a trial run?'

'That would be great Mr Brenin, I'm sure my dad wouldn't mind taking us. We could put the buggy in his trailer, and we'd all fit in his car. I'll bring my stopwatch.'

Jack forced himself to grin like the others, but he didn't feel excited.

'You can have first go Jack,' said Elan.

Jack's heart missed a beat. The last thing he wanted to do was to career headlong down a hill so close to the ground.

'It's fine, you or Techno can go first.'

'I wish I could fit into that seat, there's nothing like feeling the wind blowing in your face,' said Grandad, as he looked longingly at the buggy.

'We're going to need a helmet, it said so in the safety rules,' said Techno.

'I've got one we can use…' said Elan.

Jack's eyebrows rose. He couldn't imagine Elan wearing a crash helmet. He wondered if she might be going to magic one so he didn't say anything.

'… and I think Techno should go first, it's his design.'

Techno looked overjoyed.

'Are you sure Elan? It was your buggy that got smashed. What about you Jack?'

'Be my guest, I'll time you.'

Grandad looked thoughtful before he spoke.

'You all need to have a go. The driver's weight can affect the speed. From the trials we'll be able to work out who should drive on race day. We all want what's best for the team don't we?'

'We do,' everyone agreed.

Jack felt as if a great weight had been lifted. He knew he wouldn't have the fastest time.

'Of course the strongest one will need to go round the course. There are a couple of hills that the buggy will need to be pushed up,' continued Grandad.

Jack smiled. He knew without a doubt that Elan was the strongest.

'That's settled then,' said Grandad. 'We'll aim to have our new *Comet* finished for trials by the weekend.'

Jack looked wistfully at Nora and Elan as they said their goodbyes. He'd hoped to be able to visit Cory later but he knew that wasn't going to happen as Grandad had insisted they walk home with Techno. He said he wanted to talk to his dad but Jack suspected he wanted to make sure he got home alright. It wasn't far, and before long, they'd turned into the street where Techno lived.

'That's my house on the left,' said Techno as he pointed to a detached house with a large front garden, 'it's the one opposite the park.'

When they reached the park gates they had to wait to cross the road. Jack thought he heard whispering coming from behind one of the bushes. He didn't want to look round because he was sure the voices belonged to Max and Tank. He looked up at the roof of Techno's house. Two starlings were perched on the gable end. He was too far away to be sure but he thought they looked like Bicker and Grudge. It was a good job Grandad was there, he didn't want to think what might have happened to Techno if he'd been on his own.

Jack wasn't alone until bedtime. He was about to get ready for bed when he heard a faint tap on his window. When he peeped round the curtain he saw Camelin sitting on the windowsill. Jack opened the window.

'You took your time coming upstairs. I've been waiting in that tree opposite for over an hour now. I'm not coming in, can't stop if I want to make the chippy, it closes soon and I'll be able to have what's left if I get there in time.'

'I think Max and Tank were watching Techno's house.'

'Old news, got that covered. Nora's told the Squad to keep an extra eye out for him; he's as small as you isn't he?'

'Was there a reason for your visit?'

'Got some news for you; this afternoon I went to see Cory. She told me the large stone in the middle of the stone circle used to be called the King's stone. She thinks that's the one you need to look through.'

'That's great news. As soon as the buggy's finished we can go and see her.'

'Can't you use a bit of magic and get it finished quicker? It's no fun without you.'

Jack ignored the question. Camelin already knew the answer.

'I'm sorry. I don't like it any more than you do.'

'Aw well! See you later... get dreaming. I could do with another visit to Elidon tonight.'

'I'll do my best, see you later.'

Without another word Camelin took off and headed in the direction of the shops. Jack felt envious, not only because Camelin was free to fly when he wanted, but also because he too quite fancied some fish and chips.

When he was ready for bed Jack called downstairs and said goodnight. He lay in bed and wondered how long it would be before his grandad came up to bed and fell asleep. He wished Orin were with him. He missed not talking to her. As Jack fought to stay awake he heard a fluttering of tiny wings circling around his room.

'Dorysk? Is that you?' Jack whispered.

307

A large moth landed on the bottom of Jack's bed and began to crawl towards his legs. With each step it grew bigger and began to change shape. It wasn't long before the Dorysk stood on top of Jack's bent knees.

'You missed a treat today,' the Dorysk chuckled.

'Why? What happened?'

'Those two boys, the nasty pair, had their head's shaved. Nora asked me to keep an extra watch on them so I followed them this afternoon. Gave Bicker and Grudge a laugh too when Max took his cap off and showed Tank's mum his blue hair.'

Jack smiled. It served Max right for smashing the buggy. The Dorysk began making a buzzing sound then chuckled again.

'Cried, he did, when he saw himself in the mirror. I wish you could have seen it. Tank didn't seem too bothered. It serves them right for being so horrible.'

'Thanks for coming to tell me. Does Camelin know?'

'Can't find him, he wasn't in his loft.'

'Try the chip shop.'

'Now why didn't I think of that? I'd better be off. If I hurry there might be a few scraps left.'

Jack doubted it. Camelin didn't usually miss anything, and he could pick up the tiniest crumbs.

'See you soon,' Jack whispered as the Dorysk changed back into a moth and flitted out of the open window.

Jack lay back on the pillow and thought about Max. It was hard to imagine him without his beautifully groomed hair.

The snores coming from the end of the corridor told Jack his grandad was sound asleep. He didn't want to leave anything to chance. If he could summon the crystal and ask to be taken to Elidon he could tell it exactly where he wanted to go. He closed his eyes and thought of Glasruhen Hill. When he felt himself drifting off to sleep he opened his palm and tried to visualise his crystal but nothing happened. He tried again and again. His only hope was to fall asleep and be transported to Elidon in his dream, as he had been before. Jack felt his body relax, his arms and legs felt heavy and finally his eyes slowly closed.

'What happened last night? You didn't go back without me, did you?' Camelin asked as soon as Jack walked into the kitchen at Ewell House.

'It wouldn't work, I tried but nothing happened. I came over early to see if Nora might have an explanation. Do you know where she is? I don't think I've got long before Techno's due to arrive.'

'She's gone over to the island to take everyone their breakfast. You should see how much the goslings have grown.'

'I'd love to but not just now. I need to be here for Techno.'

'Techno this, Techno that, hasn't he got a proper name?'

'It's Praket Kawle,' said Elan as she placed a basket full of tomatoes, lettuce and radishes onto the table.

'Not salad for lunch!' grumbled Camelin.

'With homemade quiche,' replied Elan.

Jack watched Camelin's eyes grow big.

'Well that's different.'

Elan ignored him and turned to Jack.

'Is everything alright?'

'Not really, I couldn't summon the crystal or get back to Elidon last night.'

'Crystal magic chooses its own path. You'll be taken back when the time is right for you to go.'

'And me,' said Camelin, 'I get to go too, Kerne said I could.'

Jack felt helpless. There was nothing he could do to hurry events along. What if he failed? What if he never got back to Elidon? He tried to put the nagging doubts out of his head.

'When's the buggy going to be finished?' asked Camelin.

Elan looked surprised.

'I didn't think you were interested in the buggy.'

'I'm not, I just want things to get back to normal around here and the sooner the buggy's finished the sooner all the visitors will be gone.'

'Grandad says it will be ready to test at the weekend,' said Jack.

'We'd better get going,' said Elan. 'Your grandad must be on his way by now.'

Camelin looked crossly at Jack before shuffling out of the patio doors.

'He'll be fine when it's all over,' said Elan.

Jack nodded in agreement. He felt the same. He knew he'd feel a lot better when the buggy and the race were both finished, and more importantly, his quest completed. He followed Elan down the path to the shed. Grandad and Techno came through the front gate together happily chatting. Although Jack couldn't hear them, he could guess what they were discussing.

Jack offered to help Nora make lunch again. He felt more at home in the kitchen than he did in the workshop.

'Everything will be fine, you'll see,' Nora told him.

'If I knew the right question to ask my Book of Shadows I'm sure I'd get the answer. I'd just feel happier if I knew what to do or when to do it.'

'Have you got your Book with you?'

Jack nodded.

'Off you go down to the library, you won't be disturbed in there. There's a chapter about Elidon you might like to read. Just ask for information about the Land of Shadow and I'm sure your Book will give you an answer.'

'What about lunch?'

'It's fine. I can manage. If I'm running late I've got a very effective spell I can use.'

Jack and Nora both laughed. He didn't doubt Nora could have lunch ready in a couple of minutes if she needed to. He picked up his rucksack from by the dresser and made his way down the corridor to

Nora's library. He opened the double doors and stepped into one of his favourite rooms. Sunlight streamed in through the windows. Tiny dust particles danced and swirled inside the shaft of light. Jack loved the feel and smell of the old leather-bound books. He sat down and placed his Book on the table. For a few moments he let the peaceful atmosphere of the room wash over him before closing his eyes. He placed his hand on his Book and whispered.

'Tell me about the Land of Shadows.'

His hand jerked away from the Book as the cover flew open. The pages turned rapidly until they arrived at the chapter on Elidon. After a general introduction the chapter was divided by sub-headings. Jack was able to find the relevant information easily. He didn't have time to look at the whole chapter, but he knew enough from the little he'd read. To enter Elidon again he must use his crystal and he'd only be allowed to return at the same time too. Both he and Camelin were going to have to wait until Saturday night and then the Saturday after for their next two visits. This was the rule for all visitors who wished to return, and there were no exceptions. Jack sighed as he closed his book. He took one last look at the bookshelves before putting his Book inside his rucksack. He closed the library doors and went back to join Nora in the kitchen.

'Did you find the information you needed?'

Jack nodded.

'Not good news then?' asked Nora.

'We can't go back until Saturday night.'

'At least you know and won't be worrying about it now. Lunch is ready. Will you go and fetch the others?'

Jack smiled and nodded a lot during lunch as the others told Nora how far they'd progressed. He hoped the others hadn't noticed his disappointment; he didn't want them to think it was anything to do with the buggy. It was going to be a long wait until the weekend.

Jack woke early on Saturday. He spent most of the morning lost in thoughts of Elidon. After lunch, a knock on the front door announced the arrival of Techno and his dad. Jack wrote a message to Elan, in his Book of Shadows, to tell her it was time to go. He waited for her to arrive at the kitchen door. He could see she was excited as she ran up the garden. They joined Techno at the front of the house. Jack had expected they'd all be waiting for them but as he closed the gate he could see the buggy was still on the pavement. It seemed to take forever to get the buggy safely onto the back of the trailer. Jack watched as Grandad and Techno's dad secured and padded it. They pushed and shook it until they were satisfied it wasn't going to be damaged. Thankfully the journey to Monument Hill didn't take long.

Once the buggy was unloaded everyone except Techno's dad made their way to the top of the hill. He stayed at the bottom to signal to Grandad when to let the buggy go so he could start the stopwatch.

Jack and Elan insisted Techno went in the buggy first. Jack wasn't happy when he saw how fast the buggy sped down the hill.

'That should be a great time,' Grandad shouted, as Techno pulled the buggy back to the top of the hill.

'Now you Jack,' said Techno, as he passed him the crash helmet.

Jack didn't say a word; he looked pleadingly at Elan as he offered it to her.

'Thanks Jack. I won't be long.'

Elan also sped down the hill. Jack swallowed hard.

He knew he'd not be able to get out of having a go.

'Well done,' Grandad said when she reached the top of the hill. 'There you go, Jack, put the helmet on. It's your turn now.'

Jack reluctantly climbed into the seat. Grandad strapped him in and checked the seat belt was secure. He felt a jerk as Elan and Techno released the buggy. The ground rose up and down as he sped along. His stomach churned. He closed his eyes but quickly opened them again as it made him feel worse. Thankfully he was almost at the finish. The buggy was no longer pointing downwards. It slowed, and eventually stopped. Techno's dad helped Jack undo the safety belt. He could feel himself trembling as he stepped out of the buggy.

'Are you alright?' asked Techno's dad.

'I am now, thank you.'

He gave Jack a piece of paper.

'Take this up to your grandad for me. It's got all your times on.'

Jack took his time as he pulled the buggy back up the hill. That was the last time he ever needed to race. When he joined Elan and Techno at the top Grandad gave them their positions.

'You were in third place Jack, Elan was second and Techno first.'

'Well done,' said Jack, 'really well done, you deserve it.'

'Best of three?' said Grandad.

'Not for me,' replied Jack. 'It should just be between Elan and Techno.'

'Are you sure? You might pick up a bit more speed if you have another go.'

'I'm sure,' replied Jack. The thought of going down the hill even faster was not appealing.

By the end of the afternoon Techno was the clear winner of the time trials. Elan had proved herself the strongest by being the only one who could push the buggy uphill without any problems. Jack felt relieved. He also felt grateful to Techno because if he'd not been on the team Jack would have been in the driving seat on race day.

As they drove back to Glasruhen, Jack blocked out the excited chatter about the way the buggy had handled. His thoughts were elsewhere. He was impatient for the day to end. He had a return journey to make to Elidon before morning.

RETURN TO ELIDON

Jack woke with a start. He was lying on his back; he knew he was back in Elidon. He felt for the leather thong around his neck. He'd put the hag stone on at bedtime and it was still there. He was glad he'd remembered, especially since he didn't seem to have much control over when, or how, he returned to the Land of Shadow. He hoped Camelin had remembered to put his on too.

Jack lay for a few moments until he felt completely awake. As he moved slightly he heard the rustle of dead leaves underneath his back. Was he in Newton Gill forest again? The only way to find out was to open his eyes. He expected to see bare branches but above him was the canopy of an enormous tree. Through the dense leaves he could see a darkened sky.

Jack stood up and visualised his black tracksuit and trainers. His pyjamas and slippers transformed instantly. He wondered if he ought to materialise himself an umbrella too but decided he'd leave that to Camelin. Jack tried to orientate himself and work out his exact position. He was somewhere in Glasruhen Forest, but he didn't know exactly where. It was time to summon Camelin. He closed his eyes and whispered his name but nothing happened. How had he summoned him before? He'd wished for him to be there. Again Jack closed his eyes, and said the words in his head, *I wish Camelin were here by my side.* A rustling of leaves and a jolt on his arm told Jack his wish had been granted.

'You took your time,' grumbled Camelin as he shook his hair and straightened his back, 'I've been up for hours, waiting for you to call me.'

Jack watched as Camelin visualised his clothes. He was relieved to see the yellow sou'wester hadn't re-appeared even though the wellingtons had. Jack tried not to laugh when he saw Camelin standing in a pair of black leather trousers, a jacket that was zipped up to his neck and matching gloves. Jack thought it was an improvement on the previous outfit until the umbrella appeared, swiftly followed by a clothes peg on the end of Camelin's nose. Jack burst out laughing.

'What's so funny?'

Jack laughed even harder. The peg had drastically altered Camelin's voice.

'The peg,' Jack managed to blurt out as he clutched his sides.

'Why? Didn't you bring one?'

Jack managed to compose himself so he could speak again.

'No, what would I want a peg for?'

'You said we've got to go to the cave at the bottom of Glasruhen Hill, you know, the one where the Hag lives. I'm not going in any Hag cave without some body and nose protection. I've got a spare if you want?'

'It's OK thanks. Why don't you take it off for now and you can put it back on later if the cave smells.'

'If! What d'you mean *if* the cave smells? It's a Hag cave, it IS going to smell.'

'Maybe the hag stone will stop the smell.'

'Humph! Please yourself, I'm keeping mine on.'

Jack didn't speak for a few moments until he was sure he wouldn't start laughing again.

'Do you know where we are, or more importantly,

do you know where we have to go?'

'Didn't you ask your Book of Shadows? You've had all week and you didn't find out where the cave is.'

'Did you?'

'I didn't but I already know where it is.'

'Do you think you could lead the way? I did hope we might be able to get this piece of the torc back tonight.'

'If we do, can we come back and have a bit of fun next time?'

'This isn't the kind of place to be having fun. Don't you remember what Kerne said, we don't want to meet any men here, especially one man in particular.'

'I know, but you get to be a boy and a raven. I had to choose. These three visits are my only chance to be a boy again; we didn't get to have any fun last time. Please, Jack, if we get the torc tonight, please say we can come back again.'

Jack felt awful. Camelin was right. He could transform into a raven at any time. He had the best of both worlds but Camelin didn't.

'Alright, but only as long as we choose somewhere safe to visit.'

'Aw Jack! You're the best pal in all three worlds.'

'Lead on, we're wasting time.'

Camelin licked his finger and held it up above his head.

'This way,' he pronounced as he spun around.

'Are you sure?'

''Course I am.'

'And you can tell from licking your finger?'

'Naw, I've seen people do it when they're testing which way the wind's blowing; I know which way to go, follow me.'

Camelin chose a path through the trees. Occasionally Jack caught a glimpse of the top of Glasruhen. They seemed to be walking around the base of the hill in an anticlockwise direction. The only sound was the crunching of old leaves and twigs beneath their feet, and the squeaking of Camelin's leather clothes.

'Are we nearly there?' asked Jack.

'We'd have been here a lot quicker if you'd known where we were going. You could have just wished us there.'

Jack made a mental note to plan more carefully in future. Camelin stopped suddenly, held his finger to his lips and pointed towards a rock face that was partially hidden by a tangle of brambles, and some small bushes.

'It's over there,' he mouthed.

Jack nodded and made his way towards the brambles. The entrance had to be somewhere in the rock face. As soon as he stepped around the thorny thicket he could see an opening. He approached the entrance as quietly as he could. Even though he knew he was going to be invisible, he didn't want to make the Hag suspicious. He inched his way along the wall then listened carefully. A rasping sound echoed around the inside of the cave. The Hag was at home. Jack took one step in front of the entrance and gagged. The smell coming from the inside was revolting. He swallowed hard and made his way back to Camelin as quickly as he could.

'I think I'll have that spare peg, if you don't mind.'

Camelin smirked as he partially opened his umbrella, fished inside and triumphantly produced the peg.

'The Hag's asleep,' Jack whispered, once the peg had clamped his nostrils together. 'With any luck, we'll be able to find the piece of torc and be out of there before she wakes up. Come on, I need your help.'

They retraced Jack's steps. Before Jack stepped inside he took a deep gulp of fresh air. Once inside the cave, it took a few moments for their eyes to adjust to the darkness. The only light was coming from a badly made stone hearth. A few embers still glowed inside the circle of large stones. The snoring came from the left-hand side of the cave. Jack doubted the Hag would sleep with the torc in her hair and reasoned she'd probably have put it on a table close to the bed. He started walking in the direction of the snores. Camelin followed. The squeaking sound from Camelin's leather trousers seemed louder inside the cave, it could quite easily have been mistaken for a mouse. Camelin stopped abruptly and stood very still when the Hag stirred. She coughed noisily as she rose before shuffling towards a huge pile of rubbish. She cocked her head on one side and listened intently before her long nose began twitching.

'Mmm! I hear meeses… must be breakfast time! Here meesy, meesy, meesy,' the Hag cackled as she searched underneath a pile of bones.

Jack and Camelin froze when she moved closer to them. She sniffed the air close to Camelin's head before turning her attention back to finding what she thought was a mouse. She kicked the debris on the floor and bent over to sniff around the bed. Jack was grateful Camelin had brought the pegs; even in the dimly lit cave he could see clouds of dust rise. He knew the smell would have been unbearable. He also knew he needed to take another lungful of air. His plan had been to return to the cave mouth each time he ran out of breath but he didn't want to move and alert the Hag to his presence. He took a deep breath, then immediately wished he hadn't. The taste of rotting fish and mouldy mushrooms in his mouth made him want to cough. His cheeks puffed out as he choked back the taste. Jack could see Camelin was having the same problem.

'Come out little meesy, Devorah Dytch wants to meet you!'

The Hag almost kicked Camelin's wellington as she continued to disturb the rubbish on the floor with her long toed boots. Jack put his hand over his mouth and crept over to where the Hag had been sleeping. It was too dark to see anything. He contemplated trying to summon the crystal but then the Hag would know they were there. As she neared the entrance, a shaft of moonlight shone onto the cave wall. Devorah stood in front of a stone basin full of water and peered into it. As she looked at her reflection she stroked her cheeks.

'Oh! My hair band! I can't go out without it.'

Jack watched as Devorah shuffled over to the darkest corner of the cave. He heard a chest open, then shut. As the Hag returned to the entrance, she cackled happily to herself about how beautiful she looked. She went back to the basin, and peered at her reflection again. It took Jack by surprise when she started to chant in a high-pitched voice.

'*Basin, Basin, in the wall,*
Who's the prettiest Hag of all?

Jack tried not to laugh as Devorah began to jig around the mouth of the cave. She returned to the basin and answered her own question in a deep gruff voice.

'*You are Devorah, with your band,*
You're the fairest in the land.'

Jack put his hands over his ears when a high-pitched cackling echoed around the cave. He watched as the Hag smoothed her long tangled hair and fluttered her eyelashes at her reflection before chanting again.

'*Basin, Basin, in the wall,*
Who's the prettiest Hag of all?

Before the Hag could answer, Jack removed the peg from his nose and spoke. He tried to make his voice deep and gruff.

'*You're not the fairest in the land,*
Whilst you wear that hideous band.'

The Hag's mouth dropped open. She stood for a

few seconds and stared at the water.

'Who said that?' she screeched.

'I did,' Jack replied, in the same gruff voice. He put his finger into the water and swirled it around. 'You looked far prettier when your hair was over your face.'

'Why didn't you say so before?'

'I've been thinking about why you looked different, it's the band, it really doesn't suit you.'

The Hag screeched again, even louder than before. Jack's ears hurt. His throat felt sore from the horrible fumes, and from trying to make the gruff voice. He could see Camelin was standing outside the cave, presumably to get some fresh air. Devorah leant over the basin of water and waited until the ripples settled. She looked carefully at her reflection.

'You're right,' she screamed, as she grabbed the band from her hair and flung it out of the cave. 'Now, let's try that again shall we…

Basin, basin in the wall,
Who's the prettiest Hag of all?

Jack tried not to laugh as he replied.

'*Devorah Dytch, Devorah Dytch,*
Now you're prettier than any witch.'

'I never liked that stupid band anyway, don't know

why I ever thought it looked good, I'm so much prettier without it, you're right basin, you're right. Now… where's that meesy?'

Jack waited until the Hag started rooting through the pile of bones before tiptoeing out of the cave. He hoped Camelin had seen where the band had landed because he'd not been able to see a thing from where he'd been standing.

'Did you see where it went?' he mouthed.

Camelin stuck his thumb in the air and patted the umbrella on his arm. Once they were clear of the brambles Camelin removed his peg and began running. Jack followed. They ran as fast as they could away from the cave.

'We didn't have to run so far,' gasped Jack, 'I could have wished us home.'

'Oh we did! That was a brilliant run. I haven't been able to do that since we were in Annwn.'

'I need to sit down, at least until I get my breath back.'

Camelin pointed to a large boulder in the grass. When Jack's heart stopped racing he was curious to have a closer look at the piece of torc.

'Where did it land?'

'Land! I caught it in the brolly. I told you, umbrellas always come in handy.'

'Can I see it?'

Camelin opened the umbrella a fraction before producing the piece of torc from its folds.

'It'll look great when you've remade it.'

'It's lucky she threw it away, she'll never know we've got it and won't come looking for it.'

'You were brilliant in there. All that stuff with the mirror, where'd you learn to do that?'

'I didn't, and I don't ever want to have to talk like that again, my throat still hurts. We ought to be going.'

'Aw Jack!'

'I promise we'll come back next Saturday night, as long as we can find somewhere safe to have some fun.'

Jack was about to stand up, but before he could he slid off the rock. Camelin slid off too and almost fell on top of him.

'What happened?' asked Jack.

'I think we chose the wrong rock to sit on, look, it's not a rock at all, it's a big toe and I think the giant it belongs to is up there.'

Camelin pointed upwards. A dark shape towered over them. Jack didn't dare move.

'What's it doing?' he whispered.

'Probably thinking,' Camelin whispered back.

'About what?'

'Whether we're worth eating.'

'Time to go home I think!'

Jack was about to wish them back to their beds when the giant bent over and began to rub his ankle. Jack could see lots of tiny red marks all over his feet. A great tear rolled down the giant's face and almost dropped onto Camelin's head.

'He's hurt,' said Jack.

'He nearly wet me through,' grumbled Camelin, 'come on, let's go.'

'He looks sad. We can't just leave him like this.'

'Yes we can; you might not have noticed but he's a giant, he's big enough to take care of himself.'

'Nora would help him.'

Camelin sighed.

'Hello,' Jack shouted. 'Do you need any help?'

The giant looked down at them. He didn't say a

word, but as he sat down the ground shook.

'Don't bite me, please don't hurt me,' wailed the giant.

Camelin looked surprised.

'We won't hurt you. What's wrong,' shouted Jack.

'You're not Hags then?'

'Absolutely not,' replied Camelin. 'We don't like Hags, they're smelly, horrid, nasty little creatures.'

'And you're not going to hurt me?'

'No,' said Jack, as he bowed. 'We're raven boys from Earth, I'm Jack and this is my best friend Camelin.'

'A friend, you're lucky to have a friend. I wish I had a friend. It gets lonely on your own.'

'Aren't there any more giants in Elidon?' asked Jack.

'Only me, Judd's me name. Used to live on Earth myself, in Glasruhen Forest, but it's hard to keep out of sight when you're this big. The Lord of Elidon let me pass into the shadows so I'd be safe, and I was till a Hag moved in.'

'I don't understand,' said Jack.

'It's that Hag, Devorah Dytch. She bites and scratches and torments me. Just look at my poor feet and ankles.'

Camelin laughed.

'You could squash that Hag if you trod on her. What's the problem?'

'I couldn't! I wouldn't! I've never hurt anything in my whole life.'

Camelin rolled his eyes.

'But she's tiny and you're huge.'

'She makes me give her some of my eels, she loves them but she's afraid of the water, Hags don't swim you know. In return she's promised not to tell the Spriggans where I am.'

Jack frowned.

'Why wouldn't you want the Spriggans to know where you are? They could shrink you back down to your proper size.'

'I'm afraid of the tunnels.'

'All Spriggans are afraid of the dark,' said Camelin.

'I'm afraid of the dark as well, I don't like being in small spaces, I need to be in the open air. I can't live on Earth; men just don't understand giants. When I lived there a long time ago they stared at me, some called me names, some screamed and ran away, and worse still, some tried to kill me. That's why Kerne let me come to Elidon.'

'But I still don't understand why the Hag bites

and scratches you.'

'It's to let me know she's hungry. When I feel the pain in my leg I go down to one of my traps, catch an eel and bring it back for her supper.'

'Why don't you hide?' suggested Camelin.

'It's not easy when you're this big.'

'Well why don't you make yourself a rowan berry necklace?' asked Camelin. 'They keep Hags and Witches away, they can't stand rowan trees.'

The giant sighed.

'A long time ago there were lots of rowan trees in Newton Gill forest, but now they're gone, all dead wood. When the last tree died the Hags moved in.'

A sudden thought struck Jack.

'If you had a hag stone you'd be invisible.'

'I would if I had a hag stone, but I don't.'

'You can have mine,' said Jack as he took the thong off his neck and offered it to the giant.

'You'd give me your stone?'

Tears welled up in the giant's eyes again.

'Please don't cry,' said Jack. 'It's fine, you can have it if you'd like it, and consider us your friends from now on.'

The giant held out his hand and Jack dropped the stone into his palm. The thong had been far too long for Jack and he knew it wouldn't fit over the giant's head, so he slipped it onto his wrist. Jack hoped it would work, the stone looked so tiny now as Judd stroked it.

'Thank you, this is the best present anyone could ever have given me.'

Camelin frowned at Jack.

'What are you going to do if we meet that Hag? She'll be able to see you now.'

'I'm hoping that's not going to happen but if it does I'll share yours.'

Jack smiled at Judd.

'We've got to go now, I hope we meet again, and I hope you don't get bothered by any more Hags.'

Camelin rolled his eyes.

'When you two have finished, you were saying we ought to get home.'

'Why the rush now?' asked Jack.

The growling from Camelin's stomach gave Jack his answer.

'Pass me the end of the umbrella,' said Jack.

'Goodbye Judd, we really do have to go.'

The giant stood and smiled at them both.

Jack made sure he had the torc securely in his other hand before closing his eyes.

'I wish we were both home in our beds,' he said slowly and clearly.

It was late when Jack woke the next morning. In his hand was the second piece of the torc. He felt a great sense of relief. He was making progress, only one more piece to go and his quest would be complete. He needed to go and see Cory as soon as he could and look through the King's stone. The rest would be easy, once he knew where he had to go.

THE KING'S STONE

The buggy was ready to be painted. Grandad thought there'd be time to give the new *Comet* two coats of paint. At least it meant Jack would be able to help, painting was something he was good at. They'd looked at the route around the bridleway together but the only part of the race Jack was involved in was at the end. He had to be at the bottom of Monument Hill for when Elan and Techno arrived there. They needed him to help Elan push the buggy up to the top. The race ended when all the team members had crossed the finish line. The buggies went down the lane while the other two team members ran down the grassy hillside. Jack knew he and Elan were fast runners and the downhill sprint didn't worry him in the least. He'd felt a lot better about the race since he'd known he wasn't going to have to drive the buggy.

Jack looked across to Ewell House. He searched the sky in the hope of seeing Camelin but there wasn't a bird to be seen. He was about to lie on his bed and look through his Book of Shadows when he saw Elan come through the hedge at the bottom of the garden. She made her way to the greenhouse, where Grandad was potting up seedlings. Jack raced downstairs and arrived in time to hear part of the conversation.

'That's fine,' said Grandad.

'What is?' asked Jack.

'Nora wondered if you'd like to come and see the goslings. She'll be going over to the island soon and thought you might like to see how much they've grown.'

'I'd love to, thanks.'

'See you later then,' said Grandad. 'Don't be too late, we've got an early start in the morning; we need to get the first coat of paint on the buggy as soon as we can.'

'Nora's expecting you early,' Elan told Grandad. 'See you tomorrow.'

When they were out of earshot Jack was able to

ask Elan about Camelin.

'Is he alright? I've not heard from him since we came back from Elidon.'

'He's been in the library.'

'The library!'

'He asked Nora if he could look at the map of the whole area.'

'Did he say why?'

'Something about finding somewhere to go to have some fun.'

Jack groaned.

'I promised him that if we found the second piece of torc we'd go back and have some fun in Elidon on our final visit. He doesn't get the chance to be a boy any more.'

'You'd be safe if you stayed in the meadow near the fairy mound. You'll not come to any harm in there.'

'I'm not sure that would be Camelin's idea of a fun place to go.'

'You might want to mention it to Nora.'

Jack nodded. He wondered why Camelin was taking so long to decide where to go, and what kind of fun he was expecting to have.

'Come on, race you to the lake,' said Elan, 'we can get some running practice in.'

He didn't even wait for Elan to say *go*. He set off at speed and didn't stop until he reached the edge of the lake. Elan was a fraction of a second behind him.

'You cheated, you started before me,' she panted.

Jack was too out of breath to speak.

'Breathe though your nose,' advised Nora as she joined them. 'When you can, hop into the boat and I'll row us across the lake.'

They were nearly at the island when Jack saw Camelin flying towards them. He landed gracefully next to Jack.

'Mission accomplished,' he announced before giving Jack a slow nod and a nudge.

Jack didn't answer; he knew Camelin wouldn't say any more while Nora was there.

As soon as the boat reached the island, Medric came hurrying towards them.

'All present and correct, Gerda's just got the youngsters ready for inspection, they're all inside.'

Camelin bustled ahead and poked his head in the doorway. Medric wasn't far behind and pushed him out of the way with his outstretched wing.

'Guests first, in you go Jack.'

Camelin frowned but he didn't argue with Medric.

Jack was amazed by how big the goslings were. He could see how proud both Gerda and Medric were.

'Have they been given names yet?'

'They have,' said Nora. 'When they come over to the garden they'll introduce themselves.'

'They didn't like my suggestions,' grumbled Camelin.

Nora gave him her disapproving look.

'We'd better be getting back; this was just a quick visit. After lunch tomorrow your grandad has to go over to Beconbury. Once the buggy's had a coat of paint there won't be anything else you can do until it dries. I suggested you might like to stay. It will give you chance to go and see Cory. What do you say?'

'Thanks! That would be great. Can Camelin come too?'

'I don't see why not.'

Camelin looked pleased. It would also give them plenty of time to chat about their return visit to Elidon. As Nora rowed back across the lake, Jack's thoughts wandered. He still didn't know the area well enough to choose a safe place to go. It was going to be a hard task to persuade Camelin to stay in the meadow.

The following morning Jack woke early. He wondered what was different, until he realised sunlight was streaming in through his curtains. He quickly drew them back. The blue sky confirmed it was going to be a lovely morning. He felt excited. This afternoon he was going to look through the King's stone and see the place where the final part of the torc had been hidden.

Jack had already laid the table for breakfast by the time Grandad entered the kitchen.

'You're up bright and early. Exciting isn't it?'

Jack could feel the colour rise in his cheeks. Did Grandad know where he was going later?

'Nothing like the first coat of paint, it'll transform what we've built into a something like a racer.'

Jack grinned and nodded. He was relieved Grandad had been talking about the buggy.

By the time Techno arrived at Nora's everything was ready. Between them they'd finished painting by lunchtime. As they stood back and admired their morning's work. Nora joined them.

'You must all be really pleased. The buggy looks brilliant.'

'It's going to be really fast too,' said Techno.

Grandad didn't say anything. He had a faraway look in his eyes and a huge grin.

'You'd better go and get cleaned up,' said Nora. 'There are towels and plenty of hot water in the bathroom.'

Elan raced Jack and Techno to the house. It didn't take long for them to get cleaned up and soon three loud knocks on the door announced the arrival of Techno's dad.

'I'll be off too,' said Grandad, 'see you later.'

As soon as the front door closed, Jack heard Camelin calling from the kitchen.

'Are you ready?'

'We are,' Elan shouted back as she winked at Jack.

There was silence. When they entered the kitchen Camelin was perched on the windowsill with a very grumpy look on his face.

'What's wrong?' asked Jack.

'You didn't tell me Elan was coming too.'

'I'm only going as far as the meadow. I need to visit Jennet.'

'Well that's different. Are you ready?'

'What's the rush?' asked Nora.

Camelin didn't answer but Jack wondered if it might have something to do with food.

'I'll walk with you to the edge of the meadow,' said Elan, 'and meet you there later so we can walk back together.'

'I'll fly on ahead and meet you there,' Camelin croaked once he was airborne.

When Jack and Elan reached the bottom of the garden they both raised their arms at the same time to open the hedge. They broke into a fit of giggles as the trees parted for them. As they strolled through the tunnel they chatted happily about anything and everything except the buggy race. Jack was happy his world was beginning to return to normal. When they reached the edge of the meadow, Jack was expecting Camelin to greet them with his usual grumble, but instead he shuffled over to them without a word.

'See you in a bit,' Jack said to Elan as she set off through the meadow. When he turned back to Camelin he realised why he hadn't spoken.

'You're eating aren't you?'

Camelin tried to give Jack his most innocent look as he swallowed hard.

'Just a snack. If they'd let you fly, you could have had one too. You won't tell Nora will you?'

'I won't. Come on, we'd better find Cory.'

'She's waiting for us by the bushes, can't you see her?'

Jack couldn't see the nymph. He looked for her pale green face and long chestnut hair but she blended in perfectly with her surroundings. Jack only saw her when they got closer and she waved.

'The field is very muddy after all the rain, be careful not to slip,' Cory told Jack.

He looked down at his trainers; they were already caked in mud, so a bit more wouldn't hurt.

'Do you know anything about the Lost Treasure,' Jack asked her.

'Only what I've been told, but I do know about the King's stone. If you look through the hole at the top towards Glasruhen Hill it shows you the way to a burial mound. It's where the people who wanted to go into Annwn at Samhain would have gone. The mound was one of the portals open to anyone for that one night of the year. The passage leads into the King's tomb inside the mound in Annwn. The fair folk used fairy mounds, and the Druids would have opened their gateways, but ordinary folk had their own doorways too.'

'And what will I see when I look through the hole in the stone the other way?' asked Jack.

'What you are supposed to see. According to Elan, it will point towards another stone, one that will lead you to the place where a part of the King's torc was placed for safekeeping.'

Cory parted the bushes and then closed them again once they were inside the clearing.

'We went to your old home the other night,' said Camelin as they made their way to the stone circle.

'Oh my beautiful tree, I loved that tree but alas, all that's left is dead wood now.'

'Jack made it live again with his magic.'

Cory stopped and stared wide-eyed at Jack.

'You made my hazel tree live again?'

'Only for a short while, it was when we were in Elidon. I needed to eat some hazelnuts and drink from the well.'

'Ah! The tree of knowledge it was called; many sought that tree but very few ever found it or ate the nuts. I'm sorry, forgive me; we have more important things to do. Those days are gone.'

Jack had trouble keeping his balance in the muddy field. Camelin took off and landed on top of the King's stone. Cory didn't seem to be having a problem. Her feet hardly touched the ground as she made her way gracefully towards the circle. As soon as Jack joined the others he knew he'd got a problem.

'I'm too small, I can't see through the hole and I haven't brought my wand.'

'Use your crystal,' said Camelin.

'It doesn't work like that.'

'Summon it; tell it you need to see through the hole. It's supposed to help you isn't it? There's no point in knowing everything about crystal magic if you're not going to use it.'

Jack thought Camelin might have a point. There were no stones around to stand on and even if there were, he'd need a very large one, and without his wand he wouldn't be able to move it. Jack closed his eyes, took a deep breath, held out his hand and willed the crystal to appear.

'That's it Jack, you did it, tell it what you want.'

Jack transferred his thoughts into the crystal. He suddenly felt lighter and when he opened his eyes he could see both his feet had left the ground. He rose slowly in the air until his face was level with the hole in the stone. He was propelled forwards until he could see through it.

'No! That can't be right,' he wailed.

'What's wrong?' asked Cory.

'I'm looking at Monument Hill, there's no room to move my head so I can't see anything else. There's no stone like this on top, there's only the Monument we saw when we did the trials. The stone's gone.'

Jack lost his concentration and with a sudden rush of air he landed hard at the base of the King's stone.

'You should have told your crystal you wanted a soft landing,' said Camelin.

'I didn't have much choice, it just happened.'

'Are there any other standing stones in that direction?' Jack asked Cory.

'I wouldn't know. You need to ask a Bogie or a Water Nymph for that kind of information.'

Jack sighed.

'We were doing so well. We're going to have to go Cory; I need to get back to Ewell House. Nora might know the answer.'

'I'm sorry Jack, but I don't know what else I can do to help.'

'Nothing I'm afraid, but thank you for everything

you've done already.'

Camelin yawned loudly.

'Shall we go?'

Jack and Camelin hurried to the bottom of the meadow. Elan was already there and with her was Peabody.

'A Bogie!' cried Jack. 'You're just what we need.'

'I don't think this Bogie is going to be able to help,' replied Elan. 'He's coming home with us until all this has been sorted out.'

'Why would you want to invite a Bogie to stay at Ewell House?' asked Camelin.

'Nora asked me to fetch him. The Dorysk told her he'd been traumatised.'

'By what?' asked Jack.

'We think it's Velindur, he won't leave him alone, he's reaching out from the Land of Shadow and the only way we can help Peabody is to bring him back to Ewell House. Velindur will not tread the earth where a Druid lives.'

'You'll have to bring him yourself,' grumbled Camelin. 'I'll see you back at the house.'

'Nora says to go straight home,' Elan called after him.

'You didn't see the stone did you?' said Elan.

'Only the Monument.'

'Nora and I suspected as much. There used to be a stone circle on the top of Monument Hill but that was a long time ago. None of us knew how important it was. Many circles have been destroyed over the years. There wouldn't have been anything we could have done to stop the stones being removed. If Arrana was with us she might have known where you needed to look. That's why I went to see Jennet but she doesn't know the whereabouts of the stone either.'

'Couldn't we ask Peabody?'

'I'm afraid not, he's in no fit state to talk at all.'

'What am I going to do? How am I ever going to find out what the inscription said? Without it I'll never find the other piece of torc. I can't fail now.'

'When you return to Elidon you'll have to go back and see Sabrina, she might know something about the other stone.'

'Camelin won't be pleased.'

'Go to Sabrina first and then when you've got the information you can let Camelin have some fun. Her island might be the safest place for you in Elidon.'

'Thanks Elan, that's a great idea. We'd better get Peabody back. You don't think Velindur is watching us now do you?'

'Nora's not happy about any of us straying too far from Ewell House at the moment. He can't escape from Elidon but she's worried about what he's planning. We all need to take extra care. Gwillam says he's a very vindictive man and he doesn't like any of us, not after what happened at the trial in Annwn.'

They walked back to Ewell House in silence.

The next few days seemed endless. The buggy looked great after its final coat of paint. Grandad and Techno had made some last minute adjustments then agreed there was nothing more to be done. They were ready for the race.

When Saturday finally arrived Jack knew he should have been excited but he felt apprehensive. If Sabrina couldn't help him his quest would be over. Grandad had arranged to pick up Nora and Elan so they could all go over to Lillerton Fair together. It was wet and dull when they set off. The day dragged. Normally Jack loved the sights, smells and sounds of the fairground, but it wasn't anything like the one he'd been to in Annwn. There

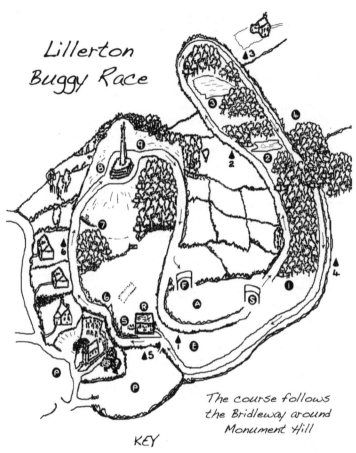

Lillerton Buggy Race

The course follows the Bridleway around Monument Hill

KEY

- **P** Car parks
- **E** Exhibition field
- **S** Starting point
- **F** Finish
- **A** Award Arena
- **▲** Marshall's tables and First Aid point
- **R** Refreshments and toilets

351

Lillerton Buggy Race

Teams park in the Cricket Club car park.
Register at table 1 in the exhibition field.
Judging and safety checks will take place
prior to the race in the exhibition field.
There will be a staggered start.
Wheel your buggy to the starting line
when the team is called and not before.
Follow the route.
The marshalls will tick off your buggy as
it passes each table. Any team failing to
do this will be disqualified.
The third team member must sign in at
table 6 and make their way to the foot
of monument hill to await their buggy.

From the start pass Bankside Plantation ❶
then Pitchcroft Pool ❷ Up the hill past
the Old Quarry Lake ❸ Round the bend
and down the hill through Wild Moor
Woods ❹ At the car park follow the
path past Lillerton Cricket Club ❺ and
then the Cemetery ❻ Meet your third
team member at the foot of Monument
Hill ❼ Push the buggy to the top ❽ and
release it downhill ❾ for the race to the
finish. Buggies must keep to the track
and the runners must keep to the grass.
When all three team members cross the
finish line the time will be recorded.
Spectators-please do not enter the Arena
until all the buggies have finished the race.

weren't many stalls and every time the drizzle became a heavy downpour they had to run to find some shelter. Grandad thought the bad weather had probably put a lot of people off. One of the stalls had programmes for the buggy race. Grandad collected one for each of them. In the middle was the map of the route around the bridleway. Grandad eagerly looked at the map and pronounced there'd been no last-minute changes. After they'd eaten, they'd decided to go home.

Grandad had been worried that if the rain continued for another week the race might be cancelled, but he'd spoken to one of the other organisers and they'd said the forecast was alright and the race would almost certainly go ahead.

Grandad chatted happily all through supper about the races he'd been in when he was a lad, and how the new *Comet* was the best buggy he'd ever seen. Jack hoped for Grandad's sake that they won but he doubted they would, especially since Max and Tank's buggy had been made for them by mechanics.

It was a relief when Jack finally got to bed. It wouldn't be long before he was back in Elidon. He'd carefully rehearsed what he wanted to say so he could ask Sabrina the right questions. Before closing his eyes he reached over to his bedside table and picked up his small silver dolphin, the one he used to have on a key ring. This time he wasn't going unprepared. He thought the dolphin would be something Sabrina might like. He knew she'd told him he needn't bring a gift but he thought it would be rude not to give her something in exchange for the information he so desperately needed.

RACE DAY

Jack became aware of an indistinct voice inside his head. Was he in bed or in Elidon? He sat up and opened his eyes. It wasn't his bedroom, but it wasn't the place he'd willed himself to either. He was expecting to be beside the river, opposite Sabrina's island, not inside a cave. The voice that had woken him spoke again. The familiar harsh tone sent a shiver down his spine. The sudden realisation of whose voice it was made his heart skip a beat. He looked around for a means of escape but the cave was in shadow. It was too late to move. He heard a cruel laugh. Jack put his hands over his ears. He knew the words about to be spoken would echo around the walls. *Now I'll have my revenge… revenge… revenge.*

The sound of glass shattering against the rock told Jack the diamond key had once more been smashed. A figure lunged at him, *Vengeance is mine… mine… mine.* Jack held his breath. He instinctively closed his hand around his golden acorn. As the shadowy figure threw his head back and laughed again, Jack could see, without a doubt, that it was Velindur who stood before him. This had to be a dream. He couldn't possibly be inside the Caves of Eternal Rest; he was at Brenin House in bed. He closed his eyes and wished with all his might for Velindur to disappear.

Jack listened intently. The only sound he could hear was his heart pounding in his chest. He didn't dare open his eyes. *Take me to the Gelston River, take me to the coracle*, he wished. He heard the sound of rushing water, and knew his crystal had transported him back to Elidon. He cautiously opened his eyes. He could see Sabrina's island in the moonlight. The coracle was on the grassy bank and the swollen water of the Gelston River rushed past him. He made the wish that would bring Camelin to him.

'What's wrong with you?' said Camelin, as he shook his hair and wiggled his shoulders. 'And more to the point, what are we doing here? I've got plans for tonight.'

'And I've got a problem.'

'You look like you've seen a ghost. Aren't you going to change your pyjamas?'

Jack took a deep breath and visualised his tracksuit and trainers. He knew Camelin wasn't in the right frame of mind to listen to his nightmare, nor would he be pleased when he learnt Jack needed him to row the coracle over to the island.

'I have to speak to Sabrina again before we have some fun.'

'Why?'

'Elan thinks she might be able to tell me about the missing standing stone from the top of Monument Hill, unless you know where I can find it?'

Camelin scowled.

'You promised.'

'When I've seen Sabrina I'll go wherever you want.'

Jack hoped Camelin had chosen somewhere safe, preferably well away from any kind of cave.

'You'll need a pair of wellingtons, long ones.'

Jack looked at Camelin's choice of outfit. He was wearing the same bright yellow jumper he'd worn the first time they'd come but instead of trousers, he had a pair of shorts and bright green wellingtons. The umbrella was securely hooked over his arm.

'Why do I need wellingtons?'

'And a couple of nets too.'

'Nets?'

'Yeh! We're going pond dipping. I thought about it when we were talking to Judd, you know, when he was saying about the eels. I've seen lots of people with jam jars and nets going to the big pond on the far side of Glasruhen Hill. It looks like fun. I can tell you exactly where we need to go. I've looked at the map.'

'Will we need jam jars too?'

'Naw, we'll put them back if we catch anything. What d'you say? It'll be fun won't it?'

Jack couldn't see any harm in going pond dipping. He knew it would be fun. There were so many things they could do together as boys and a few hours just didn't seem long enough. He could see Camelin was impatient for an answer.

'Agreed.'

'Aw Jack! I'm so excited. Come on. Let's get in the coracle. I'll have us over to the island in no time.'

It wasn't easy getting the coracle into the water. The river was swollen with all the recent rain and the current was a lot stronger than before. Once they were on the river the little boat rocked and swayed. It wanted to follow the swirling flow of the water. Camelin had to work hard to steer the coracle towards the island.

'What's that?' said Camelin as he nodded towards the shore.

Jack looked around. A large rowing boat had been pulled up onto the grass. He felt uneasy. It meant someone was on the island and that someone was probably man-sized.

'We can't land there. Paddle round to the other side. We don't want anyone to see us. Maybe whoever's here will leave soon.'

Camelin nodded and steered the small craft away from the boat. Jack signalled to Camelin not to speak. The quieter they could be the better. They kept close to the water's edge to avoid the strong currents. A sudden jolt made Jack lose his balance. He thought at first they'd hit a rock but when he felt the boat being dragged to the shore he turned around. The one face Jack didn't want to see was grinning at them.

'We meet again. How nice to have some company,' said Velindur, as he held the coracle fast with a hooked pole. 'You wouldn't be looking for the same thing I'm looking for, would you?'

Jack shuddered. The voice was soft and friendly but Velindur's eyes were cold and hard. He looked directly at Camelin and held him in his gaze.

'Let's get you and your little friend ashore where I can deal with you properly.'

Camelin didn't hesitate; he stood and used the paddle like a bat. The coracle swayed precariously. Velindur dropped the pole in order to defend himself but Camelin's arms weren't long enough. He yelled as Velindur reached out and wrenched the paddle from him. Jack tried to dislodge the pole but as he pulled it upwards he tore the side of the coracle. Without the oar to steady them the little craft began to rock violently from side to side. Water rushed into the boat. Velindur gave the coracle a hard prod with the paddle.

'Now it's your turn to suffer; you made a fool of me in Annwn. This will be the last time I ever have to look upon your face.'

Jack could hear Velindur laughing as the current swept them away from the island.

'The river will take you to your doom and save me the trouble,' he yelled after them.

Jack swallowed hard. He could see fear in Camelin's eyes as the coracle swirled and spun around; water poured in through the tear in the side. They were slowly beginning to sink. Camelin grabbed his umbrella. At first Jack thought he was going to try and use it as a paddle, but instead, he opened it up and tried to use it as a sail. Without any means to steer or paddle they were at the mercy of the river. The coracle sped along. Jack and Camelin clung to the sides. There was a sudden jolt, which nearly tipped the coracle over. Jack could see they'd struck the side of a fallen tree that jutted out from the bank. He felt dizzy as the little craft spun around. He could hear something loud ahead of them. Camelin grabbed his arm.

'Time to go home! Wish us out of here!'

'But I've got to speak to Sabrina, we can't come back to Elidon again before Samhain.'

'We need to go now. I know where we are. That's Brion Ridge rapids up ahead, you can hear them. If we don't go soon we'll be in the river.'

'No you won't little one,' a loud voice shouted above the roar of the rapids.

The coracle rose as Judd scooped them up in his cupped hands.

'Dangerous place for little boats, this river. Dangerous place for anyone.'

Camelin looked very relieved.

Jack was unable to speak. He sat very still, trying to get used to the swaying motion as Judd carried them back to the shore. From this height, Jack could see the tree they'd struck formed the boundary of one of Judd's eel traps. A feeling of relief washed over him. Now they were safe, Jack tried to make some sense of their encounter with Velindur. He'd seen the hatred in his eyes as he'd stared directly at Camelin. Did he think Camelin was *The One* destined to be the King of Annwn? Velindur had never seen them together before as boys. At the trial Jack had been a raven and Camelin a boy. Jack didn't think Velindur would ever forget, or forgive anyone who'd been at the trial in Annwn, especially since that was the day he'd lost everything.

Jack held on tightly to the side of the coracle as Judd lowered it to the ground. He was grateful to be on dry land again. As he stepped onto the grass he shouted up to the giant.

'You saved us. How can we ever thank you?'

'You're my friends now,' replied Judd, 'there's no need for thanks.'

Camelin looked very pale as he turned and glowered at Jack.

'You know I can't swim.'

'I know, but this is the last chance I've got to speak to Sabrina. I'm really sorry and I wish none of this had happened.'

As soon as the words had left his mouth, Jack

realised he'd said something foolish. The soft mattress under his back told him he was back at Brenin House. He heard a moan and opened his eyes. Beside him was Camelin.

'What did you do that for?' he grumbled. 'You promised we could have some fun. There was no reason to come back once we were on dry land.'

'It just happened, I only realised what I'd said when it was too late. I'm sorry but you know what this means, don't you?

Camelin shook his feathers and glowered at Jack.

'It means I'm not a boy any more and I'm not going to get to go pond dipping.'

'It means I might never find the missing piece of torc. You heard what Kerne said: once I was crowned we could go back to Elidon any time we want. We could have been boys together and had so much fun, but now, the lost treasure might be just that... lost forever.

'You'll be fine, you're destined to be king, they all think so and you said that's what you saw in the Stone of Destiny.'

'I also saw Velindur shaking a book.'

Jack watched Camelin hop onto the windowsill

and fly off in the direction of Ewell House. He felt overwhelmed with sadness. There was a week to go until the race. He'd do his best to try to find out what had happened to the standing stone from Monument Hill. If he was destined to be crowned king there had to be a way to find the missing piece of torc. He stood for a long time looking at the sky before he got back into bed.

'Rise and shine, it's race day! Come on sleepy head, up you get. It's a lovely morning.'

The last thing Jack wanted to do was get out of bed. Grandad sounded so excited. This was the big day they'd all been working towards so it was only fair to put his heart and soul into making the buggy race a success.

'Eat your breakfast,' said Grandad as Jack walked into the kitchen. 'We'll leave the washing up for later. I'll do one last check to make sure we've got everything and then we'll be off.'

Jack had never seen his grandad with such a spring in his step. As they arrived at Ewell House, Techno and his dad were dropping the back of the trailer down.

'It's going to be a great day,' said Techno.

'Yes,' replied Jack with all the enthusiasm he could muster.

With everyone helping, the *Comet* was safely loaded on the trailer in no time. Jack sat on the back seat between Elan and Techno. It was the first time he'd seen Elan all week. Nora had said she'd had something important to do but she hadn't said what. He managed to catch her eye and mouthed *sorry* to her. She nodded and smiled encouragingly even though she looked sad. There was nothing either of them could say or do until later. Jack tried to put everything except the race out of his mind. He listened and tried to join in with the excited chatter going on around him.

It took a while for them to reach the car park. There were hundreds of people milling around the village. It seemed everyone had made their way to Lillerton for the race. At least the sun was out and the forecast was good for the whole day. Unfortunately the grass was muddy. Pushing the buggy up the hill wasn't going to be easy. Once the *Comet* was off the trailer, Grandad helped Techno and his dad push it over to the starting line. Jack smiled when he saw how proud they looked standing next to it. The buggy glinted in the sunlight and looked as good as any of the others in the race, except for one bright red racing car at the end of the line. Max, Tank and Benbow stood next to their custom-made buggy having their photographs taken. The reporter and photographer from the local paper didn't seem interested in any of the others. Jack looked up at the trees. He wondered if the starlings would be there. It should be Crosspatch, Grubber and Snaffle, as they always had the first watch of the day. Movement in a tree opposite the refreshment tent caught his eye. There were three groups of starlings, each sitting in neat rows of five. It looked like the whole Flying Squad had flown over to see the race. Jack was left in no doubt as to who they were when Camelin landed beside them.

Elan came over and nudged Jack. She nodded towards Max and what was left of his gang. An argument seemed to have broken out.

'What's happening?' asked Jack.

'We'll know in a few minutes, the Dorysk's over there somewhere,' Elan whispered.

Before long a ladybird landed on Elan's hair. Jack could see the tiny insect had a minute pair of glasses. When he'd gone Elan smiled.

'You'll never believe it; they haven't even tried

their buggy out. Benbow was supposed to be driving but he can't get into the driver's seat. Neither can Tank, his legs are too long. They've even spelt the name of the buggy wrong, they've got *Terminater* on the side. Wait until Techno finds out, that'll make him laugh. If they'd used his plans it would have been built to fit. It looks like Max is going to have to drive and the Dorysk tells me he's not happy about it. Benbow is riding on the back and Tank is doing the uphill push. I don't think we've got much to worry about. Neither Benbow nor Tank can run very fast.

The loudspeaker calling for all competitors to take their places interrupted their conversation.

'See you at the bottom of the hill,' said Elan as she went off to join Techno at the starting line.

Jack made his way to a table where the uphill pushers had to sign in. He waved to Grandad then followed the other boys to the far side of Monument Hill. Jack wished he'd paid more attention to what had been said earlier in the car. He knew it was a staggered start and the first buggy over the finishing line would not necessarily be the winner. It all depended on the final time but he had no idea when the *Comet* was setting off. He could hear the loud crack of the starting pistol at intervals but it was impossible to see the starting line from where the pushers were standing. Most of the boys seemed to know each other. They were gathered in groups chatting and laughing. Only he and Tank stood alone. One by one the buggies arrived. The third team member raced over to help push their buggy to the top of the hill. Jack could hear the cheers and shouts as each buggy was released from the top for the downhill finish. He began to feel uneasy. There were very few boys left and one of them was Tank. A buzzing in his ear followed by a hurried whisper didn't help.

'They've been held up,' the Dorysk shouted. 'Elan said to tell you not to worry, she's dealt with it and they aren't hurt.'

'What happened,' Jack whispered.

'A couple of boys were hiding in the bushes on one of the uphill stretches. One of them grabbed Elan and the other pushed the buggy into the hedge.'

'Are you sure they're alright?'

'Elan and Techno are fine but the two boys will think twice about messing with Elan again.'

Jack was too busy talking to the Dorysk, and looking for their buggy down the track, he didn't see Tank come over.

'Talking to yourself, are you, Pixie Boy?'

Jack ignored him and kept looking towards the track for the *Comet*.

'Oh look! Here comes the *Terminator*, this is where you get a nice surprise from me.'

Without warning he pushed Jack hard on the shoulder. Jack stumbled back but Tank pushed him again, and again, until Jack's legs came to a halt against something solid. Tank sniffed the air around Jack.

'Something smells. Must be bath time, don't you think?'

With one final shove Jack fell backwards. He anticipated a bump on the head but instead he felt the shock of icy cold water. Tank had pushed him into a horse trough. He struggled to climb out but each time Tank laughed and pushed him back until a loud honking sound made Tank turn.

'Time to go Pixie Boy, you'll have a long wait for your friends, I think they might have got a bit tied up!'

Jack watched Tank run to his buggy. Benbow got off the back and the pair of them began pushing the racer up the hill. Now Tank was gone, Jack tried to get out of the trough but his legs kept slipping from under him. The bottom and sides were too slimy. He tried again but it was no good, he needed something to hold onto. On the back of the trough was a bronze horse's head. Water trickled through its open mouth into the trough. The only thing Jack could see that might help him lever himself up was a ring through the horse's mouth. He grabbed it with his left hand, put his right hand on the side of the trough and heaved. He'd got one leg onto the side when the ring broke and he crashed back into the water. He could see the *Comet* racing down the track. He waved and shouted to attract Elan's attention. She leapt off the back and dashed over to help him.

'Did Tank do this?'

Jack nodded.

'Thanks,' he said, as Elan helped him out.

'You OK?' shouted Techno.

Jack put his thumb up and then showed Elan the broken ring.

'I'd have got out if this hadn't come away in my hand.'

Elan stared at the metal loop. She took it from Jack, plunged it into the water and tried to remove some of the grime from its surface.

'You know what this is, don't you?'

Jack looked closer. Under the layers of dirt he could see a glint of gold.

'It can't be? How?'

'It is! As soon as I touched it I knew what it was. You've found the last piece of the torc.'

Jack's mouth fell open. Elan passed it back to him. He'd like to have examined it more closely but they were wasting precious time. He grinned at Elan as he zipped it into his tracksuit pocket before taking up his pushing position next to her at the back of the buggy.

'Come on, let's get the buggy over the finishing line; we've wasted enough time. We can catch them if we try,' said Elan.

Jack looked up. There were still two buggies being pushed up the hillside and one of them was the *Terminater*.

'Ready?' said Elan.

'Ready,' replied Jack and Techno.

The ground had been churned up and it was muddy underfoot. Jack's arms and legs ached as they pushed the *Comet* up the hillside. With Elan's strength and their combined effort they gained on the others bit by bit and reached the top before either of the other two buggies.

'Race to the finish,' cried Elan as she took off down the hill.

'To the finish,' Jack shouted as loudly as he could.

The cheers and shouts of encouragement were

deafening. Jack felt the wind in his hair as he ran faster than he'd ever run before. As they sped down the grass he could see the *Comet* cross the finish line. Seconds later he heard a loudspeaker announce the *Comet* team were home. He collapsed panting next to Elan on the sodden grass. Jack didn't care – he was wet through already. When he managed to sit up he could see the red racing car was halfway down the hill. Benbow and Tank were struggling to run down the slippery grass. The other team were a little way behind but were gaining fast. Unexpectedly the red car swerved. Instead of heading towards the finish it veered off towards a waterlogged part of the field that had been roped off. A spray of mud erupted as the racer swept under the rope and plunged into the mire. It came to an abrupt halt. Tank and Benbow, along with several marshals, ran over to the car.

Max stood up in the driver's seat and removed his splattered helmet.

'Get me out of here,' he yelled at no one in particular.

Some of the crowd giggled as Max tried to get out of the car, followed by loud peals of laughter as he slipped and fell in the mud.

'The *Terminater* is disqualified for leaving the track,' the loudspeaker announced. 'The driver is unhurt.'

They waited eagerly for the results of the race. Eventually one of the organisers stepped up onto the stage and spoke into the microphone. He thanked everyone for coming and began reading the results in reverse order. Jack knew they hadn't won. They'd lost too much time thanks to Max and his friends. He could see Grandad eagerly waiting to see how they'd done. Even though they'd had some hold ups, Grandad was still confident they'd be in the top ten.

They all cheered really loudly and congratulated each other when they found out the *Comet* was in fourth place. Techno whooped for joy and did a victory dance with his dad. Jack looked over to the tree where the starlings and Camelin had been perched but they'd all gone.

'That's a really great result,' said Techno.

'It is considering the problems we had,' Jack agreed.

'Max only has himself to blame for losing the race,' said Elan.

Jack smiled as he looked over at the roped-off area

where the *Terminater* had been abandoned. It didn't look too good now. Max was nowhere to be seen. The photographer and reporter from the local paper, along with a huge crowd, were gathered around the winning team.

'I think we need to get you home and out of those wet clothes,' said Grandad. 'Lying on the wet grass probably wasn't a good idea, you're soaked though.'

It didn't take long to load the *Comet* onto the trailer.

'I'm sorry we didn't win,' Jack said to Techno as they arrived at Ewell House, 'it was a brilliant design.'

'There's always next year. I don't think Max or Tank will be bothering us again. Danny's left the gang too you know, he wants nothing more to do with them.'

'Did you see Max's face when he realised everyone was laughing at him,' said Elan.

'Serves him right,' laughed Techno.

'I hope you'll be able to put your bike back together again,' said Jack.

'Dad says I don't have to, he's going to get me another one. We can keep the *Comet* as she is, we'll be able to have some fun with her during the holidays if you'd like?'

'We'd love to,' said Elan, 'wouldn't we Jack?'

Jack nodded. He'd be happy to watch the others if they wanted to go downhill but he'd like to take his turn on the flat.

Techno grinned.

'Do you two fancy a game of football, when the field's dried out a bit?'

'You bet,' Jack said without any hesitation.

'Count me in,' said Elan.

Jack could see his grandad and Techno's dad shaking hands.

'Are you ready son?' his dad called.

'See you soon,' called Techno from the open window as they drove away.

'See you soon,' Jack and Elan called after him.

Jack glanced up to the roof of Ewell House. Camelin didn't look too pleased. Jack made a mental note to invite him for a game of *Beakball* on Nora's lawn, when the weather was better and the ground had dried out. Making the buggy hadn't been such a bad thing to do after all. He'd made a new friend, and more importantly, he'd managed to find the last piece of the torc. In the morning when he went over to Ewell House he'd see if Orin wanted to come home. Jack unzipped his pocket and put his hand around the twisted piece of gold. Camelin had been right, everything had turned out well, and he'd completed his quest. Now he had all three pieces he could be crowned King of Annwn at Samhain.

'We'd better be getting home too,' Grandad said to Jack.

They said goodbye to Elan and walked along the back lane to Brenin House.

'Quite a day, wasn't it?'

'It was,' agreed Jack.

When Jack was back in his room he heard a tap on his window.

'Sorry you didn't win,' said Camelin.

'It's fine, I'm just glad Max lost and ended up in the mud.'

'With a little bit of help from yours truly.'

'What do you mean?'

'Max sent two of his friends to ambush Elan. I was watching from one of the trees. I tried to warn her but I'm not sure she saw my ravenphore. There was nothing

376

I could do, not that Elan needed any help, so I followed Max. You didn't see my signals either. I knew Tank was going to do something.'

'So did I, but even if I'd seen you there was nothing I could have done to stop him.'

'I knew Elan wasn't far behind so I hung back and watched Max's team struggle to push their buggy up the hill. It must have weighed a ton with all the metal they'd used to build it. Anyway, when he came down the hill I had a little flyover and gave him a surprise parcel, right on his visor. When he tried to wipe it off he smeared it all over, couldn't see a thing, he hadn't got a clue where he was going and shot straight into the mud. It was no more than he deserved.'

Camelin exploded in a fit of chuckles. Jack laughed too.

'Can I see the torc?' Camelin asked as he hopped onto Jack's table.

Jack laid the three pieces of the king's torc on his bed. He took out his wand and pointed it at the last piece.

'*Expolio*,' he commanded.

They watched as the grime slowly dissolved. Jack lowered his wand and smiled when the gold shone brightly.

Camelin nudged him.

'Didn't I say you could do it?'

'You did but I don't understand how the torc ended up as a bit in a horse's mouth.'

'Peabody told Nora there used to be a small pool at the bottom of Monument Hill. He said the torc had been given to a nymph for safekeeping but she obviously didn't take it with her when she lost her home.'

'Did Peabody say which water nymph used to live there?'

'He did, it was Uriel.'

Jack felt a shiver run down his spine as he remembered the visit they'd made to Uriel's well. Camelin coughed and pointed his wing over to the three pieces of gold on Jack's bedspread.

'Aren't you going to remake it then?'

'I'll try.'

Jack ran his fingers over the twisted pieces. He concentrated and visualised the torc he'd seen around Kerne's neck. A bright light shone from above his hand as his crystal appeared. When its rays fell on the pieces of gold, they rose from the bed. In mid-air they twisted around each other. A golden glow filled his room before a beam of light burst from the crystal and fell on the bare ends of the torc. Two golden acorns began to grow from the twisted metal. When the torc was complete it fell back onto the bed with a dull thud.

'You really are a natural you know, Gwillam was right when he said you were worthy. No one can doubt that now.'

Jack picked up the torc. It felt heavy now all the pieces were entwined. The two acorn finials were beautiful; their cups contained all the colours of autumn. He was tempted to try it on but it didn't really belong to him until he'd been crowned. Finding somewhere to keep the torc was going to be a big responsibility.

'I've just got to keep it safe until Samhain.'

'You can do that, you're Jack Brenin.'

'I hope so. We've gone through a lot to recover this.'

'But we did it together.'

'We certainly did.'

Camelin hopped back onto the windowsill and was about to go when Jack's Book of Shadows began vibrating.

'You've got a message. Who's it from?'

Jack opened his Book on the first page and watched the writing appear.

'It's from Nora.'

'And… what's it say?'

Jack felt the colour drain from his cheeks as he read the message.

> *Whatever you do, don't remake the torc.*
> *Gwillam was overjoyed to hear you'd recovered*
> *all three pieces of the Lost Treasure*
> *but also afraid Velindur might try to steal it.*
> *If Camelin is still there get him to fly it*
> *over to Ewell House one piece at a time.*
> *It will be safer here.*

> *It seems the King's torc wasn't the only Treasure*
> *lost from Annwn.*
> *What you saw in Velindur's hand is the*
> *Book of Sorrows.*
> *Elan and I are needed in Annwn and have*
> *to return immediately.*

Jack sat down heavily on the bed. His joy had turned to despair.

'What's the Book of Sorrows, and why would Velindur want it?'

'I've no idea but you'd better unmake that torc quick. You don't want to lose it, not after all we've been through.'

Jack held out his hand for his crystal but it didn't reappear. He quickly flicked through his Book of Shadows until he got to the spell page. It didn't take him long to find what he was looking for.

'*Retexo*,' he commanded as he stretched both his hands over the torc.

There was a flash of light. When Jack looked, the two acorns had disappeared, and the golden strands were untwisting themselves. When the spell had finished three separate golden pieces lay on the bed. Without a word Camelin picked one up and set off towards Ewell House. Jack hoped that once the pieces were with Elan and Nora they'd be safe until Samhain. It wasn't long before Camelin was back and on his way with the second piece. As Jack watched for Camelin's return a large beetle, wearing a pair of spectacles, flew in through the open window with Twink on its back. Jack held out his palm for the Dorysk to land.

'Elan sent me,' said Twink. 'She says not to worry, everything will be alright. She's asked us all to keep a watch over Glasruhen. Velindur can't leave Elidon but if he so much as takes one step towards Brenin House we'll raise the alarm. You can sleep easy until Samhain, you've got a lot of friends who won't let you down.'

Jack sighed with relief.

'Thanks Twink, and you too Dorysk, I know I'm very lucky to have such good friends.'

There was a loud cough from the windowsill. Camelin had obviously overheard this conversation.

'And even luckier to have Camelin. I couldn't have found the lost treasure without him.'

Jack smiled as Camelin puffed out his chest feathers.

'Ready to take the last piece?'

'Ready.'

When Jack was alone he thought about everything he'd been through in the last few weeks. The Stone of Destiny had given him a vision of what was to be. Now he'd completed his quest and the Lost Treasure of Annwn had been found, he'd be crowned king at Samhain. He could rest easy knowing the three pieces of the torc would be safe at Ewell House. He was sure, now Gwillam knew it was the Book of Sorrows Velindur had stolen, he'd be able to find out the reason why he'd taken it. Both the buggy race and the quest had given him a sense of achievement. Seeing the torc remade, no matter how briefly, had been thrilling. What everyone had been telling him was true; he really was destined to be king. At last he felt excited.

He looked over at his calendar. At least the summer wasn't over. There was still plenty of time to have some fun with Camelin.

RAVENPHORE

UP   RIGHT   HELP

DOWN   LEFT   LOOK OUT

FORWARD   BACKWARD

FLYING SQUAD WATCH ROTA	Max Wratten MAX	Frank Smedley TANK	Benjamin Archer BENBOW	Daniel Westbrook DANNY	Praket Kawle TECHNO
FIRST WATCH	CROSSPATCH	GRUBBER	SNAFFLE	CHORTLE	SNATCH
SECOND WATCH	BICKER	GRUDGE	DIGGER	MUMBLE	TWIZZLE
THIRD WATCH	DAZZLE	PIPPA	BEAKY	TWEEK	GROUCH

Alphabets
and
Runes
for the
Humankind
of
Glasruhen,
for the
Fair Folk
and
Not So
Fair Folk,
for the
Druids
of
Annwn,
and
for the
Dragons
of
Long Ago

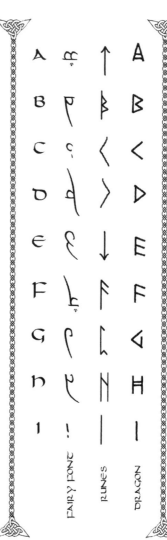

FAIRY FONT

RUNES

DRAGON

FAIRY FONT   RUNES   DRAGON   FAIRY FONT   RUNES   DRAGON

WHO'S WHO, WHAT'S WHAT
and
WHERE IS IT?

Here are the additions to my glossary from my fourth adventure. Although Catherine Cooper has been helping me write my memoirs, any comments in brackets have been added by me.

WHO'S WHO

Beaky – Starling from the third watch of the **Flying Squad**, his watch is **Benbow**. (*A well-known nickname for any bird who likes to stick his beak into everything.*)

Benbow – Nickname of **Benjamin Archer**.

Benjamin Archer – Known as **Benbow** and a member of Max's gang. (*Hee hee! Ben short for Benjamin and Bow because his surname is Archer.*)

Bicker – Starling, and leader of the second watch of the **Flying Squad**, his watch is **Max.** (*Doesn't matter what you say, Bicker will always argue, even when he knows he's wrong.*)

Chortle – Starling from the first watch of the **Flying Squad**, his watch is **Danny**. (*A great starling, always laughing.*)

Cloda – A **Sylph**. Nymph of the air and librarian at Falconrock. Her official title is Archivist, Guardian of Ancient Knowledge, and Keeper of Secrets. As a nymph of the air, Cloda takes the form of a falcon. (*Librarians and archivists can be fearsome creatures, especially if you're noisy.*)

Crosspatch – Starling, and leader of the first watch of the **Flying Squad**, his watch is **Max**. (*You can guess how he got his name.*)

Danny Westbrook – Known as **Danny** and a member of Max's gang. *(His dad owns the Music Shop in Glasruhen.)*

Dazzle – Starling, and leader of the third watch of the **Flying Squad**, his watch is **Max**. *(Always has the most beautifully groomed plumage, a credit to the starling world.)*

Devorah Dytch – A **Hag** living in **Elidon**. *(Like all Hags, she's bad tempered and smelly.)*

Digger – Starling from the second watch of the **Flying Squad**, his watch is **Benbow**. *(He always has his beak in the ground.)*

Frank Smedley – Known as **Tank** because of his size, and a member of Max's gang. *(He's the goalkeeper who pushed Jack and wrecked Elan's bunch of flowers. His dad has a scrap metal yard in Newton Gill.)*

Grannus – Guardian of the well, stream and spring at **Falconrock.**

Grouch – Starling from the third watch of the **Flying Squad**, his watch is **Techno**. *(A really grumpy starling if ever there was one.)*

Grubber – Starling from the first watch of the **Flying Squad**, his watch is **Tank**. *(Like Digger he's always got his beak in the ground looking for his favourite food.)*

Grudge – Starling from the second watch of the **Flying Squad**, his watch is **Tank**. *(He's got a long memory and doesn't forgive very easily.)*

Judd – The Glasruhen Giant. *(He's the giant in the story told in Annwn.)*

Max Wratten – Known as Max. Leader of a local gang. *(He's the boy Jack accidentally gave a bloody nose to with the football when he first arrived in Glasruhen. Max has had it in for Jack ever since.)*

Netty – A Fairy from the **Meadow Mound**. Representative of the meadow and wayside **Fairies**. She likes to sleep in the nettles in the **back lane**. *(Like all fairies she talks too much.)*

Pippa – Starling from the third watch of the **Flying Squad**, his watch is **Tank.** *(Always first, likes to beat everyone at everything.)*

Praket Kawle – Known as **Techno** and a member of Max's gang. *(He's brilliant at designing, drawing plans and making things work.)*

Rhoda – A Fairy from the **Meadow Mound.** Representative of the garden **Fairies.** She sleeps in the rhododendrons in Grandad's garden. *(Also talks a lot.)*

Sabrina – **Water Nymph** of the **Gelston River.**

Snaffle – Starling from the first watch of the **Flying Squad**, his watch is **Benbow**. *(He's great at finding things and hiding them away.)*

Snatch – Starling from the first watch of the **Flying Squad**, his watch is **Techno**. *(None of the starlings have any table manners but this one is the worst.)*

Speedy – A Fairy from the **Meadow Mound** whose real name is **Veronica**.

Tank – Nickname of **Frank Smedley.**

Techno – Nickname of **Praket Kawle.**

Tweek – Starling from the third watch of the **Flying Squad**, his watch is **Danny**. *(Always preening himself and never ready on time.)*

Twink – A Fairy from the **Meadow Mound** whose real name is **Twinkle**. Representative of the moor and mountain **Fairies**. She lives in the eyebright flowers on **Glasruhen Hill**. *(Another talkative fairy.)*

Twinkle – A Fairy from the **Meadow Mound** known as **Twink**.

Twizzle – Starling from the second watch of the **Flying Squad**, his watch is **Techno.** *(He finds it so difficult to keep still you'd think he'd got ants in his feathers, which isn't good when you need them to stand to attention.)*

Veronica – Fairy from the **Meadow Mound** known as **Speedy**. She sleeps in the speedwell flowers in the meadow. *(Never call her Speedy to her face or you'll suffer the consequences… she's got a very short fuse.)*

WHAT'S WHAT ?

Fairy – Another name for a type of **Sylph**; Nymphs of the air.

Flying Squad – A group of 15 starlings enlisted to spy on the five boys in Max's gang, consisting of three groups of five, for 24-hour surveillance. *(They were very undisciplined until I formed them into three efficient squads... just shows you what natural leadership can do.)*

First Watch
Crosspatch watching **Max** – Max Wratten
Grubber watching **Tank** – Frank Smedley
Snaffle watching **Benbow** – Benjamin Archer
Chortle watching **Danny** – Danny Westbrook
Snatch watching **Techno** – Praket Kawle

Second Watch
Bicker watching **Max** – Max Wratten
Grudge watching **Tank** – Frank Smedley
Digger watching **Benbow** – Benjamin Archer
Mumble watching **Danny** – Danny Westbrook
Twizzle watching **Techno** – Praket Kawle

Third Watch

Dazzle watching **Max** – Max Wratten

Pippa watching **Tank** – Frank Smedley

Beaky watching **Benbow** – Benjamin Archer

Tweek watching **Danny** – Danny Westbrook

Grouch watching **Techno** – Praket Kawle

Gnarles – Are dying trees, no longer under the protection of a **Hamadryad**. They still have some life in them but the **Dryads**, who once tended and looked after them have left the forest and the Gnarles are left to slowly turn into dead wood. *(They don't seem to appreciate my singing.)*

Sylphs – Nymphs of the air. They can shape-shift into creatures that fly.

WHERE IS IT?

**The Map of Glasruhen – (pronounced *glass-rue-hen*
meaning *ancient green hill*). From *The Golden Acorn*
– *The Adventures of Jack Brenin* Book One.**

Brenin House – The house where **Grandad** and **Jack**
live. It's been in the Brenin family for generations.

Elidon – The Land of Shadow.

Falconrock – A rocky outcrop to the north-west of
Glasruhen where an ancient Druid's library can be
found.

Gelston River – The home of the **Water Nymph,
Sabrina**.

Hazel Well – Located in the heart of **Newton Gill
Forest.**

Lillerton – The next village to **Glasruhen** where
Monument Hill can be found.

Meadow Mound – A Fairy Mound in the meadow not far from **Brenin House**.

Monument Hill – A large hill to the south-west of **Glasruhen**, on top of which stands a tall obelisk. The monumental obelisk was erected in memory of a local duke who once lived in **Lillerton**.

Newton Gill Forest – Once a great forest of oak trees but now most of the trees have become **Gnarles**. The **Dryads** no longer live in the trees and the whole forest is slowly dying. The old **Hazel Well**, and the **Gnori**, home to the **Bogie**, **Peabody**, are here too.

My Who's Who, What's What
and Where Is It?

can be found on my website at

www.pengridion.co.uk

ACKNOWLEDGEMENTS

I'd like to thank everyone at Infinite Ideas
for all their help and support,
my friends and family, and a very
special thank you to Ron.

I'd also like to thank all the members of the
Shrewsbury Canoe Club who helped me with
my research. In particular, Nigel Baker, for
his in-depth navigational descriptions of the
River Severn, its islands and character.